I0691228

TRUTHTAKER

A DISPLACED HISTORY NOVEL

TRUTHTAKER

A DISPLACED HISTORY NOVEL

LYSANDRA JAMES

RADIANCE

RADIANCE

An Imprint of Roan & Weatherford Publishing Associates, LLC
Bentonville, Arkansas
www.roanweatherford.com

Library of Congress Cataloging-in-Publication Data
Names: James, Lysandra, author.
Title: Truthtaker/Lysandra James | Splintered Regency #1
Description: First Edition | Bentonville: Radiance, 2025.
Identifiers: LCCN: 2025947302 | ISBN: 979-8-89299-100-1(trade paperback) |
ISBN: 979-8-89299-101-8 (eBook)
Subjects: BISAC: FICTION / Fantasy / Historical
FICTION / Fantasy / Action & Adventure
FICTION / Fantasy / Women
LC record available at: https://lccn.loc.gov/2025947302

Radiance edition December 2025

Cover Design by Casey Cowan
Interior Design by Natalie Brianne
Editing by Addison Gardner & Lisa Lindsey

For my boys.
I love you to infinity and beyond.

ACKNOWLEDGEMENTS

THOSE WHO BELIEVED IN ME.

My husband, Jeff. He gives me space, time, and chocolate so I can work my magic. He lets me rant when my characters are misbehaving and talk through plot holes even when what I'm saying doesn't make any sense to him. He brings me food and caffeinated beverages when I'm deep in the writing zone and endures my getting up at five most mornings. He's the one who sent me to my first writing conference—the one that started it all. For that and more, I'll be forever grateful.

My boys—Bryant, Corbin, and Darien. They're the best kids a mom could have. Always and forever. They've always taken it for granted that I would be published someday and I couldn't let them down. What kind of mother would I be?

My sister, Amber. She is the most amazing dragon slayer as well as one of my favorite beta readers. She calls me out on my crap and sends boxes of sunshine when I need it most. She also lives too far away, which means I have to drive nearly five hours to see her. So rude.

THOSE WHO SUPPORTED ME.

My writer & artist friends. There are too many to name individually, but you know who you are. Without you, I wouldn't have made it this far. I love being part of the most wonderful and uplifting community of creatives. Each time we're together, I feel like I'm coming home.

My non-writer friends. We've laughed. We've cried. We've sassed and vented. They're characters in their own right, which is why I adore them. They may not always fully understand me, but they love me anyway and that's what matters most of all.

My role models and mentors. They paved the way and showed me it was possible to chase my dreams and slay my dragons. Some even had the audacity to later tell me I'm an inspiration to them. How dare they?! (I'm not crying sappy tears, you are.)

THOSE WHO HELPED MAKE IT HAPPEN.

Lindsay Flanagan—my editor and friend. I never would have followed this path if she hadn't pioneered the way. I wouldn't have continued on this path if she hadn't fought for me. She's fierce and determined and I would be incredibly fortunate to be anything like her when I grow up.

Casey & Amy Cowan. I had no idea I was pitching to a publisher when we first met. To me, they were just a couple of authors at a writers conference asking me what I wrote. Best mistaken identity EVER. I'm so glad they took a chance on me. I hope to make them proud.

My beta readers—Katie Lyon, Sarah Earl, Jenny Rudd, Charity Keyes, and Emily Powell. Truthtaker wouldn't be what it is without their feedback and input. Or their excitement and anticipation for the next book to be written so they can get their hands on it. I'm working as fast as I can!

AUTHOR'S NOTE

I have a confession to make. I am not a historian. In fact, my history class in high school was my least favorite. Researching historical names, places, and events gave me headaches. I swore I would never write in a genre that required doing extensive research.

And yet . . . here we are. And I'm now obsessed.

Having caught the history bug later in life, I know I'm going to get things wrong. It's inevitable. No matter how many books I read or documentaries I watch or papers I peruse, I'm going to mess up some of the details.

But it's also fiction. Fantasy. Make-believe. A world of "what-ifs" that I get to play in and twist and adapt to fit the vision inside my head.

The story is what matters. My characters and what they experience and become matter. Lifting my readers up and helping them believe that anything is possible matters. Teaching them they can chase their dreams and slay their dragons matters.

Not obscure details that most people won't know are wrong.

And any naysayers or nitpickers can be Snatched.

So there.

PROLOGUE

VERITY COVINGTON LEANED OVER THE side of the *Atlantia's* oak railing and closed her eyes, relishing the feel of the sea breeze rustling through her hair. The wind had teased most of her hair pins out, but she didn't care. She would repair it as best she could and put her bonnet back on before going back below deck. No one would be the wiser. For now, though, she clutched her bonnet tight with both hands, or the wind would surely send it flying over the ocean, never to be seen again.

"What are you doing on deck again, Miss Covington?"

Though the words were scolding, the tone was not. Verity hid her smile and turned to face the handsome lieutenant that was part of the reason she escaped her cabin whenever possible.

"Lieutenant Saunders, how lovely it is to see you as well. I thank you for asking after my family." She attempted to keep her face passive, but she feared there was a twinkle in her eye. How could there not be when someone as handsome as he was speaking with her?

Lieutenant Saunders touched the brim of his hat and flashed her a smile that left her knees weak. She gave herself a silent reprimand for allowing herself to respond to him in such a manner. After all, she was promised to a man she'd never met.

"Once again, you chastise me to fulfill my duty, Miss Covington." He joined her at the railing and peered over the water. "I assume your family is well."

Verity looked toward the ocean. It was easier to pretend she didn't have a flutter in her stomach at his proximity when his gaze was focused elsewhere. "Mother is still confined to bed. My father is tending to her as best he can, though he leaves it to our maid whenever possible." With a single arm—the other lost to a war injury—there was only so much Father could do. He wouldn't join her on deck, though. There were too many eyes to see his lack.

As if reading her thoughts, Lieutenant Saunders bowed his head. "I am sorry the crew has not been kind to him. They're a superstitious lot. They've not been unkind to you, have they? A woman on deck isn't seen as a favorable sign."

Something Verity learned quite well early on in the voyage. "They leave me be."

Well, they did now. After Lieutenant Saunders and the captain had lectured them soundly about treating a paying passenger with proper respect. They still pressed their luck whenever they thought they could get away with it.

There was a reason the lieutenant often found his way to her when she was on deck.

She shouldn't love it as much as she did.

Verity cleared her throat. "Tell me again about India."

"Again?" Lieutenant Saunders chuckled. "I've told you at least a dozen times over."

He could tell her a thousand times more, and she would never grow tired of it. "If it's to be my home, I must know as much as I can. Please?"

Lieutenant Saunders clasped his hands together and closed his eyes, as if imagining himself in that foreign land. "India is far different than anything you've ever known. The air is thick with spices, heavy with heat, and wildly exotic."

He painted a vivid picture of her future home, weaving tale after tale in his deep, smooth voice. Verity closed her eyes as he spoke, trying to imagine everything he described. Some things were easier than others, as she had seen paintings and drawings of elephants and flowers and other flora and fauna. Others she could only gather the vaguest images.

"And my future husband?"

Verity wished the words away as soon as she spoke them. Her arranged marriage was a topic they avoided, though they talked around it often. Father had once mentioned her betrothed's name at a supper they'd shared with the officers only to discover a distant familial connection between the as-of-yet unknown man and Lieutenant Saunders. She had hoped she'd only imagined the crestfallen expression on the lieutenant's face when he learned she was to be married almost as soon as she debarked. Verity scrambled to think of something to say, anything to say to change the subject, but her mind drew a blank.

Lieutenant Saunders straightened and tugged on his jacket—deep blue like the deepest depths of the ocean. Trimmed in gold and fitted to his figure. There was a reason young women swooned at the sight of a naval man. "I've only met the man once. Though he seemed like a nice enough chap."

Nice enough. That was all she could ever get from anyone. No one wanted to talk about whether Mr. Garvey was handsome or tall. Or how he preferred his tea. Or if he was kind and generous and would overlook Verity's eccentricities or Father's missing arm. Or if he would actually listen to what Verity had to say as so many others refused to do.

Instead of attending balls and sipping tea with eligible young ladies on the hunt for a mate, she was now on a ship to India, along with other misses who had failed to catch husbands during their London seasons. Rejects, all of them. Along with the hundreds of convicts sailing in the belly of the ship, far below her feet—both men and women, being transported to distant shores.

They were the ones who didn't fit in. Who didn't belong.

England had decided they weren't welcome any longer.

Verity flinched. That wasn't entirely accurate. Father had decided that after Verity's third season without her receiving even an offer to ride in the park, it was better to seek for Verity's husband elsewhere. Somewhere far from the prying eyes of a judgmental society.

She would have preferred to choose her husband herself, but options were becoming more and more limited, and Mother's woebegone weeping had worn on them all. Even now, confined to her bunk with a weak stomach, Mother bemoaned their fate to any who would listen.

So be it. When Verity was wed, she would never hide herself away like Mother often did. She would not complain about the smallest stomach twinge or press the back of her hand to her forehead as if she was about to faint.

Verity would live. A married woman had more leeway to act as she pleased than an unmarried miss. Living in India would grant her some freedoms she wouldn't find anywhere else. Even if her intended was a bloated whale with more pockmarks than sense, she would find happiness. She knew it.

She turned to the lieutenant. An errant breeze caught a strand of her hair and whipped it into her mouth as she opened it to speak. She spat it out, but not quick enough to prevent the sea salt that had coated her hair from touching her tongue. She coughed, trying to dispel the foul taste.

Lieutenant Saunders gave her a knowing glance, one that spoke of suppressed mirth. "You could put your bonnet on, you know. Or go below with the rest."

Below deck where the other ladies pretended the dining room

was a drawing room in London, speaking of trivial matters while embroidering handkerchiefs and linens to prepare for their married lives.

Verity hated embroidery. And gossip. And everything else London society enjoyed. Like her name implied, she trusted only in the truth. Truth and integrity held value beyond compare. If one was to be the truest to their own person, they had to live their own truth rather than stuff it away where it would never see the light of day.

A shout from the front of the ship—the bow?—brought Verity's attention back to where she was. The proper terminology for the ship baffled her at times. None of it made sense. Bow, stern, jig . . . It was almost like a foreign language, though she would gladly learn it all if it kept her from the prison of her cabin below.

"Storm abrewing!"

Storm? The sky had been clear and blue only minutes before. Lieutenant Saunders gave her one last glance before he rushed off to where the captain stood near the bow.

Verity looked to where the increasingly anxious men pointed. A towering bank of angry black and gray clouds barreled toward the ship. Almost as if the sea knew when she spied the storm, the waves increased, and the ship bucked, nearly knocking Verity off her feet. Her grasp on her bonnet failed, and it flew off over the white-capped waves, tumbling upon the winds. Rain fell, lightly at first, but soon it was thick, sodden drops that splashed as they hit.

She grabbed the railing and held tight. Someone yelled at her to go below deck, but fear kept her grip ironclad. The swells rose higher and higher until Verity was certain the ship would take flight and dash itself to pieces in the raging water below. Water poured from the sky, drenching everything. The wooden deck grew more and more slick until Verity's precarious perch threatened to give way.

She was going to be thrown overboard. Her life would end before she saw the dinner-plate-sized blossoms or touch an elephant's trunk. She would never experience anything from the lieutenant's tales. She would never be free.

In a moment of relative calm, she readjusted her grip and wrapped her arms around the most secure-looking bit of railing.

Despite her heart racing and the blood pumping through her veins, Verity could not regret her place here on deck. Not when she could see what they faced.

The rain let up enough for Verity to peer ahead past the front of the ship to the roiling seas. Men scrambled about, shouting orders and responses Verity could barely hear. If she wasn't so exhilarated and terrified, she would have blushed at some of the language the sailors used. Some of the phrases she could only guess at their meaning.

A sea bird dove through the winds and whipped past Verity toward the bow. It twisted and turned with each gust like a dancer upon the storm's blustery stage. It flew toward the deepest, darkest part of the storm, a dark circle of nothingness that loomed ahead. The bird's white plumage contrasted sharply against the black void that swirled in the sky, a void that rose higher than the ship's tallest mast and spanned nearly as wide.

The bird gave the ominous darkness no heed as it continued its dance. Up, then swooping down, then back and forth.

And then it vanished.

Verity stared at the spot where it disappeared, heedless of the rain and sea water plastering her hair to her face. She hadn't seen the bird fall to the waves, she was certain. Yet it was nowhere to be seen. Had the storm . . . eaten the bird?

She cried out as the ship fell down the slope of a particularly large wave. Her stomach roiled as hard as the ocean, threatening to cast up her accounts. She felt as ill as Mama claimed to be. Worse, if that was even possible.

She was going to die here. Eaten by the storm just as the bird had been. Eaten before she was wed to a stranger whom everyone deemed merely "nice."

Perhaps she preferred to be eaten.

The dark, swirling circle neared with each passing wave. Closer and closer. Verity watched the crewmen to gauge their reactions. Lieutenant Saunders had disappeared, lost in the scramble of men in striped pants and checkered shirts. The captain seemed to be arguing with another uniformed man. All scuttled about the ship, almost as if part of a choreographed dance—part madness, part fluidity.

Yet no one panicked. Surely this wasn't normal. This couldn't be a typical storm. Even as she held on for dear life, eyes wide and breath catching, no one else seemed to see the impending danger.

Verity wanted to scream a warning, but words escaped her.

What was that thing? What would she say? Shouldn't someone be tightening something? Or cutting something? Or steering the ship in another direction, away from what was certain death?

If she knew how to do any of it, she would. If only to save those below. There were men, women, and children who would taste the bottom of the ocean this day. Hundreds of souls. Lost.

Without tearing her gaze away from the monstrous void that grew larger with each passing moment, Verity uttered a prayer. What she prayed for, she could not say. Only that every ounce of her being went into those words. If there was a God, and if that God cared one jot for their lives, they would be saved. She would even marry her bloated whale if it meant saving everyone on board.

The bow of the ship lifted with the next wave. As it descended again, the figurehead slipped into the darkness. The next wave pushed the ship farther in.

Yet no one screamed in fear. No one sobbed in terror. No one leaped over the side to escape their fate.

No one seemed to pay the void any attention at all.

Why couldn't they see?

As Verity watched, frozen and unable to so much as breathe, the void swallowed the ship as a snake swallowed its prey, a yard at a time. Time itself seemed to slow. Verity tried to scramble back, away from the oncoming onslaught of midnight death, but the slick deck prevented any progression. Before the darkness took her, she squeezed her eyes shut and ducked her head, all courage failing her. She sucked in a breath, her first in forever, though how that would help, she didn't know.

A light tingle touched the tip of her head and spread to her extremities. It felt like a shroud of death.

The winds abruptly died, as did the rocking of the ship. An eerie serenity as opposite the storm as it could possibly be.

Stillness.

Calm.

Was this what death felt like? Rain and sea water still clung to her skin, hair, and clothing. Verity shivered but didn't dare open her eyes. She was dead. She knew it. Had she ascended to heaven, or had her wicked ways condemned her to an eternity of hellfire and torment as the vicar had always claimed?

Did she have to find out? She had to open her eyes eventually. She couldn't stay here with her eyes squeezed shut, clinging onto the railing as if the storm still raged.

Or could she?

Cries of amazement filled the air—a sharp contrast to the shrieks of pain and horror she'd expected. That boded well. Surely the men would be in agony if hell had been their final destination.

"What the blazes?"

The voice was practically in Verity's ear, as if someone had stepped to her side at the ship's rail. It wasn't the lieutenant. This man's voice was more gravelly and coarse.

Verity pried one eye open, then the other. She peered over the railing toward the sea.

Or, rather, where the sea should have been.

Instead of the endless horizon of an open ocean, blue-hazed hills and a mountain of ice rose in the distance. Verity looked to the other side of the ship only to see another shoreline, this one lower and more even. Large creatures that looked like hairy elephants stared at the ship, then moved as one away with slow, lumbering gaits.

While Verity was no expert in the art of sailing, she did know that a ship in the middle of the ocean should not find itself suddenly surrounded by land on all sides. Not even after traversing a storm as wild and chaotic as the one they'd survived.

A storm that was nowhere to be seen.

"What the—"

"You said that already." Verity couldn't take her eyes off the shoreline, not even to berate the spellbound sailor. This couldn't be India. Not with the cliffs of ice and snow. Besides, they still had weeks yet to go on their journey. It couldn't be a French port. England was at war with France. The crew would have given their shores a wide berth. Could this be the Spanish coast? Had they entered an inlet somewhere?

"I'll say it again until my eyes stop showing me falsehoods." The crewman shielded his eyes and leaned over the railing.

Not France or Spain then. This crew had seen both shores multiple times. Verity looked to the crewman, hoping to glean some understanding from him, but he appeared to be as lost as she felt. He stared toward the ice cliffs, unblinking and jaw agape.

His astonishment didn't inspire confidence. If such a widely traveled man could not believe what he was seeing, things were strange indeed. Verity tried to catch the eye of another sailor or even the captain to regain a semblance of peace or security, but they all stared toward the land.

"Where are we?" Verity whispered. She was now convinced

something had gone very very awry. God or the devil or some dark magic was at work, and none of it good.

A chill wind blew, prickling her wet skin. She brushed the excess water from her arms and hugged herself in an effort to ward off the cold. It hadn't been this cold before the storm. Chilly, yes. Not bitter cold as it now was. Nor should winter's chill occur at the end of summer. She huffed, only to see the puffs of breath billow before her.

The crewman placed his hands on his head and muttered a few words Verity knew should put the blush to her cheeks. If she didn't agree with his sentiments, she very well would have flushed as red as a rose.

"Language." It was the only thing Verity could think to say. What else should one say when they were mysteriously transported from the only world they'd ever known?

The crewman frowned and gave himself a little shake as if he'd only just realized she was there. A shake and a scowl, accompanied by a small growl Verity would not have heard if they'd still been upon the ocean. "Apologies, miss. I will guard my tongue more closely."

A lie if she ever heard one. She wished these men would simply speak the truth. She was experienced enough in the world to take it.

The crewman turned to her. Whatever else he was about to say died on his tongue as their eyes met.

Time stopped.

Something tugged at Verity's soul, some invisible cord that she could only feel but not describe. It unloosed something.

Then something . . . clicked.

The crewman's eyes darkened, just as the storm had darkened the sky. A malicious grin spread across his face, and he dropped his hands to his sides. There was a predatory gleam there, one Verity's sheltered life had kept from her. She inched farther away, seeking for someone to notice, to save her.

The crewman looked about him, his grin widening when he too noticed the distraction about them. No one was paying them any mind whatsoever.

He licked his lips, his gaze traveling the length of Verity's body. She shuddered, wishing she could scrub the sensation of being evaluated from her skin. Never before had she felt so dirty, so foul.

She stepped back, but he matched her movement, coming ever closer.

Then, he lunged.

Like a rabbit fleeing a fox, Verity leapt away, scrabbling for purchase upon the wet boards beneath her feet. She slipped. Then fell. She pushed backward, desperately trying to put some distance between them.

Still he advanced.

Before his hands came into contact with her dress, Verity kicked toward his face, feeling a satisfying and sickening crunch beneath her foot.

The crewman cried in pain and grabbed at his now bloodied face.

Lieutenant Saunders rushed forward, determination in his stride. He had protected her from the worst of the worst upon this ship. Sheltered her, befriended her, and gave her hope. Help had come at last. Verity reached for him, desperate for his aid, grateful for a savior, practically begging for relief.

Their eyes met . . . and time stopped once again.

As the lieutenant's expression shifted, Verity gasped. Where there had once been kindness, there was now something else. Something that struck fear in the depths of Verity's soul. An anger. Raw and savage. He turned that anger not on her, but on the man who attacked her, who continued to advance on her.

She screamed.

And the eyes of every man on deck turned toward her.

Time stopped once more.

CHAPTER 1

THREE HUNDRED YEARS LATER

LILLIA PENNYWORTH, HIGH LADY OF the Little Realm and Truthtaker to the Lady Regent, was late. Terribly late. She'd taken a slight detour on her way here to purchase a sweet roll from her favorite baker's cart and to inquire after his wife, who had recently had her first baby. Their conversation had run longer than she'd expected. At four and twenty, she should know better than to trust her inner clock.

Though, if she was completely honest, she would rather be among the common people who had enough troubles of their own to worry about her lack. Or her fallen state. She felt she belonged with them more than with those of her same status.

Pity that.

She stepped from the muddy street onto the stone pavers of the palace courtyard, grateful to no longer have to navigate puddles and animal droppings. If only they would finish cobbling the roads instead of refinishing the hull of the *Atlantia* again, perhaps Lillia could have gotten here even faster. Society may have come a long way since the Arrival, but it was only in the last decade that the last of the animal hide roofs in New London had been replaced by slate shingles.

As Lillia hurried through the courtyard, she kept her head low and clutched her pocketbook close to her chest, trying to keep from drawing any eyes to herself. It was hard enough to remain undetected as it was, thanks to the blinders on her face marking her as Gifted and the light blue and white uniform she wore as a Truthtaker. Even her layered cloak was marked with the Guild's insignia. There were eyes everywhere. Gossip to share. Secrets to ferret out. And she was often the target of such things. Her every move documented and analyzed by those who believed themselves better than her. Lillia ducked her head and kept moving, determined to arrive as close to on time as she could manage. With as little notice drawn as possible.

However, an increasingly loud conversation between a guard and a particularly insistent man caught her ear. She slowed ever so slightly.

"I must see the Lady Regent," the man was saying. This wasn't the first time Lillia had seen him in the vicinity. He dressed as the dye traders did, primarily in furs and skins, though his clothing wasn't nearly as colorful. An explorer perhaps? Or a hunter? He flung his hand toward the courtyard entrance. "Colonization to the south is the only chance we have to evolve as a society! We are penned in here like animals, while those beasts prowl the fences, waiting for them to fail. We must establish a colony we can truly protect. A place we build, grow, and thrive."

Not a Preservationist then. Preservationists sought the Lost Passage that brought their ancestors here, not new lands to settle.

The guard shrugged half-heartedly, her round cheeks rising and falling with her shoulders. She wasn't Gifted, based on her lack of blinders. Either that, or she tested so weak in her gift, she didn't need any protective eyewear. Lillia suspected it was the former. Many women who grew up in the Academy of the Gifted took on roles to keep them close to their childhood home, even if they weren't granted a gift.

"Take your Novationist propaganda somewhere else." The guard gave a long, drawn out sigh. "The Lady Regent has no time for it." She sniffed and rubbed her mittened hand across her pinked nose and turned her gaze elsewhere.

The would-be colonist clenched his jaw. His voice grew steely and even. "But having those resources more readily available could . . ."

The rest of that particular conversation was lost to Lillia as she rounded a corner and slipped through the double doors that gained her entrance into the Guild's headquarters. It was the fastest path to the courtroom, though it would force her to pass other Gifted. Most days, she avoided such a route, but time was not on her side.

She would have preferred to eavesdrop on the argument in the courtyard. The constant battle between Novationists and Preservationists had become more heated as of late. Novationists favored innovation and progression, while Preservationists leaned more toward traditional beliefs and seeking a way back to Mother England. Both had valid arguments. They also had very strong, and sometimes loud, opinions. Their continual bickering often gave Lillia a headache, particularly when nothing seemed to ever be resolved.

This new cry for colonization was intriguing, though. She would have to ask around to find out more.

Lillia stepped to the courtroom door, only slightly out of breath. She firmed up her shoulders, trying to work up the courage to face what waited for her on the other side.

Conducting this trial was her duty, her Soulmaker-given responsibility, and she was expected to take it seriously. If she hadn't spent so much time talking with the baker's wife, she could have taken the time to center her thoughts in one of the common rooms before approaching the courtroom. She could have reviewed the notes she carried in her pocketbook rather than rely upon her memory of her initial reading of the case.

She could have braced herself for being stared at. Again.

On display for all to gawk at.

It was humiliating.

She touched her blinders—indigo-tinted spectacles with side shielding to prevent accidental Revealing—to ensure they were firmly in place. She must have waited in front of the courtroom door too long. The Soulseer Guild guard, clad in an amber uniform trimmed in red, gave her a long, speculative look, her gaze lingering on Lillia's left hand.

Or rather, where Lillia's left hand would have been if she'd been born with one. Normally, Lillia was better able to hide her lack, but she had rushed through getting ready this morning and hadn't thoroughly tightened the laces that fastened her false hand to the leather shoulder brace she wore under her clothing for that purpose. The false hand holding Lillia's pocketbook in place against her chest hung slightly askew at an unnatural angle, drawing undue attention to it. She'd have to be careful not to dislodge the prosthetic lest it loosen entirely and fall. The false hand would not be easy to replace should it break, particularly on Lillia's limited funds.

Mama had ensured it was crafted from the finest ivory available. It wasn't the most practical material, but Mama had insisted on quality. Appearances mattered, even if the hand was normally gloved. For the price, Lillia would have preferred a prosthetic with articulating fingers. She'd seen one like that once, though it was only a partial hand to make up for three missing fingers. The man who wore it had patiently answered her endless questions. In the end, though, the price was too dear for her slim pocketbook.

And what would she tell Mama, who had spent nearly a month's allowance on the ivory one Lillia now endured?

She pulled at the hand to straighten it. The laces were of finest wool from the undercoat of a muskox. Soft against Lillia's skin, but not terribly sturdy. She'd had to replace them frequently to prevent them from fraying. They were yet another thing Lillia didn't feel she could change. Mama would notice for certain, even if leather or a stronger twine would be more durable. The risk was too great.

Once the trial was over, she would find a quiet corner where she wouldn't be disturbed to secure the hand more firmly. For now, she would manage as best she could.

"Name?"

The disdain in the Soulseer guard's expression was not new. It wasn't the first time one of Lillia's supposed "sisters in the gift" thought poorly of her. Nor would it be the last. This Soulseer was too old to have been in the Academy with Lillia, but rumors of the one-handed Truthtaker who gained her gift too early still ran rampant throughout the community.

Lillia cleared her throat. "I am the High Lady Lillia Agathina Constance Faith Pennyworth, Truthtaker to her Majesty, the Lady Regent." Lillia tried not to allow the embarrassment at having such a pompous name bleed through into her voice. Though now fallen in grace, Mama had once held high hopes for both herself and Lillia and had named her only daughter accordingly, despite Lillia's missing hand. Or perhaps because of it.

Lillia gripped her split overskirt tight enough to wrinkle the fabric. She was an imposter. A fraud. She knew it. The guard knew it. Anyone watching must have known it. Lillia would be denied entry and sent to work the southern farms where the rest of society's rejects were hidden away.

She deserved as much.

The Soulseer guard, low in both rank and ability, wasn't powerful enough to fully See a fellow Gifted's soul, or she wouldn't be standing guard at the courtroom chambers. It didn't matter. One didn't need to have such a gift to see through Lillia's facade. Lillia would be turned away for certain. Shamed and rejected.

The guard lifted a single brow. She sized Lillia up once more before silently opening the door and allowing her entrance. Lillia slipped through, flinching as the door shut firmly behind her. She'd passed muster yet again. Yet it didn't feel like a victory. More like a sentence.

How long had it been since she'd conducted a trial? Weeks? Months? She couldn't recall. Thank the Soulmaker, serious crime was not a daily affair.

The other Gifted were already in place, a testament to how late Lillia was. Lillia nodded her apology and stepped to the podium, feeling heat rush to her cheeks. They were judging her, she knew. Her tardiness was yet another strike against her.

She paused to assess who was participating in today's trial.

Two of the Soulseers were older, closer to Mama's age, and well-known to Lillia—Lady Shelley and Lady Madeleine. They were the Visual and Temporal Soulseers, respectively. She'd conducted trials with them before. While they conducted themselves with decorum, they had never been overtly kind or friendly with her. Once the trial was over, they would escape as quickly as possible as they had always done. Likely to avoid having a conversation with Lillia. She didn't blame them. She wouldn't want to associate with someone as tainted as she was either.

The Aural Soulseer was new, though. Fresh from the Academy and newly Gifted. Lillia strained to remember the girl's name. Alice? Annabelle? She was fairly certain it began with an *A*.

Whatever the name, the girl obviously knew who Lillia was. Her lips quirked, and she leaned to whisper to Lady Shelley, who sat next to her. The older woman glanced toward Lillia and nodded. The girl's expression darkened, and she openly scowled. There would be no friendship from that quarter.

If Lillia knew there were no spectators behind the tinted glass of the observation room, she would have allowed the prickling of her eyes to evolve into actual tears, to make the women see how their whisperings affected her. If they knew, would they still say and do the same things?

As Truthtaker, however, she had to maintain decorum. No one would take seriously a Gifted who burst into tears on the courtroom floor, no matter how powerful in her gift she may be. Besides, she knew that even if they were alone, she still wouldn't allow the tears to fall. Tears were a sign of weakness to these women. She could not cry. Not where anyone could see.

Lillia checked the clock above the observation window. Three minutes to eight. Three minutes to compose herself and prepare her mind for what was to come.

Rather than read through her notes, like she should have done, she took time to study the prisoner. The accused men at each trial intrigued her. Each so different from the rest, yet all had been accused of horrific things.

What had brought them so low they felt the need to resort to violence or other heinous misdeeds? Their people had come a long way from the days of the Arrival where all men were considered evil based on the actions of a few. Yet these men and their criminal actions kept those memories alive in the hive mind of society. Why?

This man, whose life would shortly be decided, sat in a sole chair in the center of the room, his arms and legs shackled with strong chains bolted to the floor. The security measures seemed excessive now, but Lillia was grateful for their presence. She knew very well what could happen after a Revealing.

The man's breathing was raspy, audible even from where she stood several feet away. She could make out his features clearly, thanks to the light streaming in the high windows. Lanterns lit up what the windows didn't. The white walls, the charcoal gray stone floors, the dark woods, the tinted window to the observation room next door. It felt stark and sterile. A blank canvas suitable for deciding this man's future. What occurred within these walls would determine his life's course.

Lillia took in the man's torn and stained shirt, open at the collar. His trousers were equally rumpled and stained. He wore no shoes or belt. Nothing that could be construed as a weapon, as much for his safety as for hers.

Despite the chill in the air, a trickle of sweat hung at his brow. He must have fought being chained. Many did.

The minute hand on the clock struck the hour.

Eight o'clock. Time to begin.

Lillia cleared her throat, and all eyes were upon her. Suddenly, it felt as if she was the one on trial instead.

"Mister Gregory Phillips," she said in a voice that held the slightest quiver, "you are accused of theft, malicious intent of bodily harm, and the resulting death of an innocent man. How do you plead?" Thankfully, she could read most of her part. If she had to rely upon her memory, she would have been sent to the farms long ago.

No. She was too strong for that and would be, even when her vision began to fade. She would have been placed in isolation until her gift claimed the last of her sight. It was the only fate allotted to a Truthtaker who was no longer of use.

Mr. Phillips licked his lips. His eyes darted toward the darkened glass of the observation room, then to the other Gifted seated on the opposite side of the room.

"I didn't do it." His voice sounded harsh and rough. It grated on Lillia's ears. She tried to keep her discomfort from showing in her expression. Her efforts must have failed as Lady Shelley gave her a pointed look before giving a small shake of her head.

A chastisement. And not a subtle one either. The Aural snorted softly and smiled to herself.

Lillia fumbled with the pages in front of her. The words refused to settle so she could read them. She was a fraud. An imposter. And everyone here could see why. She used her false hand to hold the papers in place as she thumbed through them. The weight of the ivory was good for something, at least.

When she found the page she was searching for, she tugged it out and set it on the stand where she could see it. Everyone watched her expectantly.

She was failing. Again.

Lillia touched her brow. Not enough perspiration to trickle into her eyes. A small blessing, but a blessing, nonetheless. "I have the testimonies of three witnesses. These statements have been verified by Soulseers, who were present when said testimonies were given. I shall read them for the Guild of the Gifted and for those who have chosen to observe."

Thankfully, her voice held strong as she read the words. According to the witness reports, the accused had attacked another man, intent to rob him of his money. The victim had been killed in the process. Witnesses placed the accused at the scene of the crime. One even called the accused by name.

Mr. Phillips scowled as Lillia spoke, no remorse in his expression. He slouched in his seat, clutching the armrests of his chair. Each time he shifted, the chains holding him in place clinked and clanked against each other.

Lillia finished reading the testimonies, and there was another awkward pause, one she was to fill with her next part. She fumbled through the pages again to find her script. If she had been on time, she could have arranged them how she pleased to make this process go more smoothly. Each second she delayed was another strike against her.

Those strikes, though imagined, felt heavier and heavier with each thudding beat of her heart.

She cleared her throat again. It was a habit she truly did need to break. "I ask that the Aural Soulseer now approach the accused. See and speak truly."

The young Aural rose with grace and poise and glided across

the room. She gave Lillia the slightest curtsy, barely enough to qualify as such, before facing the accused.

"Mister Phillips," the girl asked in a youthful voice that seemed better suited for a classroom, "are you guilty of the crimes of which you are accused? How do you plead?"

"Not guilty, ya twit." He glared at her. "How a child such as yourself dares to be let off your mother's apron strings, I do not know."

The Aural gave a high-pitched squeak. She glanced back at the more senior Soulseers, who gave her encouraging nods. She pursed her lips and took a deep breath. "Thank you, Mister Phillips." Her tone took a condescending quality to it as she addressed Lillia. "I See darkness about him, Truthtaker. It swirls and changes, indicating he is speaking falsely."

She curtsied—again as shallow as possible without being disrespectful—and made her way back to her seat, clasping hands with Lady Shelley.

Lillia noted the young girl's vision in her report, ignoring the near slight. She was used to far worse than what the girl could dole out. "I ask that the Visual Soulseer now approach the accused. See and speak truly." She set down her pen and gave Lady Shelley her full attention.

This was the Soulseer gift that intrigued Lillia the most. A Visual Soulseer could See a miniature version of the person whose soul they Saw. The actions of that avatar could be more readily interpreted than the vague colors of an aura. Mama was a Visual, though she rarely shared what she Saw with anyone anymore. Nor did she wear her blinders unless her headaches were too bad to go without.

Lady Shelley gave Lillia the proper respects before speaking to the accused. She repeated the same words the Aural had spoken, but with a more sincere inflection. "Mister Phillips, are you guilty of the crimes of which you are accused? How do you plead?"

The accused shook his head and lifted his lip in a sneer. "As if you care. You've already determined my guilt. Not guilty."

His accusation didn't seem to ruffle Lady Shelley's composure. She merely watched him, tilting her head slightly. "Truthtaker," she said after a moment, "I See his avatar clutching a coin purse to his chest. His hands are stained with blood. He tries to wash the blood away, but it remains. I believe him to speak falsely."

She gave one last searching look to the accused, then curtsied to Lillia and returned to her seat.

Things were finally moving along smoothly. For that, Lillia was incredibly grateful. As long as the trial concluded in a satisfying manner, her reputation would not suffer. Much.

She cleared her throat, reprimanding herself silently. "I ask that the Temporal Soulseer now approach the accused. See and speak truly."

As Lady Madeleine gave her respects and approached the accused, Lillia noted Lady Shelley's remarks. She wasn't nearly as invested in what the Temporal Soulseer had to say. Temporals were notoriously inaccurate. Their visions spoke either of the past or the future, but rarely did they know which.

"Mister Phillips, are you guilty of the crimes of which you are accused? How do you plead?"

The accused slumped in his seat and raised a shackled hand. "How many times will ye ask me the same thing, witches? I am not guilty. I didn't do it. Release me and leave me be." He sounded weary. Lillia understood that feeling all too well. He didn't have much longer. Then, he would earn his rest, whether guilty or not.

Lady Madeleine, whose strength and seniority was well known despite her variable gift, did not hesitate to speak. She held her head high, as did one who held favor with the Lady Regent. "Truthtaker, I See that this man has attacked and will attack again. Or he has attacked more than once. Or will attack more than once if freed. He has no remorse. He speaks falsely."

Lillia barely had time to thank her before Lady Madeleine swept back to her seat. The consensus of the three Soulseers was that the man was guilty. However, testimony of the Soulseers was not enough to sway a verdict. There had to be sufficient outside evidence to support their visions, which they had in the witness statements.

That was the last page. The one Lillia now had to wrestle from the bottom of the stack. Her false hand shifted as she tugged on the page, and several papers fluttered to the ground. Lillia dropped to her knee to retrieve the pages. Curse her tardiness and the resulting rush this morning! Nothing was going as it should.

The tittering of the Aural could not be of Lillia's imagination. Or the murmuring of the observers behind the glass. Or the pounding of her heart thrumming in her ears.

She arranged the pages upon the podium, then squeezed her eyes shut long enough to plead the Soulmaker for strength. When she opened her eyes again, the words on the page remained steady enough for her to read clearly.

"Along with testimony from both witnesses and Soulseers alike, the accused was discovered with a coin purse identified as belonging to the victim."

"I found that purse on the ground." The accused directed his voice toward the viewing windows. "On the ground, right there on the road." He gestured to the floor, the chains on his wrists clinking. "And if it's on the ground, it's fair game."

Lillia ignored the interruption. "My fellow Gifted," she said, allowing her gaze to encompass all three Soulseers and the currently silent Witwraith, "I ask that you deliver your verdict."

Each of the Soulseers stood, one at a time, and declared a single word—guilty.

Lillia made a note of the individual votes. Her hand shook as she wrote. Thankfully, her notation remained legible. She would hate to have to rewrite it. Every second she remained here was another second she was under close scrutiny. Who knew who had decided to observe this trial? She couldn't make out faces through the observation window. What if it was the Lady Regent herself, come to decide if her Truthtaker was indeed worthy of the role?

She looked to the Witwraith.

Lady Hannah.

She, of all the Gifted here, likely understood Lillia the most. Witwraiths were the only Gifted more shunned and reviled than Lillia. For good reason too. They were the final blow, the ultimate reckoning. No man's soul survived a meeting with a Witwraith's gaze.

Lady Hannah sniffed. She cocked her head to the side, then looked down the row of Gifted, then to Lillia, then to the observation glass. Her wild hair swayed back and forth, almost as if it had a life of its own. She shrugged. "Yeah, I figure he's guilty too."

Four guilty votes. If it hadn't been unanimous, it would have fallen on Lillia to provide her vote as well.

With the verdict recorded and the Gifted testimony complete, it was now Lillia's turn. This was the part she hated the most. Every time she Revealed a man, it reminded her of the first time. The Revealing that tore apart her family and marked her as a pariah. Memories of those early days surged to the front of her mind, but she tamped them down firmly. Now was not the time for self-pity.

She cleared her throat and spoke clearly enough to be heard through the vents that connected the courtroom to the observation room.

"Mister Phillips, you have been charged with theft and manslaughter. Witness statements have been read and evidence provided that supports that accusation. You have been found guilty by three Gifted who have seen into your soul. Confess now or be made to confess."

Fear now entered into the eyes of the accused. He pulled against his chains, not for the first time if the lesions on his wrists were any indication. The fear was soon replaced by resolve. Then hate. He sneered.

"Found guilty?" He spoke with disgust and loathing. "There's no real proof I done the deed. Just the words of three witches who should be burned at the stake." He spat on the floor. "This isn't justice. I demand a fair trial! Where are the men who should decide my fate?"

The accused—Lillia could no longer bring herself to think of his name, to humanize him—launched into a Conservationist diatribe about the evils of the Gifted, how they were witches and devils in disguise, and how their so-called Gifts were a form of brainwashing. How the entire trial was a manipulation of justice, and how the ways of the old world were superior, where men ruled over women as God intended.

Lillia had heard it all before. Here in this very courtroom, in fact. A year ago, Conservationist extremists had stormed a Novationist urban planning session, demanding to have a voice. While most Conservationists had remained civil, some had demanded the Novationists cease city improvements and use the funding available to discover a way home to Mother England. Never mind that none had seen those shores in over three hundred years. Find the Lost Passage, they'd insisted. Return home to England and the patriarchal society that had worked well enough for hundreds of years. Do away with the witches and their brainwashing "magicks."

The old ways were best, they'd said. Innovation and magic had no place in their society.

The Novationists who had been attacked claimed the only way forward was through progress. This was their home now, and they had to make the best of it. This land of ice and snow and mammoth beasts had more to offer than a long-forgotten homeland that was more myth than history. They sought to tame the land, to build and grow and expand. Colonization was the key to survival, they claimed. The old ways were dead, better off forgotten. And any who believed otherwise were better off forgotten as well.

Men should be controlled, they believed. Controlled and made subservient as women had been for centuries. They could not be trusted, not with the existence of abilities that only affected those of the male persuasion. Therefore, they should not lead.

Two opposing groups. Two extreme viewpoints. Tempers had flared. Fists had flown.

The resulting chaos from the riot had been brutal. Six dead, a dozen more injured. The male instigators from both parties had sat in their own chairs at trial, chained as the man in front of Lillia was. They were accused, questioned, and found guilty.

Then Revealed and Snatched.

As this man would be.

The women were sent to labor in the mining fields under close supervision of both Gifted and non-Gifted guards. They now worked in chains to dig and reinforce the trenches that kept predators from the Southern Road. The trade route between the farms and the city could not be disrupted.

When the accused's rant slowed to a stop, Lillia held up her hand. She stepped from behind the podium and approached the accused, stopping out of his reach.

"You then deny you are guilty of these crimes?"

The accused growled. "I'm guilty of nothing, witch. Unless it's the crime of listening to your drivel. Your brainwashing won't work on me. I'm stronger than that."

It was as Lillia feared. This man could not be swayed. He had no remorse. She closed her eyes to draw upon her inner well of strength. "Then, Mister Phillips, if you continue to deny your part in this matter, you must be Revealed."

She opened her eyes to see doubt flicker in the accused's eyes. He looked to the observation window, to his image imperfectly reflected there.

Behind that glass could be anyone. From the lowest layman to the Lady Regent herself. The tint in the glass was the same as in her blinders. Meant to protect those on the other side from accidentally being Revealed as the original men on the *Atlantia* had been during the Arrival.

The thought of someone watching, hidden behind that glass, always unnerved Lillia. Who knew whose eyes took in her every move, tallied her every mistake?

Oh, how she hated this.

But duty prevailed. If she did not do this, she would be placed on trial herself for dereliction of duty. Consequences for a Gifted who did not do as she must were harsh indeed. Mama depended on her. The Lady Regent depended on her. Society depended on her. She could not fail in this task or any other.

Lillia's hand trembled slightly as she touched her blinders. She took a deep breath and closed her eyes before removing the indigo-tinted spectacles. Steeling herself against the emotions that would inevitably surge through her, she blinked her eyes open.

The world around her lost its bluish tint, and she saw it all as it truly was. The white walls were whiter than ever. The flames in the lanterns were more yellow. And the sunlight streaming in was so bright and warm and welcoming. She wanted to do nothing more than to take it all in. This was how she longed to see the world. In full color before her gift stole it all away, as it did to all Truthtakers. Slowly, but surely, she would lose the ability to see these colors. And when all the world was gray and then black, then and only then would she be able to walk among men without her blinders as a blind Truthtaker was no longer a danger to anyone.

How cruel this so-called gift could be.

The scoff of the man in front of her brought her focus back to where it belonged. She sighed, soft enough to not be heard, and turned her gaze to meet his.

He met her gaze with defiance, as if he didn't truly believe anything would happen.

How wrong he was.

As his eyes met hers, time stopped. Her heartbeat slowed. Even the dust particles that danced in the sunlight paused. There was a shift within her mind. A linking of sorts. An awareness of this man. Dark, filthy, putrescent. It writhed and rumbled through her awareness, spoiling anything it touched. Lillia's soul recoiled from it, trying to push it away. With an inner strength formed by years of practice, Lillia shoved the man's filth into the furthest corner of her mind and walled it off to keep the infestation at bay.

She breathed deeply. Slowly. Achingly slowly.

Time resumed with a lurch. It took nearly everything in Lillia to not double over and empty the contents of her stomach upon the floor. This was why she rarely ate breakfast on trial days. This was why she dreaded each and every one.

The accused blinked.

It was as if the world held its breath, awaiting his Revealed self to emerge.

Lillia sensed his intentions before they took shape. She stepped back, false hand pressed to her stomach, both to keep the ivory prosthetic and her stomach's contents in place.

The accused lunged forward, pulling on his chains, practically frothing at the mouth.

"Witch!" he screeched. "I'll kill you! You and all the rest of the devil's spawn!"

Lillia retreated behind the podium, though it would provide little protection if he should break free. Her breathing came erratically, and it was difficult to think clearly. The guard outside the door would not enter unless bidden. It was simply her and the other Gifted here to manage the man.

A hand on her shoulder helped Lillia draw her attention. The Witwraith, Lady Hannah, nodded and jerked her head toward the accused.

"Is it my turn now?"

The Witwraith's approach and subsequent question weren't precisely part of trial protocol, but Lady Hannah—with her wild hair and uncouth manner—had never been conventional. Lillia nodded and gripped the side of the podium to keep from falling over. The anger and irrational passion of the accused raged through Lillia, nearly overwhelming her with its intensity, even from behind the wall in her mind. Every emotion he experienced felt heightened and unrestrained. It beat against the barrier she'd erected, desperate to break through. It was a true revelation of his inner self.

"Please." Lillia could only manage a strained whisper. She needed relief soon. She would not be able to hold him back much longer, not while standing so near to him.

Lady Hannah patted Lillia's shoulder again before marching over to the accused and grabbing his hair. She wrenched his head back to force him to meet her eyes. The unexpected motion startled him into submission. Then, the Witwraith whipped her scarlet blinders from her face and stared at him. He tried to break free, but the small woman was stronger than she appeared.

Lady Hannah began to mutter something under her breath, so low Lillia could not make it out. She'd never been able to hear a Witwraith's spell, nor did she wish to try. Their gift terrified her more than her own.

Lillia placed her blinders back on her face and steadied herself. Thank the Soulmaker the other Gifted were riveted on what was happening before them. The performance gave Lillia the time and relative privacy she needed to compose herself.

The muttering continued for what felt like an eternity, filling the room and weighting the very air. And then . . . silence.

The weight pressing on Lillia's mind and emotions lifted as suddenly as it had come. She sucked in a breath and held tight to her stomach again, which lurched and threatened, though Lillia managed to avoid further embarrassment. As the pressure in her mind released, she released her breath. Slowly, calmly.

She was free.

Yet this freedom felt stained and foul. A shadow of what the accused's presence in her mind once was.

The accused now sat silent, staring at Lady Hannah. He did not move. Nor did he speak.

Lady Hannah released her grip on his hair and studied him closely, gripping his chin to turn his head in one direction, then the other. After a full minute of silence, she gave a weary, yet satisfied nod. "He's Snatched."

Lillia made a note with a quivering hand and fixed her gaze on the three Soulseers. "What say you, Soulseers? Do you concur?" The unnecessary question kept the proceedings moving forward. Lillia clung to that, for it kept her sane.

One by one, the Soulseers vocalized their assent, confirming what Lillia already knew. They could no longer See his soul.

Despite his violent nature, Lillia felt a prick of sadness and guilt. This man was now one of the Snatched—men whose wits were stolen away. He was little more than a mindless servant, only capable of doing what he was told. As with other newly Snatched men, he would need detailed instructions on how to do everything. Walking, eating, performing bodily functions.

There were low-ranking Gifted and men employed to train these Snatched, to prepare them for whatever role they were destined to fulfill. Many Snatched were assigned to the mining fields and farmlands in the south, trained for hard labor. The more adept—and more handsome—were sold as servants to the wealthy and high-ranking members of society. The Lady Regent herself always kept a Snatched at her side. Having a Snatched as a servant provided a level of prestige that those in power often sought. Lillia had no such aspirations.

"I'm done," Lady Hannah announced loudly. She staggered toward the door with nary a look back. She waved toward the newly Snatched man. "Clean up after me, if you will."

The door opened for her, and two trainers hurried in to unlock the chains and provide the Snatched with his first instructions.

Lillia swallowed hard to coat her dry throat with any sort of moisture. Clearing her throat would do little to help. Her voice sounded more hoarse than she would have liked. Mama would see that as a sign of weakness, but it couldn't be helped. "The accused has been Snatched. He will serve his sentence as deemed fit by the Guild of the Gifted. And thus concludes these proceedings."

With that, Lillia stepped away from her podium. The Soulseers filed out of the room, one by one. Not one of them met her eye, nor did any offer assistance. She didn't expect them to. She wasn't worth their time or energy.

Lillia did not remain. Her work was done. It was now time to find a quiet corner to rest and recover.

And cry.

Oh, how she hated trial days.

But such was her role as a Truthtaker.

CHAPTER 2

DAVIN SMILED AS HE RAN his hand across the coarse winter hair of his prize mare's side. Her belly was swollen with foal and, if his calculations were correct, she would birth soon. He hoped. The temperatures were dropping, and the winters here in Lakewood were far colder than at Lake Verity's shores. The original horses brought over on the *Atlantia* could have survived in the freezing temperatures, but their descendants had lost that ability through generations of inbreeding. So-called purebred horses were little more than decoration anymore. Even mules bred from that line failed to have the constitution and hardiness needed for the inland climates so near to the ice sheets. Besides that, mules couldn't reproduce. Nor could the offspring of purebreds and the native horses the original settlers encountered on the scrub-riddled plains.

That is, until now. Serenity was the first of Davin's breeding efforts to not be sterile. It was a miracle in itself. With this foal, a thousand opportunities would open up.

Serenity nickered softly.

"All right." Davin chuckled. He rubbed her nose. "I'll get you a treat. You've earned it, girl."

Sam pulled a carrot from a sack hanging by the open door and handed it over the stall wall to Davin. He went back to mucking out the next stall over without a word, as was his nature. When Sam first joined the staff at Bradford Lodge as a young boy, that silence had bothered Davin. As a kid, Davin had wondered if the new boy had been Snatched, but he'd since accepted it as Sam's way. The quiet companionship was a welcome contrast to the squawking and screeching he dealt with elsewhere. Here in the stables, there was a peace he couldn't find anywhere else. This here was his domain.

Davin fed the carrot to the mare, running his hand over her side once more. The foal she carried had been more active today, a good sign of a healthy constitution. The sire—a native horse caught from the hunting grounds—was a sturdy sort as well. If all went according to plan, this foal would mean great things for Davin. Reliable horses that were more than show were rare. The intense cold of the long winter months made upkeep and care more expensive than many could afford. Most laymen had to rely on oxen to pull their wagons or resort to hand-pulled carts. Davin had even seen a carriage pulled by the bovine beasts. Slow and plodding.

But the foal Serenity now carried could change all of that. Davin had carried on his father's work of carefully breeding horses that could withstand the ice and wind. Their coats more closely resembled those of muskoxen and mammoths with long, coarse hairs over a soft, thick undercoat, thanks to their native horse bloodlines. Davin had even been able to comb out Serenity's underlayer and save it. While it wasn't as fine as that of a muskox, the yarn Sam had spun from it had promise. A woolen fabric made from that yarn could provide much-needed warmth.

"I think we're close, Sam." Davin opened the stall door and

slipped out, closing the door softly behind him so he wouldn't startle Serenity. "This foal may be the best yet."

"She has good bloodlines."

The comment from the otherwise reticent Sam, while unexpected, was welcome. Davin had far too many doubts regarding this venture. Father had started it when he was but a lad. No one had believed it would work, so he had carried on in secret. When he disappeared six years ago, Davin had taken over. Even his mother had no idea what happened in her stables. She rarely stepped foot into the yard, preferring not to soil her slippers or boots. If she saw Davin in his present state—dirt and straw clinging to his pants, mud dried upon his boots—she would have a fit. This was not how the son of "an almost Gifted woman" should act. After all, they had to set an example for the country gentry of the town of Lakewood.

Davin put his gloves back on to fend off the cold. The chill kept coming, stronger each minute. The leaves on the trees had already changed color and were starting to fall. This foal would come none too soon. Father's belief that late-born foals were sturdier and stronger may have been mere supposition, but Davin wasn't going to take any chances. He'd breed all his mares late if it meant getting the results he wanted.

Perhaps that was the key to bypassing the hybrids' sterility. That and the carefully measured mixture of grains and fodder Davin and Sam fed each of the horses each day. The composition was a tightly held secret. Only the two of them knew exactly what went into it.

"Have the stable boys keep watch tonight," Davin told Sam as he brushed bits of straw and dust off his pants. "If she shows signs of foaling, come and get me." He glanced toward the wood stove in the corner of the stonewalled stable. "Have the boys collect some more wood. We may need it."

Serenity would fare fine without the additional heat. She did last winter, which was promising. A newborn foal, though, may not be as lucky. Davin wasn't about to take any chances. If this proved successful, these horses may be the key to his freedom. He could finally buy his own land and live under his own roof without having to bow to his mother's every demand, of which there were many. While Davin wasn't necessarily a Conservationist, he didn't believe that a woman should lead a home when she wasn't qualified to do so.

Quick, short footsteps outside perked Serenity's ears. The mare turned her head toward the door just as Abigail strode into the stable, lifting her shortened full skirts to keep them out of the dirt. The raised hemline revealed the dyed leather breeches she wore underneath. It was a nod to New London fashion, which allowed for a full front split in the skirt that showed the breeches in their entirety. Lakewood sensibilities did not allow for such daring styles as of yet, though many younger women flaunted their under breeches as a new method of flirting. They'd also begun hemming their skirts nearly to mid-calf. Davin may have been old enough to marry, but even at the young age of twenty-five, he found such antics too immature for his taste.

"Hello, brother of mine." Abigail wrinkled her nose, her lip curling with disgust. "Playing with your pets again?" She lazily strolled through the stable, trailing a finger along the low walls.

One of the native horses blew out noisily when she got too close to his stall. Abigail shied away, clenching her skirts tight in her fists. "Infernal beast," she muttered.

Davin shook his head and turned away to hide the smile on his face. He'd warned Abigail several times most native horses weren't as mild mannered as a purebred. Serenity, once again, was the exception. As calm as her name suggested.

Unlike their mother, Abigail knew some of what Davin was doing. He'd never been one to keep secrets from his older sister. Even if he tried, she could ferret out a lie with ease. Abigail's uncanny ability to see right through him meant that he had no choice but to confide in her. Thankfully, she'd been willing to keep his secret, though she didn't fully support him in his endeavors. She didn't know the whole of it, though.

Davin scooped up a handful of grain and held it out for Serenity to take. Her velvety soft lips tickled his palm as she ate the treat from hand. When the grain was gone, Davin ran a hand through her mane and down her nose. "How are you, sister dear?" he said to Abigail. "Back from town already?"

"I am." Abigail peered over the stall wall. "Doctor Thurst has been here and gone. I paid him what little I had in my coin purse, but it wasn't the full amount. Mimi claims he's cured her yet again and insisted on paying him in full, so she gave him that ugly green vase in the entry. The one she claims once belonged to one of the previous Ladies Regent. I think we came out better for it."

"No doubt. Is he paid up then?" Soulmaker help them all if that infernal man insisted on staying for supper again. As part of his so-called payment. For what, Davin couldn't say. There was absolutely nothing wrong with Mimi that a bit of common sense couldn't solve.

"He tried to collect the remainder in the form of a kiss from me." She wrinkled her nose. "He may have been handsome when he was younger, but he's twice my age. And married at that. I've got better prospects."

Dr. Thurst tended to be more familiar with his female patients than was strictly proper, always trying to coerce a hug or kiss from Abigail or Mimi. Davin had even caught him being overly friendly with one of the maids. Since then, Davin made sure to be close by whenever the doctor paid a visit.

"You're certain he's left?" If not, Davin may feel the need to lurk in the entry until the man was gone. Abigail always insisted she could handle the older man on her own, but Davin wasn't sure he believed her. Abigail rarely told their mother of her headaches. Their maternal figure would insist on the doctor making an unnecessary examination.

Abigail waved his concern away. "I watched his cart until it left the driveway. But that's not why I'm here." She pinched her lips together. "Mimi would like to speak with you."

"What is it our mother would like to know?" The moniker was a recent development. Davin struggled to remember to use it instead of calling her "Mother" as he'd always done. Mimi was quick to remind him, particularly in company. She claimed the name made her feel young again.

Abigail wandered the length of the stable, peering over the stall walls in a disinterested fashion. "I suspect she'd like to know when you're planning on paying the dressmaker. And the other shopkeepers. She was denied credit when she tried to order a new muff and cloak. They're demanding payment."

Not for the first time either. Mimi was notorious for spending more money than the estate earned. Their herds of oxen and muskoxen could only provide so much income. It was enough for a modest lifestyle but could not keep up with her relentless efforts to keep up with New London society. Or rather, her imaginings of what New London society was, as she hadn't left Lakewood since Abigail was a babe.

Davin clenched his fists, then released them. He tamped down the first protest that sprang to his lips. And the second. He would give anything to remain out here, caring for Serenity and her unborn foal, rather than face his mother and her deluded insistence that he fix the problems she caused. If she would listen to him and utilize a budget, she wouldn't have to demand he settle their debts each month. However, as the matriarch of their home, she was well within her rights to do whatever she pleased. The law was on her side.

As a man, Davin only had rights if he owned property and had a matriarch in his home to govern the household. And even then, those rights were limited. But they were rights. As long as he walked the line and didn't get into legal trouble serious enough to involve a Truthtaker, he'd be fine.

Thus the broodmare.

This scheme of his would work. He could feel it.

"Tell Mimi I'll be with her shortly." Davin needed to change into something more presentable and brush the bits of straw from his hair. His time in the stable was done for now. Perhaps he'd be able to sneak out later, though. Serenity appreciated his company. And, if he was being completely honest, he appreciated hers as well. She was the only female in his life that didn't demand he be something he wasn't. She accepted him as he was.

Abigail watched him in that strange, searching way of hers. She'd always done that for as long as he could remember. If he didn't know better, he'd believe her to be a Soulseer, but activating those abilities required going through some sort of ritual or ceremony or something. The Guild of the Gifted was rather tight-lipped about that sort of thing, and Mimi refused to talk much about her own failed experience.

She had attended the Academy and gone through the Gifting Ceremony but hadn't received a gift. Shortly thereafter, she'd married Father and left New London to settle in Lakewood. That was the extent of the information she deigned to provide, though she was more than open about her time at the Academy itself. She enjoyed lording the experience over her peers, many of whom had never seen New London, let alone hobnobbed with any of the Gifted.

Why Abigail had not attended the Academy, Davin had never known. The potential ran in their family. On both sides. He'd asked once, but their mother had waved him away, muttering something about not being able to afford to send Abigail to New London. There may have been truth to that claim, yet she was able to purchase an entirely new wardrobe and redecorate her bed chamber at least once a year.

The woman's priorities were skewed, to say the least.

Abigail finally finished her perusal and gave a sharp nod. Her golden curls bounced with the motion. "Very well. But don't be late, little brother." She turned on her heel and strode purposefully back to the house.

Davin watched until she was out of sight, then turned to Sam. "Take care of our girl, won't you? Until I can come back out myself." He trusted Sam more than anyone else in the world. He and Sam worked together with a certain synchronism that only grew from a long-standing relationship. If anyone would care for Serenity the same as Davin would, it was Sam.

Reluctantly, Davin stepped outside, closed the stable door behind him, and trudged to the house to fulfill his role as a dutiful son.

He only looked back to the stables once.

All right, maybe twice.

CHAPTER 3

LILLIA'S HEAD POUNDED AS IT often did after a good cry. She dried her eyes and scrubbed at her face.

New London looked so small from the top of the palace proper. People were like insects, houses and carts like toys.

From where she stood, Lillia could see out over Lake Verity to the ice cliffs that towered over the landscape. The ice sheet that flowed from the pale blue cliffs snaked through the low-lying hills toward the water's edge. It all felt cold. Inhospitable. Yet her people had carved a civilization from this harsh environment. Three hundred years of perseverance and hard work.

And adjusting to a new land, void of people. Void of everything the crew and passengers of the *Atlantia* knew.

She turned and walked to the other side of the building. Up here, she was blessedly alone. Free from the whispers and stares. Lillia could see past the thatched and tile roofs of New London to the timbered wall that kept the people safe from the massive native beasts that roamed the hunting grounds.

She'd walked along that wall once with Papa. Before the accident. He'd described the history of the wall. How it had been built to keep the beasts at bay. How crews had to patrol the walls to mend any damage.

When a hairy trunk had peeked out from over the top, seeking perch on something, she'd peered through the rough tree trunks to see what sort of creature that trunk belonged to.

All she saw was a thick, hairy leg. Then a yellowed ivory tusk.

It was enough to make her shriek and scurry away like a tiny little mouse.

The mammoth beasts rarely pushed past the wall, but they weren't what the walls were meant to keep out.

Where mammoth beasts roamed, so did predators built to take down the gargantuan creatures. It seemed very much like navigating society as a barely accepted outcast.

Rumor had it that after the last breach, the Lady Regent had ordered the mining fields to extend their trenches past New London to provide a more permanent solution to keep the people safe.

Lillia couldn't see any evidence such a project had begun. Not from here. But these things took time to get approved. Time to plan. Time to implement.

And time was now getting away from her. She took a quick assessment of her overall appearance, using a small round mirror she kept in her reticule to ensure her eyes were no longer puffy. The mirrors had been all the rage a few years ago, and Lillia had fallen prey to the ingenious and tempting item.

When she was certain her face would pass muster, she moved on to the rest of her being.

The laces on her false hand had frayed. Oh, dear.

It must have happened while it had hung loose. She'd known she needed to tighten them. Why didn't she take the time to do so?

She knew the answer to that question. If she had stopped to adjust the laces, others would have seen. It would have drawn attention to her lack.

Yet now, she was in real danger of losing that hand until she could replace the laces.

Foolish pride.

Thank the Soulmaker she'd been left alone while she allowed the tears to fall.

Now that the trial was over, Lillia's schedule was her own. She would pick up her messages, respond to correspondence, and prepare her lesson for the Academy students. She'd been asked to speak on the Arrival. It was an easy lesson to prepare.

Like all good Gifted graduates, Lillia could recite the history from memory.

Their ancestors had been on a ship heading from England to India, then on to Australia from there. Nearly four hundred crew members, passengers on their way to India, and criminals being transported to the Australian penal colonies had been on board that day.

A storm arose and—according to Verity Covington, the first Lady Regent and sole woman to be on deck when the storm arose—a great swirling void appeared and swallowed the ship whole. The storm died, and the passengers and crew found themselves in a strange new land, no ocean in sight.

Not only was this new world landlocked, which later prompted the speculation of the Lost Passage, it was colder than Mother England. Massive creatures and unusual beasts roamed the plains and haunted the forests. Cliffs of ice were to the north and open fields to the south. Nothing remained of the world they once knew.

Something happened to the people in that passage, though. Something that changed the very nature of both men and women.

The first Gifted were created.

As one of the first Truthtakers, Verity Covington accidentally

Revealed a dozen men before she realized what was happening. All revealed their true natures that day. Some men attacked both women and each other. Others defended the defenseless, saving the lives and virtue of those they could.

Twenty-three souls lost their lives in the resulting skirmishes.

Fortunately, the only men who had been Revealed had been among the crew members and some of the passengers as the criminals being transported had been separated in the hold by sex. Otherwise, the numbers of Revealed, and likely those killed, would have been much higher.

In the aftermath, those Revealed who had proven themselves to be dangerous had been confined until something could be done with them. The others were watched until they were deemed safe.

The Guild of the Gifted was created soon after the Arrival, even before the first settlement was built. Verity Covington, being the highest-ranking member of society who had been bestowed a gift, led the Guild as they navigated their new reality. They learned how to harness their gifts and how to suppress them to prevent further accidents. They established rules and guidelines.

They even discovered how to bestow the gifts upon new women, though that was a closely guarded secret. Even those who went through the Gifting Ceremony didn't fully understand how it worked. A woman simply walked through an archway blindfolded. If she received a gift, she was given her first set of blinders. If no gift was given, the woman was released from the Academy and the Guild. There was no way to know beforehand if a woman would receive a gift or not, so any potential Gifted were gathered, instructed, and tested. It was all regimented and carefully monitored to prevent any mishaps.

Prevent, not stop altogether, as Lillia was very well aware.

Eventually, as the town of New London grew, the Guild was established as a formal government with the Lady Regent reigning. It was far too easy for a man's mind to be manipulated by one of the Gifted to allow a man to sit in a place of power.

At least, that was the reasoning. The Preservationists and Novationists debated that topic hotly. There were some on both sides who claimed punishing an entire sex for the actions of a few was unjust and unfair. Others advocated to have all men who held a position of power Revealed to confirm their intentions were pure. Still others feared that the Gifted abused their authority simply because they could control a select few of the population.

The politics surrounding the matter left Lillia's head spinning. There were so many opinions, so many policies and proposals. Such things were better left to those whose voices would be heard.

She was not one of those people. Nor would she ever be. As one who had been rejected by the elite and popular, she did not possess a voice others would hear. She would leave the politics to those who more fully understood them.

Her task was merely to present the history of their people to young girls who needed to know where they came from so they could fully understand the gift they may receive. The responsibility was fitting, as she was a direct descendant of Verity Covington herself. Mama was rather proud of that fact.

The lesson practically wrote itself, for which Lillia was grateful. Her head had already started to pound, as it often did after a good cry. It was time to retreat home where she could remove her blinders and her false hand and truly allow herself to be. After today, she needed it.

The only trouble was she had to pass through the courtyard to do it. The moment Lillia pushed through the exterior doors that led to the palace courtyard, she felt her muscles tense. She adjusted her glove over the false hand and tugged her lace-trimmed sleeve down as far as it would go. Her bonnet had a deep rim to help hide her blinders, but those who looked at her straight on would be able to identify her as Gifted. Here, where the public was allowed to roam, she needed to take extra precautions. Men and women alike visited the palace courtyard on matters of business as well as personal errands.

A young woman and man—both in rough-woven and undyed leather clothing that marked them as the working class—passed, giving Lillia a wide berth. They didn't quite hide the curious and possibly fearful glances they gave her. The young woman plucked at the sleeve of her companion, pulling him closer to her side. They picked up their pace and hurried past, not slowing until they turned the corner.

Were they in the observation room during the trial? This trial or any other? Did they recognize her or the insignia she wore on both cloak and bonnet?

If Lillia hadn't been a Truthtaker, would they have gawked at her, stared at her, in the same fashion? The intrusive thoughts rolled about in her brain, nagging and teasing her until she was thoroughly bothered.

She chewed on her bottom lip and stepped forward, setting her destination in mind. She merely needed to make it to the gate without incident. The stares would persist, she knew. They always did. If only everyone was as open-minded as the baker and his wife.

A loud crack drew the attention of everyone in the courtyard, though Lillia barely registered it. The ice cliffs were talking again. At least, that's how Papa used to put it. He'd once traveled up above the cliffs to the lake beyond. The waters stretched so far in each direction he could barely see the far shores. Chunks of ice floated in those deep blue waters, colliding with each other. The ice walls shifted and groaned. All harmless. They'd been doing that since the Arrival, and nothing had ever come from it. Nothing ever would.

Her distracted state placed her right into the hurried path of a passing gentleman. He collided with her, knocking his papers to the ground and her blinders askew. Lillia frantically shoved her blinders back into place. She knew well the consequences if she grew careless. As the man turned toward her, his elbow slammed into her false hand, and the already frayed laces broke. The prosthetic clattered to the ground between them, landing on some of the now scattered papers.

Lillia stared in horror as the man's gaze landed on her gloved false hand. His eyes widened. Then, he glimpsed her blinders, and his eyes widened even farther.

In another time and place, Lillia might have thought him charming and sweet in a scholarly way, with his round face, spectacles, and ink stains on his sleeves. She might have even considered him as a future marriage prospect worth pursuing. Someone who could be constant and sturdy. One who could be a pleasant constant companion. One who wouldn't mind having a blind wife when her Gift ran its course.

Instead of smiling at her in an apologetic manner as she hoped, the man's jaw trembled, though not nearly as much as his hands.

"I'm terribly sorry, Truthmaker. I mean, Truthtaker," he bumbled when his mouth finally seemed able to function. He dropped to his knees and scooped up the papers he'd dropped, taking great care not to disturb Lillia's false hand. As he picked up a page, he sent the hand rocking.

He froze.

Lillia couldn't move. The courtyard walls closed in on her, and the space now felt like a prison. A rag-and-bone man trudged past, pulling his cart of wares, the iron-rimmed wheels clacking against the cobblestone. Servants—both in livery and not—stopped in their onward progression, gathering in small groups and whispering amongst each other. A young girl, wearing breeches and a short split skirt that barely reached mid-thigh, overtly stared from across the courtyard.

The sun bore down upon them, the scant heat pressing

through the fabric of Lillia's cloak, chasing away any chill the early fall air had left behind. Time seemed to slow, and every detail about her came into sharp focus. She could hear the whispers.

"It's Lady Pennyworth."

"She's the Truthtaker who Revealed her own father."

"I heard she tried to put her mother away before stealing the Pennyworth title."

Which of the whispers were truly spoken, and which she imagined, Lillia didn't know. She snatched up her false hand and attempted to fasten it back into place, but the lacing was now in tatters. It wouldn't stay without repair. Sending it to be mended meant doing without until the job was complete. She couldn't bear to be without it. Even now, she felt naked. Exposed for the world to see.

The man continued to kneel in front of her, not daring to lift his head. He held his papers in a jumbled mess against his chest. "I'm so terribly sorry," he rasped. "Please don't—please don't report me."

Reporting him was the last thing on Lillia's mind. All she wanted now was to hide away and pretend this day had not happened. The negative spiral of mental berating began once again.

Conscious of all the eyes watching their interaction, Lillia stilled her thoughts and drew on her years of Guild training. Endless hours of meditation had taught her how to center her focus and be in the present. The practice failed more often than it succeeded. Yet she knew what it should look like outwardly. She forced a smile on her face. "All is forgiven," she said with a lightness she didn't feel. "It was an accident. No harm done."

No harm besides the lacing on her false hand and the hit to Lillia's already damaged pride.

The scholarly man kept his head low. "No harm, my lady? Are you certain?"

"No harm," Lillia repeated. She faked a laugh she did not

feel. Hopefully, it was convincing enough. "None at all. You're free to go."

Relief washed over his features. He leapt to his feet and bowed deeply. "Thank you, my lady. I am terribly sorry."

Lillia's heart thudded against her chest, and she prayed to the Soulmaker above for something, anything to grant her a reprieve from this situation. If only her gift included erasing memories. But that was impossible. Soulseers could only See manifestations of souls. Truthtakers could only Reveal a man's true nature. And Witwraiths . . . Well. Witwraiths could only Snatch a man's soul from him.

Nothing more.

Memory manipulation and healing and a dozen other rumored abilities that the commoners whispered about simply were not possible.

The rattling of a passing lady's carriage and the clip-clopping of horses' hooves on the nearby street cut through the tension, drawing the attention of many of the spectators. Purebred horses were a rare sight indeed, particularly a fine team of six. In a land too cold for horses the majority of the year, maintaining such beasts demanded heated stables and additional hands to maintain. A horse's more delicate constitution meant it was better suited for the warmer lands down south.

The original horses brought over by the crew of the *Atlantia* were said to be strong and sturdy, capable of withstanding the arctic chill of the long winters. Decades of inbreeding had paid its toll on the descendants of those steeds. Weaker constitutions, thinner coats, more sensitive stomachs. Deformities had become all too common. Horses in good condition were now a priceless commodity.

Oxen and donkeys were more hardy and tolerated the cooler temperatures but plodded along rather than trotted. Farmers and tradesmen favored the beasts for their endurance, but the gentry turned up their noses at such practicality. Native caribou and camels were occasionally used as well but were less reliable, as their domestication was still relatively recent. The closest creatures to the original horses that hunters and explorers had been able to find were native horses—smaller and more dainty than purebreds. The hybrid offspring were sterile, just as mules were.

Lillia didn't fully understand the technicalities of it all. Animal husbandry hadn't been a subject that interested her while in school.

Yet even she knew this team of six was a frivolous waste of funds. However, it served as a perfect distraction. The moment of relief was all Lillia needed to collect herself. She gave the trembling man a brief nod, then strode purposefully toward the street. She was going home as originally planned. The humiliation was too much to bear. Never mind the remainder of her duties for the day. She would claim a headache—not a lie—and retreat to her bed chamber, where she would read or sketch or do anything to forget this day and all that occurred.

She'd nearly made her escape when someone called to her. "Lady Pennyworth, please attend to me."

The deep feminine voice coming from the nearby carriage was the only thing that could stop Lillia right now. It would have stopped anyone. Even a charging mammoth or one of those long toothed tigers.

Lillia turned to face the carriage and gave a low curtsy. She was not the only one to do so. All within hearing also followed suit.

The reigning monarch leaned slightly out of the window, though her features were obscured by the shadows within. Very few people could say they'd seen the Lady Regent's face. Or recollect her features. Yet even the hint of her regal presence was enough to pause all activity. If Lillia had suspected it was the Lady Regent in the carriage, she would have retreated into the Guild headquarters. Today was not the day to accidentally encounter the elegant and highly esteemed woman.

Luck was not on her side, though. Lillia curtsied even lower. "Lady Regent."

All eyes were on them now, if they hadn't been already. The Lady Regent herself had called upon Lillia. Rumors would fly.

Lillia's face burned with the additional humiliation.

The carriage door swung open.

"Join me, Lady Pennyworth. I fancy a ride and your conversation."

If only the earth could open up and swallow her whole. Lillia could feel every set of eyes upon her back, hear every whispered question and doubt. Who was she to be shown such marked attention? What had she done to deserve this? Was this because of the nearly botched trial? Or because Lillia Revealed her father?

To refuse was unthinkable. At the very least, Mama would have her head. This was an opportunity Lillia could not ignore, no matter how very much she wished she could.

She slipped her false hand into her overskirt pocket to keep it from falling again and to hide her lack. She'd yet to inspect the prosthetic for damage, though she was certain something was now broken besides the lacing. A hand carved from a single piece of ivory should not have moving parts, and something had shifted within the glove as she pocketed the thing.

Conscious of the attention she garnered from the gossiping biddies in the courtyard, Lillia climbed into the carriage and sat on the rear-facing bench, opposite the Lady Regent and her Snatched companion.

The two wore coordinating colors, the Lady Regent in a silver gown with a full split in the latest fashion. Her black breeches were on full display, only covered by knee-high black boots. Her Snatched wore a coat and waistcoat in the same silver, trimmed with black. His trousers and cravat were also black. A beaver hat sat on his lap. He would be quite dashing indeed. If he wasn't Snatched, as indicated by the red band about his upper arms. The scarlet strips of fabric were the only color about his person.

The neutral colors of the royal household were a symbol of neutrality in the monarchy. The Lady Regent was part of all factions and political parties yet member of none, as was evidenced by the edicts and policies the crown put into place. Customs and culture from the old world to appease the Conservationists, city and state improvements to satisfy the Novationists. But only enough to keep each party at bay.

It seemed a delicate balance to maintain, and Lillia was ever so grateful that responsibility didn't lie at her feet.

There was a young Soulseer sitting on the bench next to Lillia. She had been a couple of years behind Lillia in school and had received her gift after Lillia had graduated to become an official Truthtaker for the Lady Regent. Rumors had it that this Sophie Saunders was actually the Lady Regent's daughter or niece or some other relative, though no one knew the specifics. The rumors surrounding this girl flew nearly as fast and far as those about Lillia.

All Lillia knew was that Lady Sophie spent most of her days carrying messages for the Lady Regent. It was a lowering task, left for Soulseers weak in their gift. Lillia wasn't entirely positive she didn't envy the girl, though, for her relative freedom.

The interior of the carriage felt dim, despite the shades on the windows being open. The lack of light provided a degree of imagined protection. She was out of her element, but at least she wasn't on full display. Neither was the Lady and her Snatched. Even here, sitting mere feet away, Lillia struggled to make out Her Majesty's features. Shadows flitted across her face. His features, too, were difficult to see.

The carriage lurched forward. Lillia leaned back in her seat and turned her attention to the world passing outside her window. It was not her place to speak first. If the Lady Regent merely wanted a silent companion during this ride, it was her prerogative. Lillia would be most accommodating.

She pulled her false hand back out of her pocket and set it on her lap to keep it from poking her in the thigh. It was no longer attached to her shoulder brace, but as long as there were no sudden movements, it would be fine. The lacings, however, were tangled about and would need to be cut off. When she returned home, she would send the hand for repairs. Curse her shortsightedness for not having a wooden one commissioned for moments such as this. She would cry off for the time she was without the prosthetic and claim to be ill enough to remain home. The reprieve would be welcome.

"That's a clever article." The Lady Regent gestured to Lillia's hand.

Lady Sophie peeked past her long red hair that hung loose about her face to where the hand rested in Lillia's lap but didn't say anything.

Lillia hadn't meant to draw attention to it. She only desired to be more comfortable for the duration of the ride.

"Thank you, Your Majesty." The words felt insufficient, but what else was she supposed to say? Lady Sophie hadn't spoken at all. Did the Lady Regent prefer silence?

The Lady Regent raised her brows. "I've heard it is made of mammoth ivory. Is that correct?"

"Yes, Your Majesty." At far more expense than Mama should have taken on in her reduced circumstances. Not as much as a more advanced prosthetic, but still quite dear.

"Might I see it?" The Lady Regent held out her hand.

Lillia could only stare at the Lady Regent's outstretched fingers. Was this day to be filled with humiliation at every turn? The ivory hand was a visible and tangible reminder of Lillia's lack. She rarely let it out of her sight, let alone allowed any to touch it other than her lady's maid who sometimes helped her fasten it into place.

Lillia could not bring herself to raise her eyes to meet those of her regent. "Yes, Your Majesty."

It took a minute or two to unfasten the remaining lacings.

She had a tool at home for such a task, but here, in a moving carriage, she had no such luxury. Her fingers, while nimble with experience, refused to cooperate.

When she finally released the last lace, she breathed deeply. That had taken far too long. Her fingertips felt rubbed raw from the effort.

Conscious of the Lady Regent's and Lady Sophie's eyes on her, Lillia handed over the ivory hand.

The Lady Regent took it in a reverent manner, cradling it carefully in her hands. "May I remove the glove?"

Lillia nodded. She wouldn't be able to do so herself until she returned home. When the Lady Regent was done with her inspection, Lillia could assess it herself. If she had to take it in for repair, she would like to discuss different options for the lacings. Something easier to accomplish on her own and better able to withstand everyday wear.

While the Lady Regent wrangled the glove from the false hand, Lillia took the opportunity to covertly study the Snatched man sitting in front of her. Lady Sophie's attention seemed to be completely on what their regent was doing. She likely wouldn't notice Lillia's perusal either.

Lillia had been near Snatched before. Many times. But never had she been able to see one fully trained as this one was. This Snatched sat perfectly straight, swaying naturally with the rhythm of the carriage. He stared straight ahead, never turning his head to look out the window.

His shorter dark hair and long sideburns were of the original fashion, during the time of the Arrival. While Lillia believed the style to visibly age most men, it was striking on him. She wondered at his crime. What had this man done to deserve to be Snatched? And what had redeemed him enough to be taken on by the Lady Regent? Surely it couldn't have only been his handsome face. She assumed it was handsome, at least. The rumors said as much.

Then again, many Snatched had been taken on by Gifted women for less.

If Lillia hadn't known he was Snatched, would she be able to determine it? Perhaps by the way he didn't meet her eyes. Or the formal posture that many men only assumed during formal occasions.

There was nothing in what she could see of his expression to give him away, though. He merely seemed to be a man deep in thought.

If she took on a fully-trained Snatched, would he be like this one? Not that she was truly considering it, but the idea was intriguing.

"Oh, dear."

Lillia returned her attention to the Lady Regent, then down at the false hand in the monarch's hands.

It was in pieces.

Lillia had suspected as much, but having it confirmed felt like a blow to her stomach.

The Lady Regent held up the thumb and gave Lillia an apologetic look. "Forgive me, Lady Pennyworth. I did not mean to break it. This piece fell off as I removed the glove." There was true regret in her tone.

Lillia swallowed hard. She glanced at the stoic Snatched who still hadn't so much as twitched. He stared past Lillia, unseeing. Lady Sophie had lowered her blinders but hastily pushed them back up her nose. Had she been trying to See Lillia's response to the broken hand?

Suddenly, Lillia felt overly conscious of every move she made. Even her breathing felt abnormal and off.

The Lady Regent tried to press the thumb back into place, likely knowing it wouldn't stay without some sort of adhesive. "Oh, dear," she murmured. "This won't do at all." She set the broken thumb down and sighed. "I'm afraid there's no repairing this. Not with my limited skills. You'll have to send it to an expert."

"Yes, Your Majesty." An expert would cost more than Lillia could afford at this time. It was worth the expense, but things would be tight for a time.

"Do you have a way to carry this home, Lady Pennyworth?" The Lady Regent shook her head, as if berating herself. "Never mind that. I'll have it sent by messenger. Sophie needs something to do today anyway. You don't need the burden of carrying something like this the remainder of the day." She set both hand and thumb aside, out of Lillia's reach.

Without the hand, Lillia's arm felt remarkably bare and exposed. Yes, she wore a stocking over it to protect it from being rubbed raw by her ivory hand, but it wasn't enough to hide her lack. It had been years since she'd gone out in public without a false hand of sorts to hide her deformity. First a glove filled with wool, then a crude wooden one that one of Mama's footmen had carved for her. It was only after Mama realized how much better a carved hand was than a stuffed one that she'd commissioned the ivory one. Mama had thrown the wooden one in the fire. It hadn't been worthy of the Pennyworth name.

Lillia still missed that hand.

They rode in silence for a minute or two. Lillia tried to turn her focus outside again, trying to keep the tears at bay. They were passing the original *Atlantia*, now in dry dock for scheduled repairs and maintenance. The masts rose high above the shorter lakeside buildings, bare of masts and flags. Though the ship hadn't seen the open sea since the Arrival, it was maintained as if it would set sail at any time. It was the government's nod to the Conservationists' efforts to discover the Lost Passage.

Lillia believed their efforts to be a lost cause. If there was a Lost Passage, it would have been discovered long ago.

"She's a beautiful ship." The Lady Regent lifted the curtain on her window to peer outside as well. Her voice held a tone of nostalgia. "Even if she never sails again, she's worth the effort. Our history deserves to be remembered."

"Yes, Your Majesty." Had Lillia uttered anything other than those words? She couldn't recall. She must sound like a simpleton of the worst kind.

"As does yours." The Lady Regent touched her forehead to brush away a stray strand of hair, the motion emphasizing her lack of blinders.

Rumors abounded regarding the Lady Regent's gift. Some said she was far too perceptive to be anything other than a Soulseer. Others insisted she was a Truthtaker, like the original Lady Regent, Verity Covington. A few were certain she was a Witwraith.

Yet the only blinders the monarch wore were darkened to a deep gray. Indigo would have indicated a Truthtaker. An amber tint for Soulseer. And scarlet for Witwraith. The color didn't matter other than to distinguish which gift the woman had. Tinted glass provided protection, no matter the shade.

Perhaps she wasn't Gifted at all?

That didn't seem right, though. Not with how the woman seemed to stare right through Lillia to her soul.

"You've been a Truthtaker longer than most your age, is that correct?"

It was an ill-kept and painful secret how that came about. Lillia was painfully aware of Lady Sophie's scrutiny as she responded. "Yes, Your Majesty."

"Your gift manifested when you were how old?"

Lillia closed her eyes and breathed deeply. "Eight, Your Majesty." Her history was no secret. It never had been. She could speak of this. It would not be easy, but it was hardly the first time she'd endured this line of questioning.

"And the first man you Revealed was?"

This was the part of the conversation Lillia dreaded the most. It wasn't enough that Lillia had been born with a single hand when everyone else had two. She would forever bear this black mark against her name. The shame would follow her to her grave.

Yet she had to respond.

"My father."

For most Truthtakers, their first experience Revealing a man was during a trial of law. Unlike Snatching, Truthtaking was an involuntary ability. A Truthtaker merely had to meet the eyes of a man for her gift to activate.

Men who had volunteered, or had been sold to the Guild to repay debts, to be Revealed for the sake of research spoke of a silent *click* and an invisible connection that linked them to the Truthtaker. The exact sensations reported varied, but the result was the same. Each man no longer had the ability to show restraint of any sort. Any words that came to mind spewed from their mouth. If there was anything they desired to do, they did it, no matter how crude, vile, inappropriate, cruel, or embarrassing.

In essence, their true nature was revealed for all to see.

It was the most accurate way to determine guilt. It was also irreversible.

Men who were Revealed but not deemed dangerous enough to Snatch were put to work in the mining fields. There, they were watched carefully by both guards and Witwraiths. If a Revealed's actions proved unpredictable or dangerous, he was Snatched without the benefit of a second trial. Snatched, trained, and assigned or sold.

This had been Papa's fate. And it was all Lillia's fault.

Gifts normally didn't manifest until girls participated in the Gifting Ceremony the year they reached their majority. This was to prevent accidents and to teach the girls how to control their gifts through discipline and structure. Not all girls who participated in the much revered ceremony were blessed with gifts, though. Those who failed to manifest were allowed to serve as companions or household matriarchs within a Gifted's home, should they choose. Who better to support and nurture a Gifted than one who had undertaken the training?

Others returned home to live their lives in relative anonymity.

"How did it happen?"

This was the most difficult subject to think on, let alone speak aloud. Lillia ran her fingers over the lace on her cuff, rubbing it until her fingertips felt raw and numb. She longed for the Soulseer messenger to avert her gaze. Anywhere but at her.

"I left my bed to see my Papa. He was working in his study. I wanted him to read me another story. I don't remember much. Just walking through a door. There was a light. Or a flash. Something bright. Then, I looked at him and . . ." It was too painful to continue. That moment altered her life forever.

Lillia's memories remained jumbled from that day, a chaotic mess of shouts and stomping feet. Strange women in blinders who forced a pair of indigo-tinted lenses upon her face, then rushed her out the door and into a waiting carriage. She'd been immediately enrolled into the Academy—the youngest student in more than fifty years. The older girls had made their resentment for her very clear, nearly from the start. A one-handed girl who gained her gift years before she should.

The resentment those girls held for her had carried over through Lillia's later years, even after Lillia had completed her own Gifting Ceremony to confirm and make official the receiving of her gift. Many of them continued to shun and even mock her.

Society was quick to condemn and slow to forget.

Mama had borne the blame, accused of going through her Gifting Ceremony while Lillia was in her womb. Such a thing, while not unheard of, was forbidden. Mama had been stripped of her title and dismissed from the Guild. As a Soulseer, she was allowed her freedom. If she had been a Truthtaker or Witwraith, the consequences would have been far worse. At least, that's what the gossip indicated.

Mama insisted she was innocent, but the evidence stated otherwise, despite Lillia's gift not manifesting until she was eight. That fact continually grated on Mama and had for years. She voiced her disdain for the entire situation and blamed Lillia for it all.

If Lillia had only been born with two hands . . .

If Lillia hadn't been so demanding of her father's time . . .

If Lillia hadn't been born at all . . .

That last one had never been spoken directly to Lillia. She'd overheard Mama speaking to another Soulseer in the palace courtyard, bemoaning her fate. While Lillia suspected her mother felt that way, that was the first time that suspicion had been confirmed.

At the tender age of eight, Lillia became a High Lady and the head of her household, complete with the entirety of the financial burden upon her shoulders.

It was a wonder Lillia had survived any of it with her wits intact.

"Your father. That's right. I remember hearing about that." The Lady Regent touched her Snatched's arm. A gesture of self-soothing perhaps? The man could offer no solace unless instructed to do so. The Lady Regent's gaze became distant and unfocused. "I knew him, you know. Your father. He was once one of my advisors. And a good friend. He helped prepare our Gifting Ceremonies." She sighed deeply. Remorsefully. "His contributions are dearly missed."

This indeed was news. Lillia knew so little of the man. He'd been taken from her so long ago, and Mama could not bring herself to speak of him, even behind closed doors.

"Such a tragedy, to be sure."

Tragedy? It was far worse than a tragedy. But it was Lillia's life, and she had to press forward as best she could.

She did not reply.

Apparently, she was not expected to. The Lady Regent gave herself a little shake and straightened her skirts. "I have an assignment for you."

Lillia looked up sharply, forgetting to be demure and submissive as she'd been raised to do. The Lady Regent did not give assignments. Not to one such as Lillia. That was left to the Guild. The members of the Guild leadership reviewed requests for trial and determined which Gifted were best suited for the situation.

"An assignment, Your Majesty?" Soulmaker help her, she sounded even more simple than before. "What sort of assignment?"

Once more, the Lady Regent studied Lillia, long and hard. She clasped her hands in her lap, a model of grace and elegance, even with the gentle rocking of the carriage as it made its way down the cobblestone streets.

"A trial. In Lakewood." The Lady Regent's words were short and staccato, void of the emotion she had previously expressed. It was almost as if they were spoken by an entirely different woman. "You'll leave first thing in the morning. I've already arranged transportation by steamboat. Be at the docks by eight. I've already selected the other Gifted who will accompany you." She pointed to Lillia. "Don't be late."

The instructions came so quickly, Lillia barely had time to process them. "Forgive me, Your Majesty, but Lakewood?" When had she heard of another Gifted going to Lakewood for trial? The accused were always transported to New London, not the other way around. "May I ask why Gifted are going to Lakewood for a trial?"

"No, you may not." The Lady Regent rapped on the roof of the carriage. "And you may not tell anyone else of this assignment. You are not to take any of your own servants." She glanced at Lillia's left arm. "Though, considering your . . . lack . . . I'll allow you another Gifted to serve as your companion to aid you. Sophie here would be delighted to go."

Lady Sophie gave a small jerk of her head and furrowed her brows. This assignment seemed to be as much of a surprise to her as it was Lillia. So much for her being the Lady Regent's trusted companion.

"Do not tell your mother," the Lady Regent continued. "She is not to know any of this."

Considering how far Mama had fallen and how well known she was for her continual complaints, that order was not surprising.

"Forgive me, Your Majesty, but am I truly the best fit for this role? Surely there are others more suitable." And whole. In more ways than one. Lillia had never left New London, for good reason. To do so now, when her false hand was damaged, would be humiliating. New people to stare at her and wonder what she or her mother had done to invoke the Soulmaker's wrath.

The Lady Regent gave Lillia her full attention, leaning forward and touching Lillia's knee. "You, my dear, are precisely who is needed for this assignment. It has been confirmed." She nodded, as if to herself. "Confirmed several times over."

Meaning a Temporal had foreseen it. Lillia could surmise that much. Not Lady Sophie, who was known to be an Aural. Was the Lady Regent then a Temporal Soulseer? That would explain many things.

They discussed a few more details, including the identities of the three Soulseers and the Witwraith who would also be conducting the trial. The Lady Regent emphasized that the Temporal Soulseer, Lady Madeleine, would be her voice at the trial. Any orders she gave should be followed as if they came from the Lady Regent herself.

"Remember, not a word." The Lady Regent kept her voice low. The carriage pulled to a stop in front of the palace courtyard's entrance. "To anyone."

Lillia lifted her chin in acknowledgment. Secrecy and discretion had been emphasized more times than she could count. Keeping this to herself would be easy enough. No one cared to associate closely enough with Lillia for her to let anything slip anyway.

She sent a searching gaze for her false hand and broken thumb but said nothing about them. The Lady Regent had said she would send them to Lillia's home, therefore there was no use asking for them back.

The carriage door opened, this time by the driver, and Lillia exited, giving a deep curtsy to the Lady Regent once her feet touched the ground. Her head swam with all she had to do and remember. It would take time enough to prepare for what she had to do. This trial would be different from any other she'd participated in. She would conduct it without the benefit of someone more experienced close by in the small chance something went wrong. The observers would not have the protection of the tinted glass. There were lists of things she needed and arrangements she needed to make for her absence. As well as a story to tell Mama that would satisfy her inevitable questions. Lillia's missing hand helped in that matter. Perhaps there was a benefit to it breaking after all.

Before the carriage door closed again, Lillia caught sight of the Snatched once more. He remained as still as ever. Not once during the drive did he move or blink or do more than breathe.

His eyes, which stared at nothing, appeared hollow and empty. As if his soul truly was gone.

Snatched.

Lillia shuddered and hurried toward the Guild headquarters, eager to place as much distance as possible between herself and the carriage. Having a Snatched was the last thing she would ever do. She didn't need another reminder of what she did to her father. Papa had deserved better.

If only she could undo what she had done. But everyone knew that was impossible.

Snatching was as irreversible as Revealing. And both changed a man.

Forever.

"Lillia, darling!"

Mama hurried to Lillia's side and slipped her hand through Lillia's right arm. The one with the functioning hand. Mama rarely acknowledged the other. "What a fortuitous happenstance!"

"Hello, Mama." Their meeting was anything but chance. Mama lurked about the courtyard most days, pulling Gifted aside for conversations, pretending to still be part of the Guild. She wasn't permitted access inside Guild headquarters without an invitation, which she tried to finagle out of her former sisters in the Gift. Mama's manipulative behavior had gotten bad enough, many Gifted now avoided the courtyard altogether.

Mama pulled Lillia forward into a less-than-leisurely stroll. When they were within earshot of a small group of Soulseers, Mama raised her voice. "And what did the Lady Regent want with my daughter? To be invited to ride with her in the royal carriage? What an honor!"

Her words had their intended effect. Several pairs of eyes locked in on Lillia. She burned with humiliation at her mother's blatant bid for attention.

"It was nothing, Mama." Lillia turned her head, wishing herself anywhere but here. "She wanted to speak to me about the trial. She also told me she once knew Papa and asked how I was doing. My hand broke earlier, and she offered to send it in for repairs."

"Your hand . . ." Mama pulled free and snatched Lillia's left arm. She lifted it, brushing the lace cuff aside to inspect the abrupt end of the appendage. "Why do you not have your hand?" Her words were practically a growl. She dropped Lillia's arm as if it were a snake about to strike. "Hide that thing before someone sees."

Lillia did as she was bade. Years of enduring Mama's temper had taught her to obey without question.

The other Gifted were still watching with varying degrees of interest. Mama pasted on a smile as false as Lillia's ivory hand. "Smile, dearest, lest they think something is wrong."

Smiling was the last thing Lillia wished to do. She managed a small smile. It felt forced. It likely looked forced as well.

"Was that truly what the Lady Regent wanted from you?" Mama pulled them into a walk again, this time away from listening ears. "She wasn't favoring you in some way? Rewarding you or . . ."

Or reversing Mama's sentence. That was Mama's ultimate goal with all her scheming and fawning. She longed to return to the Guild, to be part of that sisterhood once more.

"No, Mama. She wanted to speak of the trial." Not the trial from this morning, but the one to come. Mama did not need to know that, though. "She also gave me leave to go to Lakewood while I'm waiting for the repairs on my hand to be complete." Another truth, though not in its entirety.

Mama tapped a finger against her lips. "Lakewood. I assume you'll indulge in the hot springs there. The local gentry could be of benefit to you. They wouldn't have as much sway, but every little bit helps, you know." She mulled this over for a moment, as if seriously considering whether or not she should join her daughter. "I'm afraid I won't be able to come. I've got far too much to do here."

"Of course." Lillia had banked on that. There wasn't a large enough population of influential people in Lakewood to benefit Mama in any way. "I'll have a companion to help me. Perhaps you'll be able to join me at another time."

"Perhaps." Mama lifted her chin and took in the rest of the courtyard. Her face lit up. "There is my friend, Alice. I must speak with her. She says her daughter is part of that group of girls at the Academy who pretend to be the Greek Muses or some other such nonsense. They're threatening to run away, though where they would go, I don't know. The mammoth beasts outside of town will eat them up for certain. She's at her wit's end trying to straighten the girl out. I must lend her support."

Then, without even a farewell, Mama was gone as quickly as she came.

Lillia felt the weight of her mother's presence lift. Once she was certain Mama was deeply invested in conversation with her supposed friend, Lillia picked up her pace and escaped into the Guild headquarters. She had much to prepare and very little time to do so.

CHAPTER 4

DAVIN ADJUSTED HIS CRAVAT AND tugged at his jacket. He felt the fool. These clothes were from a bygone age, from a time when such a thing as prestige and poise mattered. They had no place in his life other than to please his mother. Men's fashion had evolved since the Arrival to include more comfortable items. Many men had done away with the ridiculous cloth about their neck, except to keep warm. He himself only wore a scarf on the coldest of days. It was practical.

But here, in the sweltering heat of Mimi's drawing room, the additional layers were too much. He wiped at a bead of sweat upon his brow.

If he dared, he would bank the fire to cool the room. Perhaps he could do that. Mimi always took longer to arrive than expected. He needn't do much, merely push that one log to the side. She likely wouldn't even notice.

As he reached for the poker, Mimi swept into the room like a storm of ice blue lace and ruffles. She flounced into her favorite armchair and pressed the back of her hand to her forehead.

Ah. It was one of those days. He clasped his hands together and waited for her to address him. It wouldn't take long. She was prone to attention-seeking.

When he didn't react to her entrance, Mimi glared at him. She didn't like being ignored, but as long as he could play innocent to her manipulations, he would. When he still didn't respond to her dramatics, she sighed as if she bore the weight of the world on her shoulders and cast her gaze to the ceiling, her hand still against her forehead.

"I have had the most distressing of news!" she announced. She peeked at him to see if he noticed.

"Indeed?" Davin hoped his expression was one of interest rather than boredom. Local gossip only intrigued him if it involved horses or cattle. Otherwise, he had no use for it.

If he appeared to listen carefully enough, she may allow him to escape to Father's study. Or even back to the stables or cattle pens. He hadn't checked on the musk ox calves lately. They surely had grown since the last time he checked. The wool they would provide in the spring would increase their income by a third. He wouldn't let his mother know that, though. Despite being the matriarch of the family, his mother had no head for numbers, other than how much a new frock cost.

Mimi dropped her facade long enough to wave Sam in from the hall. The man-of-all-work carefully balanced a tea tray in his calloused hands. He fumbled his way through the task of setting things up, his larger stature feeling cumbersome and unwieldy in the low-ceilinged room.

Davin wished he could take over and allow Sam the dignity of disappearing outside again. The man was better suited for working outdoors than in a tiny parlor. However, his mother's rampant spending had depleted their coffers to the point of having to let several staff members go. Sam remained, along with the cook and her children, who filled the remainder of the required roles.

"What news, Mother?" Davin didn't have all day to exchange petty stories of people he didn't care about.

His mother sniffed indignantly. "You are to call me Mimi, Davin. We've discussed this, son. I am now Mimi. Not Mother."

Fine then. "Forgive me, Mimi. I had forgotten." He hadn't. He simply didn't want to call her by such a silly name.

His lie placated her for now. He'd played dumb and slow for long enough, she no longer questioned it. So long as she believed him compliant, she left him to his own devices. He would play the part as long as he needed to make his dream come to fruition.

With his attention fully on her, Mimi grew more exuberant. She sat up and clapped her hands together, looking more like a mirthful child. "It is the best news," she said in a whisper that was not truly a whisper. "There is to be a trial."

Davin took one of the tea cakes and bit into it, not bothering to take a plate. Not until his mother glared in his direction. He swallowed hard and took up a plate to collect the crumbs. And a second tea cake. Cook had outdone herself again.

"There have been many trials, Mother." At her fierce glance, he corrected himself. "Mimi." How was he supposed to keep up with which term she preferred? The woman changed her mind twice a year, if not more often.

"Yes, I know that, Davin." She shoved a small cake into her mouth, apparently forgetting decorum herself. She infused as much doom and gloom into her voice as possible for a woman with a soprano-like shrill and a mouth full of cake. "But this one is different. They have called in a Truthtaker."

Davin set down the bite he was about to take, lest he choke on it. This was news indeed. There hadn't been an official trial here in Lakewood since before he was born, if ever. All official trials conducted by the Guild of the Gifted were held in New London. The only trials held locally consisted of someone poaching on another's land or someone accidentally taking someone's cattle. Or there had been that one woman a few years back who had been vandalizing buildings in town, then tried to frame her husband to be rid of him. She'd been found guilty and sent to work on the farms in Southland as punishment. That had been part of the rumor mill for months. Idle conversations still brought up the trial on occasion.

Local trials were presided over by the magistrate and were rarely worth the breath to relate other than to act as fodder for otherwise bored country gentry like his mother.

"Truly?" Davin set his plate aside. He tried to temper his tone, lest his mother sense his interest, but this tidbit of information was truly intriguing, unlike most of what came from her mouth. "What was the crime?"

"Murder!" Mimi giggled and clapped again. "A double murder at that. Can you believe it?"

Davin frowned as he pondered this news. One wrongful death in their community was news enough, but two? It was hardly any wonder the magistrates had called to New London for help. Something this serious had to be addressed properly.

If only they could place the infernal night beasts on trial as well. They were responsible for far more deaths and disappearances than any man or woman. Particularly in the past couple of years. Including the disappearance and subsequent death of Davin's father. Unfortunately, the talents of the Gifted were limited to the vicious creatures who walked upon two legs, not four.

Abigail entered the drawing room and began to pour the tea. "What is this about a double murder, Mimi?" She yawned on the last syllable. She must have taken a short nap. She often did that on days she and their mother went to town. The excursion tended to wear her out and give her a severe headache. Mimi bubbled with excitement now that her news was told. She continued to babble, the high intonation of her voice wearing on

Davin's nerves. "The Gifted arrive today by boat. The trial is set for tomorrow morning. No one knows when the Gifted will try to return to New London, but if we are very lucky, it won't be for a few days. To think. Gifted here. In Lakewood."

Mimi's enthusiasm for all things related to the Gifted came to light any time a Truthtaker or Soulseer or even a Witwraith was mentioned in conversation.

Strange how Mimi's claim to have no head for numbers did not apply when asked about the Gifted. She could recite the exact number of Soulseers—her preferred gift—as well as which order they belonged to. She knew each Truthtaker and Witwraith, along with their ages, how long they'd served, and how old they were when they died. She followed each trial in the newspaper and through the gossip chain religiously. More attention was paid to things happening a two-day carriage ride away than to what was happening under her own roof.

Davin rarely paid heed to her ramblings. The Guild existed in New London. Not here in sleepy Lakewood. He barely understood the difference between the gifts, let alone who wielded them.

Davin leaned toward Abigail and lowered his voice to keep their mother from overhearing. "Are you well, sister?" She was pale and drawn. Nor had she taken any tea or cake for herself. Unless Davin's eyes were fooling him, his sister's hand trembled as she handed him a cup.

Abigail gave a minute shake of her head. "I am well enough. Never you mind."

"And to think," Mimi continued, too wrapped up in her monologue to realize she was the only one paying any mind to her words, "if they choose to take the coach back to New London, they'll pass right through our lands on the way from town. I do hope they don't try to return to New London by boat. We may never see them."

If Davin knew his mother, she would contrive to be in town

for the trial and finagle her way into the inn where the Gifted would be staying. She would then wave to them and claim they greeted her as an equal.

Yet another thing she would be able to lord over the gossip-loving biddies she called friends.

"It's too bad those infernal night beasts have started attacking before the sun is fully set. Or perhaps that's a good thing. They could keep the Gifted in town longer as no one would be careless enough to travel when the beasts are active." Mimi took a large bite of cake and continued to speak, her words partially muffled by the food in her mouth. "I do wish someone would do something about those creatures, though. First they take your father, now this? It's getting out of hand."

The only remorse Mimi ever showed about her late husband was to lament her fate. Loudly. And frequently. To anyone who would listen. The attention-seeking behavior may have fooled her friends, but Davin had little patience for it.

"You could always become a magistrate yourself." Davin spoke in vain. Mimi would never condescend to such lowly work. He took a sip of his tea and cringed. Not only was it weak, it was bitter. Cook must be pinching pennies again by reusing tea leaves. Davin would have to reexamine her budget and see if he could increase it.

Abigail rolled her eyes and added some honey to his cup. Davin nodded his thanks, not that she would accept it. He took another sip. Much better this time. He set the cup down and took the last of the tea cakes. "As magistrate, you could help the others in containing the creatures, Mimi. Or hire hunters to hunt them down."

"Oh, pish." She shook her head and tittered to herself. "As if I could ever lower myself in such a way." She tilted her head to the side. "Though we could do something to make our own land safer, I suppose."

"I believe you're right, Mother . . . er, Mimi." Davin bit

into the tea cake. Was this his third? Or maybe fourth? Cook deserved more money for certain.. "Sam and I could walk the perimeter of our lands and watch for signs."

Mimi clapped her hands in delight. "That is a wonderful idea."

The idea was rather ingenious, if he said so himself. The excuse would keep him out of the house and allow him more time with Serenity. Mimi would never venture to the stables or into the woods to check on his progress.

"Oh, and Davin?"

Davin cringed. "Yes, Mimi?" Her syrupy tone meant she was about to ask him for something he'd find quite unpleasant. At least he'd gotten the name right this time.

"You'll go to town with us tomorrow to settle our debts, while Abigail and I seek news of the trial?"

Lovely.

"Yes, Mimi." Davin would have to review the ledgers tonight to ensure they had enough funds to do so. Settling the debts meant his mother and sister intended on making more purchases, something they could ill afford. He would have to sneak a few items out of the house later to sell. Particularly anything pink, as pink was now a vile color in his mother's eyes. Never mind that the dye required for that particular hue was hard to come by, as were many of the more vibrant colors. The dye traders had to travel several weeks south through uninhabited lands filled with monstrous creatures to obtain certain colors. The intense reds and yellows and blues worn by the Gifted to distinguish their different gifts were some of the hardest to come by.

Thankfully, even his mother was aware they could not afford such colors. The pastels she did purchase were expensive enough.

Yes, Davin was ready to move out. Let the women manage their finances and run Bradford Lodge into the ground. Without him. He had a far better future in store for himself.

And if he was feeling generous enough, perhaps he would allow them to live with him someday.

On his terms.

CHAPTER 5

A WALK THROUGH LAKEWOOD PROPER WAS precisely what Lillia needed to calm both her stomach and her nerves.

This was her first time venturing out of the Little Realm's capital city, and Lillia could not believe the difference. Lakewood was a far cry smaller than New London. New things to see and people who didn't know her upon sight. As long as she kept her head down, the wide rim of her bonnet would hide her blinders tolerably well. It did make it rather hard to appreciate the more rustic architecture, though. She wanted to take it all in. It felt like she stepped back in time. Very little brick and stone were anywhere. Most buildings were wood-framed, though the tavern she'd passed was still using mammoth bones. And instead of rows of shops, there were only a dozen or so along the main road. Each proudly boasted its wares with once brightly painted signs, many of which were now faded, the paint chipped.

No cobblestone either. Every road was hard-packed dirt. On rainy and wet days, it was likely incredibly muddy. The residents probably wore those raised wooden shoes to walk about. Lillia didn't own a pair herself, but her lady's maid did. The contraptions strapped on over a person's shoes or boots and allowed them to walk "above" the mud, in essence.

Despite the more rustic nature—or perhaps because of it—Lillia was charmed by this town, nestled in the depths of the forest on the eastern shorelines of Lake Verity.

If Lillia had the time, she would love to explore each and every shop to see what they had to offer. What trinkets and fashions were available out here where the latest trends were only a distant whisper?

The combination of her lack and her blinders drew the sort of attention she had hoped to avoid. No matter how much she tried to hide, whispers followed her through the shops. The ribbon shop was especially bad, as it was small and close, and Lillia had no choice but to reveal who she was.

". . . no hand . . ."

"She's that Truthtaker . . ."

". . . her own father . . ."

". . . Truthtaker . . ."

Lillia wanted to sink into the floor. Her cheeks flushed, and the shop felt much warmer than before. Lady Sophie glared at the shopkeeper, who spoke to her assistant behind her hand. Both ladies had the grace to blush when they realized they had been caught.

"Never mind these small-minded fools." Lady Sophie pressed her lips together. "They wouldn't know true worth if they saw it." She'd opened up to Lillia now that they were no longer under the watchful eye of the Lady Regent. Lady Sophie—or Sophie, as she insisted on being called—was sweet and kind. She had a light laugh and an easy smile, and Lillia immediately felt at ease in her presence. Though she had a quick tongue and a surprisingly quick, yet witty, temper.

Sophie's words, while kindly meant, did nothing to keep

Lillia's face from erupting with increasing heat. She turned to leave the shop, intent on hiding away in her room until after the trial was complete, but she was stopped by a short, slight young woman in a purposefully tattered dress in shades of black and red. Her wild black hair only accentuated the blood red blinders that obscured her eyes.

Lady Hannah, the Witwraith chosen for this trial.

According to the gossip chain, this young woman was unorthodox and quirky. Lillia had only seen her performance in court, but she could understand where the rumors had come from. The Witwraith uniform only added to that belief. Where Lillia and Sophie had chosen to dress more simply to avoid drawing attention, Lady Hannah seemed to seek it.

"Hello, Lady Lillia." Lady Hannah inspected the shop's offerings on the nearby shelf. She picked up a glove but put it down without truly examining it. "Shopping?"

"I am. I'm here with my companion, Lady Sophronia Saunders."

"Ah." Lady Hannah clasped her hands behind her back and continued to peruse the wares. When her gaze landed on the shopkeeper and her assistant, Lady Hannah glared and stuck out her tongue. The two women stiffened and backed up a couple of paces. Lady Hannah smirked, not bothering to hide her pleasure at their discomfort.

Sophie tugged Lillia to the side. "I think she may be concerned for you." She spoke low enough only Lillia should have been able to hear. Sophie lowered her blinders for a moment to look at their newest companion. "Her soul is, er, colorful in a way that says she's, um, concerned." The amber-colored spectacles were designed to inhibit a Soulseer's gift to keep it from overwhelming her senses. Seeing a soul was impossible while wearing blinders, just as Truthtaking was impossible while Lillia kept her blinders on.

Witwraiths were a different story. Their scarlet blinders were more for show. They inspired fear in men and women alike. Fear had its place. It kept people in line, people who would otherwise take advantage of situations.

It also looked incredibly lonely.

Lillia watched Lady Hannah, who now hovered nearby, acting nonchalantly, but glancing toward Lillia and Sophie in a discreet manner. Lillia had always felt a kinship with the young woman, though she'd never acted upon it. Here, in a small town where they were the only Gifted, perhaps she would do something about it.

"Won't you join us?" Lillia spoke almost before the words fully formed in her head. "We're taking in the town before the trial begins. I've never been here."

"Neither have I," Sophie added. "We would be grateful for your company."

Another thing to like about the spunky Soulseer. Not all would be as welcoming. Lillia would have to thank the Lady Regent for putting the two of them together.

Lady Hannah eyed them both like they were snakes about to strike, though the expression felt exaggerated. "You would, would you?" She tilted her head, then shrugged, almost as if to herself. "Then I suppose I should."

Sophie stood on her tiptoes to peer past Lady Hannah, though she stood half a head taller than the petite Witwraith. "You wouldn't have seen some dark blue ribbons while you were shopping? Or perhaps some feathers?" She looked in the opposite direction. "I was hoping to add something to Lady Lillia's hair for supper tonight."

Lady Hannah jerked her chin over her shoulder. "Back this way. I'll show you."

As the two walked away, Lillia overheard Lady Hannah insisting Sophie not dress Lillia like an overdressed chicken. Sophie playfully slapped Lady Hannah's arm and denied having any such intentions. Lillia nearly laughed out loud but caught herself in time.

A small boy, no more than six or seven years old, approached cautiously. He pulled his little finger out of his mouth and stared at her with wide eyes. Someone had dressed him well, with a smart-looking cap, a well-fitting jacket, and a scarf to keep him warm. He seemed to be well cared for, though he was unaccompanied at the moment.

He stopped directly in front of Lillia and stared openly at her blinders. "Are you a Truthtaker?" he asked with all the innocent bravado of youth.

Lillia hid her missing hand behind her back. If he was asking about her Gift, he hadn't seen her lack. Children were brutally honest and open when asking her what happened to her hand. Once they saw it, they rarely focused on anything else.

"I am." Lillia cast about in her mind for something, anything to say. Where were this boy's parents? "Have you never met a Truthtaker before?"

He shook his head, still staring at her. He pointed to her blinders. "Are those magic? Are you going to Reveal me? Ma said not to leave her side, but I wanted to see if they had any sweets here. I didn't mean to be bad. I can be good. See?" He folded his arms, the action looking more like he was hugging himself, and stood still, as if he was at his mother's side.

Lillia crouched down to bring herself more to his level, still keeping her missing hand hidden. How she wished she'd had a spare false hand to bring. "I think you must be a very good boy." She gave him a reassuring smile. "You told me the truth right away, without me even having to ask. That was a very good thing to do." He beamed at the praise. Lillia lifted her brow and continued to smile at him. "But you only made a mistake. I don't Reveal boys or men for making a mistake. Mistakes are how we learn." She shook a finger at him. "But now you know better, don't you?"

He nodded.

"And you'll remember to stay close to your ma, won't you?"

"I will! I promise!"

"Then all is forgiven."

The boy's eyes grew wider, if that was even possible. "Truly?"

"Truly."

"Mattias!" A frantic woman rushed to the boy's side. She snatched up his hand and yanked him close to her. "What do you think you're doing?"

This must have been the boy's mother. Lillia stood to explain the situation but didn't get a chance.

"Don't you ever wander away from me again, young man." The woman's eyes darted in Lillia's direction, but that was the only sign she acknowledged Lillia's presence. "You never know what could happen to you. Especially when there are people like her about." The woman pulled the boy roughly away, lecturing him. Lillia caught a few words of it, but the phrase that stood out was "one-handed witch."

The label stung. It also marked the woman as part of a subset of Preservationists that claimed the Gifted were of the devil. They were fanatical and staunch believers who resisted any change, claiming the old ways were the only ways.

Being called a witch hurt, no matter how misguided the woman who used it. It was a wonder the boy felt brave enough to approach her. Lillia tried to shake off the shame, but the woman's words started to repeat in her mind.

Lady Hannah nudged her arm. Lillia hadn't seen her approach. The Witwraith held out a fur-lined muff. "Put this on."

Lillia tentatively took the muff and slipped it over her lack and her hand. The muff was made of musk ox wool on the exterior and was lined with fur. It warmed her hand and the end of her arm quite nicely. Almost too well, considering the weather had yet to cool enough to wear a muff on the regular.

"It's wonderful." Lillia didn't have to pretend she liked it. It was perfect. The muff would allow her to hide her lack without resorting to a stuffed glove or keeping her arm hidden away in the folds of her dress or a pocket. She'd seen other men and women wearing them on the street. With this, she could fit in. Mostly. There was little she could do about her blinders.

Lady Hannah tugged at her sleeves, pulling them down then pushing them up again. "People like that should be sent to the mining fields until they learn to mind their manners." She grabbed a second muff off the shelf and practically threw it at Sophie. "Here's one for you as well." She took the last one and shoved it over her hand. She cooed with pleasure. "I would wear one every day, and I have both my hands."

Lillia blinked a few times, caught off guard by the outright reference to her lack. Most people preferred to pretend they didn't see she was missing a hand, though they would try to sneak glances when they thought she wasn't looking. Others outright stared.

Lady Hannah was the first to act as if Lillia's lack was natural.

Lillia wasn't certain how she felt about that. Good, perhaps?

"This is nice." Sophie pulled some coins from her reticule. "I'll take a second one for my, er, employer. She'll love this as well." She paused and pursed her lips. "You're not a witch, Lillia. Not for being a Truthtaker, and not for anything else. No more than Lady Hannah or I. If I felt it would do any good, I would give that woman a piece of my mind."

"I'll do it." Lady Hannah shoved her muff into Sophie's arms. "I'll put the fear of the Gifted into her, Lil. You just say the word."

For the briefest moment, Lillia allowed herself to imagine how that scene would play out. It didn't end well for anyone involved, though it could have been amusing to witness. "I doubt that would help. But thank you."

They settled their bills and headed outside. Lillia's new muff warded off the chill that pinked Sophie's round cheeks almost immediately. The muff was a wise purchase indeed.

"Oh!" Sophie pointed to a shop with a freshly painted sign. "That one should have some hair pins. Lady Hannah, we should get you some. Perhaps they have some combs that would work in your hair as well."

Lady Hannah scowled. "My hair is just fine as it is. And if you call me 'Lady' again, I'll slug you."

"But your hair could be so much better. It's so long and pretty. I would die to have natural curls like yours." Sophie practically skipped forward. "If you allow me to do something with your hair, I'll let you tell off anyone who even looks at Lady Lillia in a foul manner."

That offer seemed to do the trick. They both ducked into the next shop, leaving Lillia on her own. She would have joined them, but she needed a break from people. Besides, the sunshine that had finally made an appearance warmed her through her clothing.

This moment of peace was well-timed. The trial was forthcoming, and she needed time to clear her mind. The incident with the mother and boy had left her shaken.

She turned to seek out a bench or rock or something. Her blinders needed to be adjusted. The earpiece was looser than she would have liked. Another thing she needed to repair. This task was rather urgent, though. She couldn't allow them to go much longer without being attended to. She reached up to pull them off to inspect them when she bumped into something.

Or rather, someone.

Her blinders slipped from her hand and clattered to the ground.

She stared at them for a moment, not yet processing what had happened. It was like watching her false hand fall and break all over again. When had she gotten so clumsy?

"Forgive me. I wasn't watching where I was going."

Lillia stiffened. A man. Here. In front of her. And she was without her blinders. Oh, dear. Lillia kept her head lowered to hide her eyes behind the rim of her bonnet. "It was my fault. I was distracted."

Had the gentleman noticed her blinders on the ground? Based on his calm and very much not frightened tone of voice, he didn't appear to have done so. If Lillia only could . . .

"Oh, it looks as if you've dropped something."

Lillia watched in horror as the gentleman stooped down and retrieved her blinders. She caught sight of his profile before she turned her head away. Long, straight nose. Dark hair. Strong chin. Handsome. If she dared, she would stare at him until she'd memorized his features. A moment wasn't long enough to fully take them in.

He brushed the dirt off the blinders. "I don't think they're damaged. Though the coloring of the lenses . . ."

She sensed the moment he realized what her blinders meant. He quieted. Stiffened. Then, he thrust the blinders at her, thankfully within her line of sight.

"Forgive me, Truthtaker," he murmured in a strangled voice. "I meant no offense."

She accepted the proffered blinders, and their hands touched. Lillia's stomach flipped at the contact. She sucked in a quick breath.

She'd never felt that before, not when interacting with anyone from the opposite sex. It was exciting. Exhilarating. Intensely pleasurable. She longed to reach out to see if it happened again. But also feared the possibility.

Surely it was nerves. Nothing more.

Lillia slipped her blinders back on. He was correct, there didn't seem to be any damage, though they fit more loosely than before. She would have to retrieve her spare pair from her luggage, though they weren't in much better condition. When she returned home, she would have every pair of blinders she owned adjusted and tightened to keep this from happening again.

"All is well." She did appreciate that he kept his voice low, so as to not announce her presence to those on the street. There was no need to repeat the scene in the shop. "Thank you."

She dared to raise her head to meet the gentleman's eye. Her blinders tinted his appearance a dark blue, but her first assessment had been correct. He was rather handsome. Though he refused to return her gaze. She didn't blame him. Few men dared to do so.

He flinched at her perusal and took a hurried step back. "Once again, Truthtaker, I do apologize." He gave her a brief bow. "I must be on my way."

He did not wait for her response before turning and walking away. In his haste to get away, he bumped shoulders with an older woman who angrily chastised his retreating figure.

The shame Lillia felt earlier was nothing compared to the disappointment she experienced now. With her arm in her new muff, at least she didn't have to endure him staring at her lack. A tender mercy that.

"Strange how they act when you're around, isn't it?"

Lillia's face burned. Her mortification was now complete. She turned toward Lady Madeleine and curtsied, as was proper for a senior sister in the gift. "Lady Madeleine, what brings you here?"

The last Lillia had heard, the Temporal Soulseer had been taking testimony in preparation for the trial. She hadn't realized they'd completed the task already. A quick glance at her pocket watch confirmed that the time for the trial was indeed approaching faster than Lillia had realized.

Lady Madeleine gave Lillia a warm smile and looped her arm through Lillia's left arm, leaving her right hand free. Not many people thought to do that. The courtesy was touching, yet Lillia couldn't fully relax. Not until she knew what Lady Madeleine wanted.

As Lady Madeleine pulled Lillia into a stroll, her Snatched followed, keeping a respectful distance. Like the Lady Regent's Snatched, this was well-trained. His clothing coordinated with the Temporal's, even down to a pair of amber-tinted blinders perched on his nose. The gold fabrics trimmed with red set the two apart from the rest of the people walking along the street, marking them as something different. Special. The only nod to his condition was the scarlet arm band wrapped around his upper arm.

"I was hoping for a chance to speak with you, Lady Lillia." Lady Madeleine's smooth voice reminded Lillia of the Lady Regent's as well. It was the mark of elegance in the older set. Mama tried to adopt that same tone, but her eagerness to once again be accepted left her words more rushed and breathy. Lady Madeleine's words seemed to glide from her mouth. "I'm certain you've surmised this trial won't be like others you've known."

That was indeed true. Lillia had pondered that very thing this morning as she walked down the stairs into the common room of the inn. Lady Madeleine had determined that to be the best place to hold the trial, as it was large enough to hold the pro-ceedings. The public would be allowed to watch from the upper balcony and a designated area on the main level. None would be allowed to interrupt the trial. Any who caused a distraction would be summarily removed from the inn altogether. Guards of both genders had been employed to ensure all went smoothly.

The choice was strange considering how secretive the Lady Regent had been regarding this assignment. Though perhaps she hadn't wanted those of the upper class to flock to Lakewood to witness the spectacle.

"I do believe you're right, Lady Madeleine. This will be my first trial outside of New London. However, I've reviewed my notes. All will be well on my end."

It had to be. Far too many eyes would be watching this time. Eyes that would not be hidden behind a tinted pane of glass.

"Have you given any thought to how you would prevent Revealing an innocent, should it come to that? During the trial, there will be many men watching. We are quite the circus, you know."

Lillia thought back to the interaction she'd had with the young man only a few moments before. "I have. I'll keep my bonnet on. The brim is deep enough to hide my eyes from the public once I remove my blinders. We should not have any men standing behind the accused. I'm disciplined enough to not turn my head."

She would have to be.

Lady Madeleine nodded with each point. "Well done, my dear. I knew the Lady Regent chose well when she selected you for this assignment. I'll be sure to inform the guards and the innkeeper. The room will be set up as you suggest."

The compliment both warmed Lillia's heart and put her on edge. People didn't compliment her often, and when they did, it was usually because they wanted something.

"Do not worry, my dear." Lady Madeleine patted Lillia's arm. "My praise is legitimate. I've reviewed your history and Seen your soul. You've got amazing potential. Trust me." She tapped her blinders. "I know. A missing hand and a muddled past will not keep you down. My father was without his arm as well, and he was one of the greatest men I knew."

Lillia thought back to the carriage ride with Lady Regent in New London. She'd mentioned something along the same lines. Was this the Temporal who had foreseen Lillia's future?

Lady Madeleine must have sensed the shift in Lillia's emotions. She gave Lillia a kind smile and sauntered away. Her Snatched followed. He'd been so silent Lillia had forgotten he was there.

Once again, he put her to mind of the Lady Regent's Snatched.

She would almost believe they were the same man but for the fact that Snatched only followed a single master. Lady Madeleine may have been about the same height and size as the Lady Regent, but her features were darker and sharper. They were not the same woman. Therefore, the Snatched men could not be one and the same.

She was imagining things. Nerves, shame, and embarrassment were creating scenarios in her mind that could not be.

It was time to find the others and head back to the inn. They had a trial to prepare for and a man's fate to decide. And when it was all done, she could return home and deal with the difficulties she knew rather than try to navigate new ones here.

CHAPTER 6

WHEN DAVIN HAD PUT ENOUGH distance between the bonneted Truthtaker and himself, he ducked into an alleyway and leaned against the building.

That had been close. Far too close for comfort.

Davin's knees had gone weak, and his stomach felt rock hard when he picked up those spectacles and realized the lovely woman he'd run into had been a Truthtaker.

He'd never even seen a Truthtaker before, let alone bumped into one. He'd grown up thinking all Truthtakers were hags or old women. Crones meant to be feared. Used to scare little boys into behaving. This one had to be nearer his age. What little he'd been able to see, at least.

And he'd been fool enough to cause her to drop her blinders. Those blinders were the only things protecting him from her so-called gift. A curse, more like it. What if she'd looked at him with her naked eyes? He would have been Revealed. Then where would he be?

Likely Snatched and taken away.

The Gifted had arrived in Lakewood yesterday. It was all over town. Every shopkeeper he'd spoken with had confirmed it. One even hinted that she had sold something to one of the Soulseers.

Davin had dismissed it as pure gossip designed to impress and increase business. He never dreamed it to be true.

Then for him to nearly run a Truthtaker over. Of all the luck!

He could count one victory, though. He'd managed to convince each vendor Mimi and sister owed to hold off on calling in their debts for a few weeks. Abigail would certainly give him an earful as their mother would not be able to purchase anything new until then. Neither of them would be happy with what he accomplished, but he didn't care.

Davin could have settled most of the debts today. They had enough in their accounts to do so. However, that would be an invitation for Mimi to go on yet another spending spree. He, and their income, needed the temporary reprieve.

If they didn't like it, Mimi could take over the ledgers and accounts. After all, in the eyes of the law, the matriarch of the home was considered the head of the household. His mother owned the property, inherited from her own mother. Such had been their way since the Arrival.

Mimi, however, refused to take it on. Staring at the cramped writing gave her such a headache. She could not make sense of it all. Or so she claimed. She'd foisted the responsibility upon Davin almost as soon as Father was declared lost after his disappearance into the forest. Abigail had elected not to take them over, though she had every right to do so as the primary heir. Her headaches were too frequent to be able to focus on the numbers that swam upon the pages.

He'd taken the task only because no one else would do it.

If only Davin could disappear or forget his responsibilities altogether, as his mother and sister had done. Or, at the very least, not feel as if he wished the earth would swallow him whole.

His encounter with the Truthtaker left him unsettled, and not simply because of the danger she posed to him. If he was taken away without warning, what would happen to Mimi and Abigail? Sam and Serenity? Cook and her children?

Too many people depended on him for their everyday needs. The weight of that responsibility was crushing.

The Truthtaker, though . . . From what little he could see of her face, she had been youthful, with smooth skin and what could have been a beautiful smile, if her lips hadn't been turned down in a frown. The deep brim of her bonnet prevented him from making out much more. Her blinders obscured her eyes, thank the Soulmaker, but he could imagine those eyes to be quite lovely indeed. Would they be blue? Or a soft brown? Or even a gray that changed with the seasons?

He shook his head. He had to get hold of himself. What was he thinking, pining over one of the Gifted? Particularly a Truthtaker? If she were to take a husband, how would that even work? She'd Reveal him, unless she took extreme precautions. But to live in such a manner? Having to watch his every move lest he accidentally meet her eyes?

No. Davin could not imagine it. He had plans for himself. Ones of freedom and autonomy. He would be the master of his own destiny. He would extract himself from this life into one of his own making. Give Abigail the tools needed to be able to take over the bulk of the household management so he could breathe free.

And no imagined pretty eyes would deter him from it.

Speaking of destiny, the ostler's stables were down the street. He had enough time to have a conversation with the man. He'd shown interest in Davin's endeavor the last time they spoke. Abigail and Mimi had already claimed their spot at a table in the inn's common room balcony to view the trial. Davin could spare a few minutes before the proceedings began.

It was time Davin started branching out and making his pet project known. If luck was on his side, he'd walk away from the meeting with a deal. Or the potential for a deal. The foal Serenity carried was worth its weight in gold. Or ivory. Or anything else Davin could imagine. The sky was the limit. He had big dreams and even bigger ambitions. It was time to make things happen.

CHAPTER 7

LILLIA PEEKED OUT OF THE private sitting room door to the main common room of the inn. Half the town must have arrived to watch the trial. The locals were making it a boisterous social event. They gossiped and whispered and traded stories, flitting from one table or group to the next. Ale flowed like water, and vendors hawked their wares and foodstuffs. All that was lacking to make it a true party worthy of the New London elite was flamboyant decorations and chalk drawings on the wooden floors.

The guards Lady Madeleine had employed to keep the peace had been evenly spaced around a solitary chair near the far edge of the room. A makeshift podium had been constructed from a wooden crate upon a small table. It stood nearby. The central area where the trial would be held was roped off by colorful ribbon strung between the pillars that supported the upper level. Besides the guards, the flimsy barrier was the only thing keeping the crowds back.

Lillia's stomach erupted into a million butterflies. She had refrained from eating the midday meal for just that reason. It would not do for the Lady Regent's Truthtaker to cast up her accounts in the middle of conducting a trial. Her stomach growled fiercely, but she ignored it. She had to remain focused. Word of this trial certainly would make its way to New London and to the ears of the Lady Regent herself. The gossips would tear her apart should anything go wrong. Lillia could not allow herself to fail. Not today.

She and the rest of the Gifted waited here in this sitting room, normally reserved for wealthy patrons to give them privacy from the less well-to-do guests. The fire had been a blessed reprieve from the cold outside, making Lillia's nose tingle when she'd first come in. Now, it was rather warm and would likely grow warmer the longer they remained here.

The fur-lined muff Lillia purchased to hide her lack now felt excessive. If the common room was as warm, she would roast with the thing over her hand and arm. She could not slip away to her room now to change it for something cooler or lighter weight. Even if she wanted to, the way back was now blocked by people.

"Standing room only?" Lady Madeleine sat next to the fire, calmly embroidering. Her much younger Soulseer companions seemed to also be occupied with their sewing. Upon closer examination, though, Lillia spied trembling hands and shaking needles. These girls were as nervous as she was. If only that fact helped calm her nerves.

"Yes. And more coming in." So many people. How would they maintain order? Lillia closed the door and made her way to the corner of the room where Hannah sat with Sophie. Neither of them spoke. Lillia was grateful for the silence. If she were forced to speak, she would certainly fumble the words.

Sophie handed Lillia the traveling desk containing the papers and pen she would need to conduct the trial. The weight of the item upon her lap helped to ground Lillia's emotions. She would have to carry this thing to the so-called podium herself, as Sophie could not participate, and Hannah had her own role to play.

Managing the traveling desk was another thing Lillia had not considered when she brought the muff. Without her false hand, her balance felt off. She could manage. She often did at home when she was alone. But to do so in front of so many people?

"You can do this." Sophie gave Lillia a small smile. "This isn't your first trial, after all."

"Nor will it be your last." Hannah scowled at the Soulseers, then at the closed door. "But to those fools, this is the event of the century. They'll talk of this for years to come."

Not the most helpful observation. Lillia's chest tightened even more, if that was possible.

Before Lillia could respond, Lady Madeleine set her embroidery aside and stood, clasping her hands before her. Her Snatched stepped from the corner in which he stood, but she waved him back. He would not be joining them on the floor either.

Lady Madeleine looked to each of the Gifted in turn, then gave a self-satisfied nod. "It is time."

Lillia and the others stood with varying degrees of grace. The traveling desk was unwieldy, but nothing she couldn't handle, assuming her grip didn't slip. She would be the last to exit, entering the common room after Hannah. She wasn't sure if she preferred that honor or if she would rather walk in with the rest, mingling in to provide a degree of anonymity.

It was too late to debate the topic, though. Lady Madeleine opened the door and swept through, her skirts swaying. The two younger Soulseers followed in like fashion.

Hannah rolled her eyes at them. She waited until they had completely exited the room to make her appearance. While the crowd had quieted considerably with the entrance of the Soulseers, it went completely silent the moment Hannah stepped out.

Lillia took a deep breath to steady her nerves and followed.

The common room, which had felt so large and expansive when they surveyed the space to determine how the trial would proceed, almost seemed to close in on her. The heat of the collective bodies and their warm humid breaths weighed down the air and made it hard to breathe. There was an underlying stench of unwashed bodies and something else that Lillia couldn't identify. It put to mind something dead and decaying. The odor was so strong, she could almost taste it. Her empty stomach twisted and threatened to lurch. She may not be able to eat for the rest of the day.

The Soulseers and Hannah now stood on the far side of the circle, a guard at their backs. No one spoke. Lillia heard only the crackling of the fire in the oversized fireplace and the sounds of feet shifting and of chairs and floorboards squeaking.

The deep rim of Lillia's bonnet thankfully kept her from seeing the sheer number of people there all at once. She could pretend the only townspeople there were the ones she could see. Even that felt like too many.

Every eye was on her as she approached the makeshift podium and set the traveling desk upon it. The wooden crate shifted and swayed slightly, proving its instability. Lillia held her hand at the ready in case the desk fell, but the moving stopped.

She needed to get through this quickly. There was no telling what could go wrong.

The hinges on the desktop squealed as she lifted the lid and pulled out the papers within. Juggling them with a muff and her hand, she managed to keep hold of them long enough to set them on the desktop.

Thank the Soulmaker.

She'd taken the time to sort her pages prior to the trial to avoid looking the fool like her last trial. No leaving things to the last minute. Not this time.

She cleared her throat and lifted her head to speak to the guards. "Bring in the accused."

It had been decided to keep the accused out of the public eye until the trial began. There was no telling what the public sentiment was toward the man. Someone could take it upon themselves to deal out their form of justice. Such an action would likely lead to a secondary trial. Lillia had no desire to stay here that long.

Two guards—both women—marched to the kitchen door and disappeared, reappearing after a minute or so with a tall, thickly built man, bound by the wrists with sturdy ropes. He trudged toward the chair situated directly in front of Lillia.

He stumbled rather than sat. The guards quickly went to work securing him both hand and foot to the arms and legs of the wooden chair. In any other situation, the piece of furniture would be considered thick and sturdy. Compared to the size of the man it now held, it felt small and frail. Soulmaker help that it held.

Once the man was secured, the guards flanked him, joined by two others—men this time. Only the two women were armed, as was proper when a Truthtaker was present. They held their cudgels at the ready, as if the man would break free from his bonds at any moment.

Tension hung heavy in the air, thick and palpable. The beating of Lillia's heart increased in tempo. She kept the end of her left arm hidden within the muff, pressed close to her stomach. It was too hot in this room. Her arm felt slick with sweat, but she couldn't risk removing the muff now.

"Name?" Lillia's voice rang out but did not reverberate as it did in the trial chambers in New London. The bodies of the observers must have absorbed the sound and muted any echoes.

The man in front of her mumbled something. He kept his head down, his hair still obscuring his face.

One of the guards shoved him in his back with her cudgel. "Louder," she said with a growl.

When the man didn't say anything, the guard reached over

and grabbed his hair. She yanked his head back. "Speak to your Truthtaker, scum."

She released him none too gently. The man's face, visible now, scrunched in pain. He turned halfway to look at her. "Scum, am I, eh?" There was a slight lilt to his voice, like the hint of an accent. "I wasn't scum when I patched the hole in your roof last winter, Agnes. Or when I tracked down your little boy when he wandered off into the night beasts' territory when no one else dared follow his trail."

Murmurs rippled through the crowd.

Uncertainty crossed the guard's features. Someone jeered at her from deep within the spectators. Likely someone who had courage to say such things when surrounded by people, but who would remain silent if alone.

Agnes stiffened, and her expression hardened again.

"It don't matter, Adam. You're accused. That's all that matters now. Talk to her, or I'll be forced to use this." She smacked the cudgel against the palm of her hand a few times. "I never thought you could do this," she added sadly.

The accused flinched, likely more due to her words than her actions. "All right, I'll speak." He shook his head, and his long stringy hair brushed against his face. "But if they take me, who will find your boy if he wanders off again?" He raised his voice. "Is any man, woman, or child willing to enter the beasts' territory? Or is your bravery restricted to standing behind the safety of armed guards?"

The murmurs rose again, some angry this time.

This didn't feel right. This man didn't act like others she'd seen. There wasn't the same sense of guilt or flippancy here. No pride. No anger.

Instead, there was remorse and heavy-hearted acceptance.

Lillia fingered the edge of the topmost paper upon the stack in front of her. "Name?" she repeated.

The accused finally looked in her direction. There was a

sadness in his eyes. And something akin to defeat. "My name is Adam Burns, my lady." As the candlelight flickered momentarily brighter, it highlighted his light-colored eyes. In another place and time, Lillia would almost call this man handsome.

That thought didn't make any of this easier. She needed to maintain a neutral opinion of the man. "Mister Adam Burns, you are accused of murder of the vilest kind—that of your wife and her supposed lover. As well as mutilation of their bodies by fire and attempt to flee to escape the consequences of your actions." Several gasps rang out. Lillia ignored them, though she didn't blame them. It was a gruesome killing, one that trumped any Lillia had conducted a trial for. "How do you plead?"

Mr. Burns stared at her for several seconds before dropping his gaze to the ground once more. "They say I did it."

It was neither a confession nor a denial. He seemed to be distancing himself from the situation. Not damning on its own, but certainly suspicious. Or was Lillia reading too much into the situation?

She mentally reviewed everything she'd been told. A man acting out of vengeance toward his unfaithful wife. Killed both his wife and her lover. She would have expected someone with a darker demeanor. One who snarled at her. One more like a monster.

Lillia was no Soulseer, though. She could only guess at his intentions.

She glanced back to the Soulseers to ensure they were doing their part. All three women had removed their blinders and were watching Mr. Burns.

Three Soulseers, three different manifestations, three different perspectives. They would be the ones to decide this man's fate. A fate Lillia would seal.

Lillia waited for the signal that indicated Mr. Burns had spoken truly. The Visual Soulseer, who had been appointed spokeswoman for the three, nodded to indicate that he had.

So far, so good. Lillia turned the page. "We have testimony. A woman saw you fleeing the scene. This statement was verified by these Soulseers, who were present when this testimony was given." Lillia hadn't been present for that. She rarely was, so that wasn't unusual.

She kept her eyes trained on the pages in front of her, her head bowed. It felt like she was hiding in plain sight. So many observers. Here. Without the tinted glass. What if something went amiss?

It all felt wrong.

Lillia's arm continued to sweat within the muff. Why had she thought it was a good idea to wear this thing? Her lace cuff could have hidden her lack well enough to endure this ridiculous trial. Curse her stubborn pride!

She lifted her head, channeling courage she didn't feel. The Soulseers and Hannah watched her expectantly. What was she supposed to say now?

"I a-ask that the Aural Soulseer now approach the accused." She could have cried with relief when the words came of their own volition. "See and speak truly."

Lillia barely registered the movement of the young Aural as she inched toward the bound man and took off her blinders. This girl was barely out of the schoolroom and lacked the confidence of experience. She, unlike the Aural at Lillia's previous trial, clung to a timidity that would land the poor child behind a desk someday if she did not overcome it. She blinked rapidly and visibly shivered.

"Mister Burns, er, sir." The Aural touched her brow and gave a minute shake of her head. Lady Madeleine stepped forward and placed a hand on the Aural's shoulder. The girl gave her a tight-mouthed smile and nodded. "I mean, Mister Burns. Are you guilty of the crimes here? Do you plead guilty?" The last was spoken in a rush. It wasn't precisely the phrasing she was to use, but it was close enough.

Mr. Burns turned his bowed head toward the girl. His greasy hair fell about his face, obscuring his eyes. "I do not."

More murmuring. The guards stared daggers at any who spoke, but it did not stop all the whispers.

The Aural glanced toward Lady Madeleine, who gestured toward the accused. The girl swallowed visibly and did as she was bade.

"Th-thank you, Mister Burns." The Aural licked her lips. "I See, well, a swirling color of something that may be dark in color. The color indicates that his soul may be dark in color. Which means he may be speaking falsely."

"May be?" Lillia asked. She didn't want to intimidate her, but they were deciding this man's fate. There was no room for uncertainty. Especially with so many witnesses.

"Oh!" The Aural held her fists close to her chest. "I mean, er, that everything indicates he is speaking falsely." She tittered nervously. "Without a doubt."

Lady Madeleine gave the Aural's shoulder a squeeze and gestured for her to step back, which the girl did as quickly as she could.

Lillia nodded her assent, though she wasn't as certain of the validity of the Seeing as she would like to be. A novice Soulseer should have been guided by another of her same faction. Yet the Lady Regent had stressed the need for secrecy when they embarked on this mission. The girl must be one whom she trusted, as she had handpicked each of the Gifted here.

Secrecy, yet Lady Madeleine had insisted the trial be public. As per the Lady Regent's orders.

It was not Lillia's place to question a direct order.

Lillia cleared her throat. "I ask that the Visual Soulseer now approach the accused. See and speak truly."

The Visual curtsied to Lillia, then to the other Gifted, spreading her full skirts wide. Her attire was more traditional than most, without the split skirt that revealed the breeches underneath. When the girl rose, she clasped her hands together and approached Mr. Burns.

Her voice had a more nasally tone to it. It was crisp and precise. "Mister Burns, are you guilty of the crimes of which you are accused? How do you plead?"

Mr. Burns lifted his head and studied the Visual for a moment before resuming his defeated position. "Not guilty."

The Visual sniffed loudly. She tilted her head one way, then the other. Only then did she turn to the other Soulseers. The Aural had started weeping softly in her hands, but Lady Madeleine nodded. She had kept close watch on all of the proceedings so far. Little wonder with both of her sisters in the Gift being novices.

"Truthtaker," the Visual said, "I See his avatar hiding furtively behind a building, the light of a fire reflecting in his eyes. He rubs his hands in delight. These are not the actions of an innocent man. I believe him to speak falsely."

The Visual completed her curtsies as the crowd's voices grew once again. Lillia raised a hand to command silence, stifling a sigh when the people complied. She wished she could have seen that manifestation. A man rubbing his hands together could have been because of the cold, not because he was pleased with his actions.

It was not her place to question the testimony of Soulseers, though. "I ask that the Temporal Soulseer now approach the accused. See and speak truly."

Lady Madeleine swept forward with a grace that Lillia envied. She curtsied low with the proper deference reserved for those high in the gift. "Truthtaker," she murmured as she looked up through thick lashes. Eyes as light blue as the ice cliffs across Lake Verity shone, even in the dim light of the space.

Lady Madeleine turned to the accused. "Mister Burns, you have been accused of things most egregious. How do you plead?"

Even Mr. Burns seemed to be transfixed by Lady Madeleine.

He blew a strand of hair from his face and gave her his full attention. "My lady." His voice was hoarse, though whether from the oppressive heat from so many bodies crammed into so small a space, or from emotion, Lillia didn't know. "I am not a violent man. I did not kill those people."

Lady Madeleine gave a small *hmph* as she walked toward Mr. Burns. "I would believe that to be true, but for what I See. The future lies ahead of you, and if you are not reined in, you shall kill again. Many times and often in cold blood. I believe you to speak falsely."

Mr. Burns shook his head slowly. "'Tis not true, my lady. I would never harm another man, woman, or child."

Lillia raised her hand again, this time to silence Mr. Burns. She opened her mouth to continue. The deliberation on this trial would be difficult. They had to proceed with care lest someone cry foul.

"I propose we allow this man to speak his own testimony," Lady Madeleine interrupted. She glided across the remainder of the space to stand behind the chair and placed a hand on Mr. Burns's shoulder. "He deserves to be heard."

Lillia closed her mouth. While the proposal was somewhat unorthodox, it wasn't unheard of. This could be interesting. She didn't believe it would aid the man's cause, but she was willing to give him a chance. Just as not all Truthtakers were men haters, not all men were evil.

Lillia glanced toward the crowd, who seemed as intrigued as her. "He may speak."

Mr. Burns heaved a sigh and leaned back in his chair, slumping as much as his bonds would allow. He stared at the ground as he spoke. "I was in the woods north of town, tracking one of the night beasts that had roamed too close to Lakewood. They'd attacked another woman, left her for dead. It's the first time anyone had seen sign of them that far from their territory, and I wanted to make sure it wasn't going to cause trouble. They've been attacking during the day, you know. It's none too safe out there nowadays. No one else dares get near enough to the beasts to rid us of them." He nodded to himself, still staring straight ahead. "A man has a right to protect those he loves. He does."

Again, Lillia felt like something was off. His gaze was unfocused. His words almost felt rehearsed. "Continue."

Mr. Burns closed his eyes and furrowed his brow. "I came upon the barn. Not sure whose it was. It looked abandoned. The sort of place a beast would hide. I wanted to make sure the place was empty. That's when I saw them. The bodies, I mean." He shifted uncomfortably. "My wife . . . Nora"—his voice broke—"she was only partially dressed. And beat something fierce. I knew the moment I saw her, she was . . . gone." As he said the last word, his entire body slumped further, as if in defeat.

"And the other?" When Lillia had first heard the report, she'd had to breathe deeply to keep herself from losing what little remained in her stomach.

His expression hardened. "He was still alive when I got there. The man who tried to steal my wife from me. She was the love of my life, and he stole her affections. I wanted to kill him, Soulmaker take me, but I'm not a man prone to violence. He was injured, for certain, but not bad enough to die.

"We had words. He tried to attack me, even in his condition. Grabbed my leg. I tried to kick him, to get him off me, but I lost my balance and fell against the table. Hit my head. Dazed me a bit. I must have knocked the oil lamp over. It fell to the ground and lit some straw and a blanket on fire. By the time I regained my senses and realized what was happening, I couldn't get to him. He screamed . . . screamed so loudly. The flames . . . they were too hot." He hung his head. "I went for help, but he was dead before we could get back."

An angry retort sounded from somewhere toward the back of the crowd. One of the guards pushed her way through the people and disappeared. There were harsh words and a loud thud. Then, the doors to the inn opened and closed again.

Silence. As if the world held its breath.

Lillia turned her attention back to Mr. Burns. From all appearances, he seemed like a broken man, but appearances could be deceiving. His story seemed a reasonable explanation, but the guilty often sounded reasonable. It was not up to her to judge. Lillia turned to fully face her peers. The Soulseers watched her expectantly, but Hannah hung back, clinging to the shadows. Her part, if they should need it, would not come into play yet. Lillia's mouth was dry, nearly too dry to form the next words. She would give just about anything for a sip of water. "My fellow Gifted, I ask that you deliver your verdict."

If she'd thought the crowd had been listening intently before, they redoubled their efforts now.

The Aural stepped forward. "Guilty." She spoke so softly, Lillia had to lean forward and focus on the girl's lips to understand.

Her Visual sister stepped forward as well. She spoke with more clarity and volume. "Guilty."

Lady Madeleine nodded with each vote from her sisters in the Gift. She clasped her hands in front of her. "And I find him guilty as well."

Which left only Hannah. The Witwraith had yet to leave her shadowy corner. She scowled at Lillia, then to the accused. Then to the Soulseers. "Whether I find him guilty or not, they've already decided." She leaned back on her heels and folded her arms in front of her. "Even if I don't believe we have enough to convict."

Ripples of conversation raced through the room, relaying what only the people in the front could hear. The guards shouted for silence and tried to shush louder individuals, but few listened. It took several minutes for the commotion to die down.

Lady Madeleine fixed her gaze on Mr. Burns with an intensity that was almost palpable. For a moment, Lillia thought she saw another image superimposed upon Lady Madeleine's visage, but she surely was mistaken. While she believed in magic—her own abilities were proof of that—there were limits to what that magic could do.

Lady Madeleine lifted her chin. "Mister Burns, you went to that location knowing you would find your wife with another man, did you not? Mind you, I have Seen the truth."

Mr. Burns returned her stare, eyes wide. He blinked a few times and shook his head like he was shaking off a fly. "I . . . I . . ."

The Temporal Soulseer stepped forward and grabbed the man's chin, forcing him to look at her. "And when you arrived, you flew into a rage and killed them both, did you not?"

His jaw slackened, and the Temporal Soulseer released him. "I did as you say." His tone was as dead as his gaze. He seemed to awaken, squeezing his eyes shut and rocking back and forth, muttering something under his breath. He pressed the side of his head against his shoulder, straining against his bonds.

The crowd collectively pressed back. While some whispered, many stayed silent, staring at the man who had confessed.

Lady Madeleine returned to her sisters in the Gift and took each of their hands. "Sisters, you See as I do. You can See his guilt, how he deliberately beat and killed not only his wife, but the man she was with. Jealousy and rage guided this man's actions. He is not only guilty, but dangerous, and must be Revealed."

The other two Soulseers both nodded their agreement. Lady Madeleine's image seemed to flicker again. It was as fleeting as the first time, almost like the flickering of a candle.

Lillia swallowed hard. If she had been the one to determine guilt or innocence, she would not have chosen such a dire verdict. This man was broken, or seemed to be. She saw no signs that it was dangerous.

But her gift was not to See. It was to Reveal what was hidden.

As Lady Madeleine returned to her place with her sisters in the Gift, Lillia took her place in front of the accused, trying not to think how his thick, strong hands could easily snap her in two should he break free. He now breathed heavily, as if he'd run a great distance. He returned to flexing his hands to an irregular beat.

Hannah now stepped from the shadows. "And that, my sisters, is what we call a confession. Guilty."

Four guilty votes. There was nothing more for Lillia to do.

She looked to each of the male guards standing at attention behind the accused and waited. After a moment's confusion, one of the men grabbed at his pocket and clumsily shoved a pair of blackened blinders on his face. His companion quickly followed suit. While not foolproof, these blinders would protect them from her gift, assuming they were worn properly.

The guards formed a human wall behind the accused, overlapping their bodies so that no one could see past them. It would have been better to clear the room, but once again, it had not been Lillia's call. She was to do as she was instructed. That instruction included Revealing this man here, in front of witnesses. For what? To set an example? To keep the people in line so the Gifted would not be required to travel to Lakewood for a trial again?

Only when she was certain the men's blinders were securely in place did Lillia lower her head and remove her blinders. She spoke loudly enough to be heard throughout the common room.

"Mister Burns, you have been charged with murder, mutilation, and attempting to flee the scene of the crime. A witness places you there. You have been found guilty by Gifted who have seen into your Soul. You have confessed your guilt. You will now be made to confess fully."

She lifted her head enough to see the eyes of the accused. The rim of her bonnet hid the rest of the room from view. Even the guards standing nearby were obscured.

Mr. Burns struggled against his bonds, doing all he could to avoid meeting her unshielded gaze. The accused often did. But they all looked. When she didn't force them to look, when she merely stood patiently and waited, they eventually looked.

A minute passed. Then another. Mr. Burns's struggle slowed. Then stopped. She could sense when his curiosity finally won out. This was the moment.

"Mister Burns." She spoke as if to a child. Softly. Invitingly. "Adam."

His eyes flickered to hers. It was likely an involuntary movement, but it was enough. He did not look away. He couldn't.

Time stopped.

An invisible bond snaked between them, one only Lillia could feel. To the rest of the people, it would look like they were merely staring at each other.

So much more was happening unseen.

Something clicked.

Mr. Burns surged in his bonds, bringing the feet of his chair completely off the ground before slamming back down with a crack. The chair listed slightly to the side, and he had to partially support his weight by spreading his legs to create a tripod effect.

"Adam!" His given name felt strange and foreign on Lillia's tongue, but it was his proper address now that he was not whole. The name drew his attention as was intended. He locked eyes with her once more, and the world seemed to still.

Nothing existed but the two of them, staring into each other's eyes. Into each other's souls. Glimpses of fuzzed images raced past, and Lillia felt as if she might drown, trapped within this man's head. Glimpses of creatures and trees and fire. Nothing solid. Nothing distinct enough to make out, no matter how hard Lillia tried.

And then the Revealing snapped into place, weaving an invisible ropelike connection between her soul and his. Lillia reared back with a jerk, and suddenly time began to flow once more, leaving her dizzy and a little disoriented. She allowed herself the space of ten breaths before trusting herself to speak once more.

"Tell me what happened." He would not be able to hide the truth any longer.

This time, Adam's reaction morphed into something wild and savage. He snarled at her. At the other Gifted. At the guards. "They got what they deserved." He spat on the floor. "That filthy whore and her even more filthy plaything. If they weren't already dead, I'd strangle the life out of them both."

Someone stumbled into Lillia's peripheral vision.

Hannah.

The petite young lady glared back at the Soulseers through her crimson lenses. Her long, loose hair draped across her face, obscuring the rest of her features, though it was clear she was glaring back at whomever shoved her forward.

"Snatch him," Lady Madeleine ordered. "Now!"

Before the Witwraith could remove her blinders, Adam roared and rose up again, slamming back down with a crash. The chair splintered and broke, releasing his legs from their bindings. He fell back, slamming into the floor still tethered to what remained of the chair. He staggered back to his feet.

Screams erupted from the crowd. The door opened, and people began to stream out into the street. Lillia thrust her blinders back on and tore her bonnet off her head. She needed to see what was going on around her.

Adam shoved himself backward until he slammed into the wall, nearly freeing his arms as well. The guards—both male and female—scrambled to restrain the Revealed man, but he fought them off, his actions becoming more and more feral.

Hannah yanked her blinders off her face and shoved them at Lillia, who barely caught them before they could slip from her fingers. The Witwraith marched over to the man who was easily twice her size. She calmly waited for him to bend down in his struggles. When he did, she grabbed his head, fingers buried in his greasy hair to hold him still.

He stopped. And stared at her.

The sounds of feet on wooden floors, sobbing and shouting, cries for help . . . they all faded into the distance. All Lillia could see or hear over the pounding of her own heart was a soft murmuring coming from Hannah. She'd heard such murmuring before at previous trials, but she had never been able to make out the words. It seemed to be an essential part of the ceremony.

The murmuring stopped, though it felt as if it continued, like an errant tune running through her head. Hannah released the accused. He stood upright, his face void of emotion. His eyes stared straight ahead. The connection Lillia had briefly felt with this man had dissolved without a trace.

Ropes and bits of broken chair dangled from his wrists, but he took no heed. In fact, he acknowledged nothing at all.

Lillia swayed as the invisible connection between her and Adam was severed, gone as quickly as it had been formed.

His soul was gone. Snatched.

The common room was nearly empty now, save for Adam, the guards, and the Gifted. A few stragglers remained, gawking at what was happening.

Hannah grabbed her blinders from Lillia's hand and slipped them back on with a trembling hand. She then stumbled toward the sitting room door, practically throwing it open and falling inside. Sophie pulled her fully in and shut the door.

The motion woke Lillia from her stunned state. There was no time to dwell on what had happened. She had a job to complete. A duty to fulfill.

"You may leave now," she told the guards. They didn't waste any time, giving Lillia a wide berth as they scurried out. Only one of the women—Agnes—glanced back before disappearing through the door. Her expression was one of regret and fear.

The room quickly cleared of all but the Gifted and the

Snatched, leaving overturned chairs and scraps of paper, food, and fabric where the spectators had once been. The relative silence felt deafening.

"Well done." Lady Madeleine spoke with authority, as the Lady Regent had done during Lillia's audience. She walked around the newly Snatched man, examining him from every angle. "It's rather too bad the Lady Regent already has plans for this one. He's quite the specimen." Her gaze fell upon Lillia, and she grinned like a cat who had caught a bird. "You are of the age of majority, are you not? And you do not already own a Snatched?"

Lillia's mouth went dry. She silently begged the other Soulseers to intervene and prevent what was happening. Yet neither of them met her gaze. They silently slipped up the stairs toward their rooms, leaving Lillia alone with Lady Madeleine and Adam.

"No, Soulseer. I do not own any Snatched."

The Temporal Soulseer nodded. She placed a hand on Lillia's arm. "You'll take him as your servant. As per the Lady Regent's orders." There was no question in her tone. Simply confidence that whatever she suggested would be carried out, once again reminding Lillia of her audience with the Lady Regent.

Lillia wanted to protest, to provide some excuse as to why she couldn't do it. Surely, even with her deformity, she could manage. She had other servants, ones that were perfectly capable. She had no desire to change that.

Except the Lady Regent had given her an order to follow this woman. As much as Lillia did not want to do this, she knew she must. She nodded mutely, giving the consent she didn't want to give.

"Good." The Temporal Soulseer leaned in close to Adam's ear, leaning against his arm as she raised herself on her tiptoes to reach, and whispered something Lillia couldn't hear. Adam turned in her direction, but his gaze remained blank and unfocused.

Lady Madeleine gave a satisfied nod. "He's yours. He'll obey your every command. Use him wisely." She crooked a finger at him. He blinked a couple of times, then shambled forward. "I'll teach him the basics so he'll be ready to travel. When you return home, you'll want to take him to the Guild so he can complete his training."

Lady Madeleine led the newly Snatched man into the sitting room.

Lillia stood alone.

What had happened?

Soulmaker take her.

What was she to do now?

CHAPTER 8

DAVIN'S HEART DIDN'T STOP RACING until he was safe outside with his mother and sister. The rest of the people who had been inside the common room for the trial were quickly dispersing, though there were a few lingering. Several faces were streaked with tears, and not all of them belonged to women.

One man stood in the middle of the street, dazed and staring at nothing. He had been pushed out the doors by the crowd, but once the people had thinned out, he stopped moving of his own volition. If Davin hadn't seen the man standing far from the Truthtaker's field of vision, he would have wondered if the man had been Revealed.

"Soulmaker take me, I don't know that I'll ever recover from that," Mimi was saying as she fanned herself with her hand. "I've witnessed trials myself, you know. Back in New London when I was at the Academy. They were never so violent and intense. Why, that Revealed could have killed someone!"

That Revealed . . . as if they hadn't been familiar with the man. Davin had spoken to Adam a time or two. The man had a knack with animals and husbandry. It had been his suggestion to feed Serenity the same mix of herbs women took to promote fertility before breeding her to a native stud from Midland. Davin had thought to choose one closer to home as the distance made it more difficult to keep his future plans a secret from his mother.

Adam's suggestions were good. As soon as Davin had seen the sturdy, thick coat on the stud, he'd known the extra distance and effort would be well worth it. And the herbs must have done the trick. Either that, or he held some magic of his own.

That thought almost made him chuckle. Men with magic? Ludicrous.

Davin hadn't realized it had been Adam on trial. He'd never seen anything in Adam's behavior that would have led him to that conclusion. Adam had always been soft-spoken and hard-working. Quiet but reliable.

"He's going to get himself run over." Abigail watched the man still standing in the road. She rubbed her temples. Another headache must be coming on. They often did when she was around crowds. There had been a good many people in the inn. Far more than Davin thought possible. Not only had their table been filled until they were shoulder to shoulder, but people stood with nary an inch to spare.

The next table over, people had been placing bets on the verdict, the wagers growing more and more ridiculous. One woman bet a dyed bear beaver pelt, worth a fortune in the right hands. That had made Davin sick to hear, but he couldn't bring himself to speak up. His mother and sister would have made sure he never heard the end of it if he had embarrassed them in any way. He couldn't afford for them to pay him any more attention right now. Not with Serenity so close to foaling.

Davin gave the dazed man a closer inspection. It wasn't anyone he knew. He seemed to be in good health. Clean shaven, clothes in good order. He didn't look to be in his cups. That would have been unlikely anyway, as no alcohol had been served during or even before the trial.

If Davin had to make a guess, the man was traumatized by what he'd seen. Not that Davin blamed him. If he hadn't been raised on tales of the Gifted, told repeatedly by his mother, he would likely be just as scarred.

As it was, Davin would be enduring nightmares for days, if not longer. Watching Adam's transformation had been terrifying. The man broke the chair as if it had been a twig. He'd been mad. Crazed to the point of violence. Had that truly been Adam's hidden nature? Davin never would have guessed.

The galloping of hooves sounded in the distance. Muted at first but growing louder. It was joined by a second set and the sound of a man yelling.

Davin checked the road one way, then the other. At first, there was nothing to see. Then, a young man upon a horse rounded a corner farther down the road. He was followed by a larger man upon a sturdier horse, yelling something Davin couldn't quite make out. Both horses looked to be mixed breeds, though of lesser quality than Serenity. A coupling likely done by someone who didn't know what they were doing using poorer stock.

The younger man leaned low over his steed, urging speed. He looked back over his shoulder, then pressed his horse even harder. The horse struggled to maintain its speed. Its gait faltered and stuttered, even on the level road. Probably due to a deformity in one or more of its legs.

The larger man's steed wasn't much better, though it held up to the man's urging better. Neither horse had been bred to be ridden like this.

"He won't stop." Abigail had turned her attention to the young man. She squinted and patted Davin's arm. "Davin, he's not going to stop."

Based on the speed and direction, the young man was on a collision course with the dazed man.

Before he could form a full thought, Davin's feet were moving. He dashed to the man in the middle of the road and tried to pull him out of the way. The man was slow to respond. Far too slow.

The young rider's face was easier to make out now. Dark stringy hair, dark eyes. And a large grin on his face. He looked right at Davin and the dazed man, then adjusted course straight for them.

Davin did the only thing he could think. He turned to face the galloping horse and rider and raised his arms in the air, making him seem bigger than he was, and stepped in front of the dazed man. If he was right, the movement would spook the horse just enough to—

"Davin!" Abigail shrieked.

Everything happened quickly, yet so slowly as well. Almost as if time stopped having meaning. The horse dug its hooves into the ground and turned sharply. The rider flew off the saddle and tumbled onto the road. The horse trotted, now riderless, down the road. It tossed its head in seeming indignation as it passed. Davin echoed the sentiment.

The other rider slowed, then stopped. His breaths came in heavy gasps, as did those of his horse. The man slid off his horse and stomped to the thrown rider, who didn't seem to have injured himself too terribly. His horse slowly limped in the direction the first horse had gone.

Neither man seemed to notice.

"Cornelius!" the larger man yelled once he'd gained enough breath to do so. "You can't escape this, boy!"

The younger man growled from where he sat on the ground. He brushed the dirt off his trousers. "Not from lack of trying." He stood, listing slightly to the side before regaining his balance. Dirt and debris still clung to his clothes, and there was a tear in the sleeve of his jacket. "I have no desire to leave with you, Uncle."

Davin turned away from the family drama to check on the

man whose life he'd saved. The near-death experience appeared to awaken the man from his stupor. He stumbled back, tripping over his own feet. He managed to make it to the safety of the boardwalk before stumbling again. He continued in this manner until he ducked out of sight down the very alley Davin had previously found refuge in.

"Davin!"

And here came his own family drama. "Yes, Mimi?" Davin waited to face her until she rushed to his side.

She continued to fan her face but had now started bouncing and fluttering her fingers in a rhythm only she understood. The hysterics his mother portrayed felt forced, meant more for show than anything.

"You could have been killed!" She pressed her hand to her well-endowed chest, her fingers sprawled. She'd chosen her outfit to attract attention and, based on the number of appreciative looks she'd received, she had been successful. Now she wore her emotions to achieve the same result. "Killed, Davin! Then where would we be? What would people think?"

Considering Mimi held the land and manor, and Abigail was her heir, they would have been fine. Davin was merely window dressing that kept the books. The two women likely would have overspent until they had to sell much of their luxury items or had to retrench somewhere smaller. But they would have survived fine without him. Davin was banking on that.

"I'm fine." His words had no effect. He didn't think they would.

Abigail reached his side as well. "We should go." She lifted her chin toward the bickering men next to them. Davin raised his eyebrows in question. She gave a minute shake of her head. This was not a conversation they wanted to witness then. He still listened in as he waited for his mother to settle down enough for them to head back to the cart so they could head home.

From what he understood, Cornelius was to go to New

London to stay with relatives after some sort of trouble here. After witnessing the wild look in his eye as Cornelius turned his horse toward Davin and the other man, Davin could believe it. Send the hooligan off to New London and big city life. They had no need for it here in Lakewood. They had enough troubles with the night beasts.

Speaking of which, Davin would have to work with Sam and the stable hands to make sure someone was in the barn around the clock. They didn't need the night beasts catching the smell of the foal's birth. Enough livestock had gone missing due to the elusive, yet dangerous creatures. Men and women rarely ventured out of doors after dark, as that was when the beasts were most active.

Abigail looped her arm through Davin's. She leaned on him, her weight heavy upon his arm. "Come, brother of mine. I would like to return home while I can still see straight."

Her headache must have been growing then. Since Davin's business here in town was complete, he was happy to return. Eager, even, as he'd barely had a few minutes to spend with Serenity that morning before they'd set off for town.

He also needed to put space between him and the inn that currently housed the Gifted women. While he knew he was innocent of any crimes, he didn't want to risk another accidental run-in. One close call with a Truthtaker was more than enough for his lifetime.

"I'll get the cart." Davin pulled away from Abigail's grasp. Never mind that Mimi hadn't finished with her hysterics. She could calm herself on the ride home. As unsteady as the cart was, being pulled by big ol' Gabe the muskox over the pitted roads outside of town, she would have to devote her entire focus to keep from falling over. It would be a quiet ride home.

Such a pity.

As he passed the bickering pair, Davin glanced toward them. Cornelius watched him.

No. Glared at him. As if all was Davin's fault. As if the horse the idiot man had chosen would have gotten him anywhere he needed or wanted to go if only Davin hadn't stopped it.

"You did this." Cornelius pounded his fists against his thighs, then pointed to Davin. He ignored his uncle, who continued to berate him. "I would have been free if it wasn't for you. I will find a way to make you pay, Davin. I know your name. It's only a matter of time. Mark my words."

Empty words from a boy who acted more like a petulant child.

Davin could not bring himself to dispute the accusation, no matter how unfounded it was. Davin wasn't the one who couldn't control himself. That had been entirely on Cornelius, whatever he had done. All Davin had done was to prevent the reckless young man from being the next to go on trial. If the boy had any sense in his mind, he would thank Davin rather than blame him.

So, held his tongue. As he always did.

"Davin!" His mother's tone became more like that of a banshee. "We are ready to go. Now!"

As he walked away, he could feel Cornelius's gaze upon his back. It felt as if someone had trod upon his grave.

The entire journey home, Davin endured both his mother and sister berating him for his reckless actions. Reckless indeed. Yet he could not regret them. He had saved that man. And likely that stupid boy from himself. At least, for now. The risk to his own life was well worth it.

CHAPTER 9

LILLIA WAITED INSIDE THE TRAVELING coach with Sophie and Hannah, seated on one of the long padded benches that ran the width of the vehicle. They had chosen to ride in the forward-facing seats, as was fitting their positions in society, though they had dressed more plainly in an effort to travel with a relative degree of anonymity.

The padding on the bench was thin, and the fabric had faded, but it was more comfortable than Lillia had anticipated. She couldn't help but contrast the vehicle with that of the Lady Regent's. Money did afford one a degree of comfort not available to those less fortunate.

The interior, no matter how shabby, must have been more comfortable than topside. "I do hope Adam fares well up top." It wasn't the first time Lillia had fretted aloud. She couldn't help it. She'd never been responsible for the life of another. She wasn't certain how to manage it.

The coachman had shown incredible patience in helping

Adam climb up and instructed him on how to hold his seat while the coach was in motion. Lillia would have had him ride inside, but those seats were now being bargained for, and she did not have the coin to spend on a man who had no opinion of his own.

This was the last coach of the season, now that the weather was taking a turn for the worst. The purebred horses pulling the coach would not fare as well in the oncoming winter months on the frozen, snow-covered roads with drifts taller than a man. Nor would they have the fodder and feed they would need. They would need to travel south until the spring or be housed in a stable. It was far cheaper to go south, as this driver planned to do. Most people couldn't afford the costs associated with wintering horses in New London or its outskirts.

The bargaining was taking far longer than expected. Lillia and the others watched it unfold through the still open door, which let in the biting chill of the incoming storm most fiercely. That storm was the reason they were traveling by coach rather than by steamboat, which would have been much faster. Lillia would have been happy to stay until the storm passed, but Lady Madeleine had been insistent that Adam be sent to New London as soon as possible to begin his training. They did not have the resources here to do the job properly, and the first few days of a newly-Snatched man were crucial to his training. A poorly trained Snatched only had one future—the mining fields.

Lillia could not do that to Adam. Something about the trial still felt off, though she couldn't place a finger on it. The more she thought about it, the more she believed he may not have been as guilty as he'd been charged. She would have to talk it over with someone more senior in the gift to sort it all out and determine if there was something she missed.

Hannah had opted to join Lillia and Sophie rather than stay behind with "the nitwits," as she called the other Soulseers. The term was an accurate description of the younger two Gifted. Lillia had been relieved when they had elected to remain with

Lady Madeleine in Lakewood until the winds settled enough to take the ferry. She couldn't handle riding in a small space for two full days with the immature young women.

Lillia nestled her hand deeper into her muff, even more grateful for the article today than she had been when she first bought it. The ride home would be cold indeed. Though riding between both Sophie and Hannah would provide a little additional warmth as they sat shoulder to shoulder on the cramped bench.

"We need to get to New London as soon as possible," an older, more rotund man was saying to the driver. He looked and sounded more refined. A country gentleman perhaps. Or one who had grown up in the city. "But I refuse to be gouged for the price. No more than half a guinea. For the both of us."

The driver snorted. "A full guinea. That's my price. Unless you only wish to go to Midway. I'll be happy to leave you there if you continue to argue with me. Or you can wait for the storm to die down and take a boat. I'll not be back this way until May. Your choice."

The would-be passenger looked to his younger companion, a surly dark-haired man with sallow cheeks and a brooding expression. The bargainer stroked his thick chin as if considering. "We can't wait for the ship. We need to leave today. What if we were to pay half now, half when we arrive in New London?"

"And stiff me when we get there?" The driver shook his head. He tipped his hat to the man and adjusted his short cloak. "Try again in the spring, when you're serious about the ride. Until then, enjoy your time with those night beasts. I hear they took another victim. A child this time. In broad daylight too. If it were me, I wouldn't stay here another day, no matter the coin." He moved to climb to the top.

Lillia pressed her hand to her heart and took a deep breath. They were to be on their way, and not a moment too soon. The two men had delayed their scheduled departure by nearly half an hour. If they had any hope of missing the worst of the storm, they had to be down off the mountain soon. She prayed the horses would be able to convey them in a timely manner. They weren't the most feeble of steeds she'd seen, but neither were they the strongest. A mere team of four to pull the coach when the Lady Regent had six. It would be a miracle if they made it to Midway before nightfall.

"They're not done." Sophie peered over her blinders to where the two men stood outside. "Though I wish they were. The younger one has a darkness to him I don't like. A darkness that brightened when the driver mentioned that child."

The common room had been all abuzz about the disappearance and subsequent finding of the missing boy early this morning. It had been the son of the guard, Agnes, having wandered off again. This time, there was no Adam to find him and bring him home. He'd been torn apart by the night beasts.

Already, the ripples of Adam's Revealing and Snatching were taking effect.

"I'm not Snatching anyone else until my headache subsides," Hannah mumbled. She sat to Lillia's right, leaned up against the padded wall. No one looking at her would mistake her as a Witwraith today. Sophie had wrangled Hannah's hair into a fashionable knot, now hidden beneath a simple bonnet that matched an equally simple traveling dress. Hannah's blinders were tucked away in a small bag that now rested on her lap. She wouldn't need them while napping.

Lillia and Sophie had both opted to dress as simply. It was better to try to blend in on this journey. The trial had taken much out of them all, and they did not need the attention on them. The only item Lillia still wore that marked her as a Truthtaker was her blinders, and she hid those with the deep rim of her bonnet.

"Wait!" The older man reached a heavy arm out to the driver. "I'll pay." He glared at the younger man before plucking the coins from his pouch and handing them over. The driver counted them carefully before pulling the coach door fully open and ushering the men inside.

Lillia checked that her left arm was securely within the muff. She didn't need any awkward conversations regarding her lack on this ride. It was bad enough she couldn't remove her blinders with the two men riding with them. She would have to keep her head lowered so they did not see the indigo-tinted lenses. Better for them to believe her shy than to know the truth.

The coach rocked heavily as the older man entered and scooted to the end of the rear-facing bench. His younger companion flopped down next to him and crossed his arms across his chest.

"I don't know why we have to leave now, Uncle." The young man slumped in his seat. He didn't sit back up, even when his knees brushed up against Lillia's and Sophie's skirts.

"You know why, Cornelius." The uncle gave a shaky laugh and smiled at Lillia and Sophie. He shot a quick glance at Hannah, who was already asleep and softly snoring. "Truthtaker. Soulseer. I didn't realize we'd be sharing a coach with Gifted. And your companion, I assume."

Lillia ducked her head, though not in time. Curse her blinders for giving her away. She hadn't realized she'd lifted her head to see the two men. At least Hannah's identity remained hidden. Not only did she still need time to recover, Lillia wasn't certain either man would survive an encounter with a Witwraith who was out of sorts. Particularly this one.

The man continued to ramble, speaking quickly and stumbling over his words. "I'm Mister Dunlap. This is my nephew, Cornelius Dunlap." He nudged the younger Mr. Dunlap's arm. "Greet the ladies, boy."

The younger Mr. Cornelius Dunlap merely grunted and turned away. He sank lower in his seat.

Mr. Dunlap scowled at his petulant nephew. "Be on your best

behavior, young man." He looked at Lillia and shrugged, as if that would be apology enough for the rude behavior.

Lillia didn't press the issue. It would be difficult enough to travel with these two for the duration of the ride. No need to increase the strain with uneasy conversation.

With a shout from the driver, the coach rumbled into motion. The swaying wasn't as bad as a boat would have been, but Lillia's stomach still didn't enjoy the motion. She tried to see past either of her companions to the windows, but craning her neck caused her uneasiness to increase. There was nothing for it but to look across the space to their travel companions.

Mr. Dunlap was a heavyset man. The sort of build that would have been more muscular in his youth, but now padded with the softness of easy living. Bald with at least a double chin, if not more. Based on his clothing, he was one of the gentry, though perhaps a country lord rather than of noble blood. Lords were rare now that the role of leadership was generally bestowed upon the highest-ranking female of the family. Lords, however, were not unheard of, particularly in families where women were scarce.

One of Lillia's favorite historical figures had been Lord Child—a baron who had helped build the Academy for the Gifted. According to the histories, Lord Child had been one of the men on the *Atlantia* who had been Revealed, yet not Snatched due to the integrity of his nature. His portrait hung in one of the Guild common rooms, memorialized forever.

This Mr. Dunlap, however, possessed a calculating nature, one that took in everything around him. Lillia could almost envision him counting the cost of everything he saw. If he hadn't been so desperate to get on this very coach, Lillia suspected he would have bargained his way to a better price.

His nephew, Mr. Cornelius Dunlap, by contrast was everything his uncle was not. Surly, unwilling.

Dark.

Mr. Dunlap smacked his lips and settled more fully into his seat. "Cornelius here is off to New London for schooling. And to catch the eye of a young lady, should he be so lucky." He nudged his nephew with his elbow and gave an obvious lift of his chin in Lillia's direction. "Isn't that right, Cornelius?"

Certainly, the man was not suggesting a match between Cornelius and Lillia. She exchanged a wide-eyed glance with Sophie, who gave the slightest shake of her head. A two-day ride with these two? Soulmaker help her survive this.

"This was your idea to leave, Uncle. Not mine." The younger Mr. Dunlap shifted away from his uncle. "I have no desire to leave Lakewood. I'm more than happy to remain." His coat sleeve hitched up, revealing a bandage about his lower arm.

Mr. Dunlap flushed a deep red before pulling at his nephew's sleeve to cover up the bandage. He laughed nervously. "It's not safe here, boy. Not with those blasted night beasts roaming about. You were lucky to escape as you did."

"You were attacked?" Sophie reached up as if to lower her blinders, but dropped her hand back to her lap instead. "I thought all who were attacked didn't live to tell the tale."

Mr. Cornelius chuckled humorlessly and pulled his sleeve up to show off his bandaging. "And yet here I am. Alive and well. And off to New London to be sold to the highest bidder, like your new toy riding above."

Lillia cringed. A Snatched was not a toy. He'd been a man once. A criminal, yes. But a man, nonetheless. She wouldn't sell Adam, but other Gifted had been known to do so. She also didn't know what she would do with him once he was trained. What did a person do with a Snatched man? Put him to work cleaning the fireplaces? Make him move furniture? Or . . . something else? Another thing she would have to research.

Mr. Dunlap cuffed his nephew alongside his head. "Watch it, boy. I control your inheritance. You'd do well to remember that."

Mr. Cornelius rubbed his head where he'd been struck. "As if you'd ever let me forget, old man. The sooner you expire, the sooner I'm free."

With that, the conversation ended abruptly, which was just as well. Though the silence was easily as uncomfortable and tense.

Lillia tucked her arm and her hand deeper into her muff, trying to find comfort in the soft fur within. She longed to speak with Sophie, who now stared out the window. The Soulseer companion's head rested against the padded wall, her amber-colored blinders now secured in her hand. If Sophie was lucky, she would fall asleep as Hannah had done and avoid any more conversation with these two vile men. Lillia would not be as fortunate. Her churning stomach would not allow her a moment of peace.

As the coach rocked on over the pockmarked road, Lillia retreated into her own mind. She had to unravel what had now become of her life. A companion of suspected royal blood, who was well on her way to becoming a friend. A Witwraith—unusual even among her own kind—who seemed to have adopted them both.

And a Snatched gleaned from a most peculiar trial in the middle of nowhere.

What would people say?

What would Mama think? That was the far better question.

Actually, Lillia knew precisely what her mother would think. She'd be pleased Lillia was doing something to better herself and establish her position in society. She'd crow victory, claiming Lillia had found favor in the Lady Regent's eyes to earn such an honor.

That was all Lillia was good for in Mama's eyes. A way to undo the damage of Mama's tattered reputation. A reputation Mama denied she earned, no matter how many facts had been placed at her feet.

Lillia's eyelids grew heavy with the swaying of the coach. Perhaps she could nap after all. She had allowed her eyes to close for a brief respite when a howl punctuated both the air and the awkward silence within the coach. Lillia's eyes shot open, and she peered past Hannah to the window.

Mr. Cornelius leaned close to his window, pressing his forehead against the wavy glass. "The night beasts." His dower expression brightened to something akin to excitement. He turned his head one way, then the next, straining to see farther. "Can you see them? Are they out there?"

"No one has seen them, you fool." Mr. Dunlap smacked the young man across the back of the head. "And those who have are dead. Do you wish that upon us as well?"

All were dead save Mr. Cornelius. Unless that was a lie.

It likely was.

Lillia tried to see anything outside, but they were moving too quickly. "The beasts only attack at night, do they not?" It was barely midday, if the position of the sun was any indication. Predators could be territorial, though. If the driver pressed the horses fast enough, they could escape before there was any chance of real danger.

At least, that's what Lillia hoped.

Almost as if the driver heard her thoughts, the conveyance picked up speed. The jolt nearly tossed Lillia from her seat.

The increased speed came with increased bumps and swaying. The motion roused Hannah from her sleep. Her eyes were wide and as wild as her hair would be unbound. The bag containing her blinders slipped to the floor, but she made no move to retrieve it.

Sophie's blinders seemed to have disappeared as well. The companion Soulseer was too focused on keeping her seat to search for them.

Lillia prayed her blinders would not dislodge. She pushed them back up her nose, cursing herself for not getting them repaired sooner. When they arrived in New London, she would not only have every pair repaired immediately, she would have straps added to the earpieces to keep them on her face no matter what she encountered.

Merciful heavens, if she survived this, she would never travel from New London again. Not by boat, not by coach or carriage. She would rely only on her own two feet to get her where she needed to go.

Mr. Dunlap groaned as they hit a particularly large pothole that lifted them all from their seats for a terrifying moment. "Soulmaker, take me now." He groaned again and held his stomach, his face taking on a slightly greenish hue.

"Shut up, you fat tub of lard!" Mr. Cornelius cried. He no longer watched out his window, diverting his entire attention to holding fast to his seat.

Another howl carried over the clamor of pounding hooves and rattling coach, louder and closer now.

Mr. Cornelius tried to turn in his seat. "They're here!"

"Sit down, boy!" Mr. Dunlap tried to grab at his nephew's arm, but Mr. Cornelius jerked out of reach.

"I've got to see!" Mr. Cornelius leaned across the coach, pressing against the glass above Lillia and Sophie. He was so close, Lillia could smell the acrid odor of his sweat and feel the humid heat radiating from his body. She tried to shift away, but being wedged in between the other two Gifted, found she could not budge an inch.

Mr. Cornelius laughed. He lifted his head and released an eerie howl, loud and long. It mimicked the howls of the beasts. So much so, one would think this young man one of the beasts himself.

The horses screamed in fear, as did Lillia and Sophie. Hannah gritted her teeth and held on tight, looping her arm through Lillia's to help keep her in place as well.

"Cornelius!" Mr. Dunlap screeched. The coach increased

even more in speed, then lurched to the right. It hit a particularly large bump.

The coach began to tip, the motion feeling as if time itself had slowed.

Hannah's bag, Sophie's blinders, the ends of Lillia's hair . . . they all rose into the air. Floating at eye level. Suspended for the briefest moment.

Instead of terror, Lillia felt a sort of detachment, as if watching it all unfold from outside of her body.

As she fell from her seat and tumbled to the side, she thought how odd it was that falling felt very much like a Truthtaker's Revealing.

CHAPTER 10

D AVIN'S BACK AND FEET ACHED, but mucking out the stalls was honest work, so he couldn't complain. He'd done it since he was old enough to hold a shovel. The physical labor centered his thoughts and strengthened his body. The rhythmic motion served as a form of meditation.

The chore also allowed him to check on Serenity and her ever-growing belly. She nickered at him and playfully pulled at his sleeve. He shoved her nose back and scolded her with a smile.

"Let me finish, girl. Then, I'll get you a treat."

Once he was done here, he would need to engage in a more urgent task.

The news of the butchered child had made its way to Bradford Lodge and had been the topic of conversation over their midday meal.

Mimi, of course, was delighted to have yet another piece of gossip to indulge in. She'd insisted on having Sam hitch up the wagon to take her to her sister's immediately. Abigail had only been able to beg off going with her since her headache from the day before had yet to ease. She'd turned down Mimi's offer to send for Dr. Thurst, thank the Soulmaker.

Mimi dismissed Abigail's pain and flitted out the door, eager to share in the latest news and to speculate upon every detail, whether it was true or not.

Davin, however, was not delighted to hear of the demise of a young boy. It only spurred his fear that Serenity could be next. The mare was showing signs of nearing her time. With so much riding on this foal, Davin could not take any chances.

Sam was currently occupied and would be for some time, so Davin was on his own to search for signs of the beasts. It was for the better, as Sam had been reluctant to aid in the search to begin with. He didn't believe the beasts would be a danger to any at Bradford Lodge.

Davin felt otherwise. Beasts that would kill a small child wouldn't hesitate to prey upon a newborn foal. The most likely place to start was a section of land on the west, bordering the New London road first. The beasts were known to prey along the roads. Their known territory lay to the north of the Bradford lands on the other side of the river, so he would check that border next.

Sam would join him once he returned from ferrying Mimi back and forth. He'd grumble about the necessity of the endeavor, but he was loyal enough to do as asked.

Davin had nearly made it to the road when a howl cried in the distance. The sound lent truth to his fears. He tried to determine distance. A mile? Two? Only if luck was with him, which it often was not.

Another sound, similar to continually rolling thunder, crept into his awareness. The worst of the incoming storm had yet to hit, though, and wouldn't for a couple more hours. Only the scarcest of rainfall had begun. Not even enough to wet Davin's hair.

The sound grew louder. Davin broke into a near run. That sounded like a coach traveling far too fast for these roads. No one should be moving that fast. Not unless they were being chased.

He didn't know what he could do, but he moved without thinking. Just as he had in town when Cornelius nearly ran the catatonic man down.

Davin reached the road only to see a rising cloud of dust filtering above the treetops past where the road turned toward town. The rumbling evolved into the tumultuous rattling of a horse-drawn coach racing down the uneven road. The driver whipped the beasts, yelling obscenities to urge them even faster. The horses looked to be of inferior stock and labored to keep up the pace set by the frenzied driver. Fear filled their eyes.

The driver kept looking behind him, terror evident in every motion. The man sitting next to him swayed but did nothing else. He was likely holding on for dear life.

The coach shot past him, spewing dirt and rocks in every direction. Davin raised an arm to keep the projectiles from hitting his face.

Another howl cried, but it sounded as if it came from the coach itself. The horses screamed and jerked to the right, but the speed proved to be too much for such a maneuver. The horses broke free from the tumbling coach and disappeared down the road, running even faster than before. The harness and chains dragged behind them.

One of the coach's wheels hit a deep pothole, the force of momentum sending the coach tumbling end over end in a crunching, crashing fashion. Trunks and bags flew off, tumbling and coming to rest in various stages of destruction. Splinters and twigs and leaves ricocheted, and a thick cloud of dust billowed about, obscuring Davin's vision.

The coach finally came to rest against the trunk of a sturdy pine. It now resembled more a heap of firewood than the conveyance it had once been. Davin froze, horrified at the scene that had unfolded before him. Thought ceased to function for what seemed an eternity. Davin blinked in disbelief. The possibility of anyone surviving such a mess seemed remote indeed.

Breath and brain power returned to him in a rush. Sounds and sensations as well. He ran to where the driver and the passenger who had been riding on top had fallen. Both had been thrown from their perch. The passenger lay nearby, his neck and arm twisted in awkward angles that no man could have survived. The dead man's face pressed into the dirt, obscuring his features.

Death must have come instantly, which was a blessing.

The driver lay nearby. He still lived. Blood gushed from his side, hot and red against the pale brown of the road. Davin knelt by him and pressed his hand to the wound to try to staunch the bleeding. The driver grabbed at Davin's arm, frantic at first, then weakening. Davin pressed harder, desperately wishing there was more he could do, someone he could call for. No one was in sight, though. None living, at least.

Still, he looked.

Movement drew his eye. A woman rose from the ground nearer the wreckage. She listed to the side before regaining her balance and picking her way through the remains. She limped as she walked, her foot or leg obviously injured in the crash. Her light-colored hair had worked its way from whatever pins or fasteners it had endured and stood at odd angles. The sun, now lower in the sky, lit up the stray hairs like gold.

Odd what one noticed in a situation like this.

Another lady stood, as unsteady and untidy as the first. Spots of blood marred her skirts and her face. She stood shorter than the first, her stray hair lit up like ebony rather than gold.

They assisted a third lady to her feet, though this one still retained her bonnet. She was more stout than the other two but still cut a pleasing figure.

All were young, dressed in simple traveling clothes. Likely on their way to New London to seek husbands or attend school. A journey that was cut short before it even began.

A forlorn moaning carried through the air—evidence yet another passenger still lived, if gravely injured.

Davin could have cried with relief. He had been certain none had survived the ordeal. He opened his mouth to call for help when another figure emerged from the wreckage and yelled angrily. The blood rushed through Davin's ears far too loudly for him to comprehend the words, but he suspected none were proper for civilized company.

He recognized the man. It was Cornelius, from the street after the trial. His uncle must have coerced him onto the coach to New London after all.

This did not bode well for Davin.

Cornelius approached the first young woman, calling for her attention. She kept her face averted as he spewed at her.

"We lost them," he screamed, those words loud and distinct enough for Davin to hear. "They're gone for certain. I'll never find them now!"

Davin pressed his hands harder against the driver's side. If he drew attention to himself now, Cornelius may decide to take his frustrations out on him, leaving this poor man to die.

The blonde woman continued to keep her face averted, which seemed to rile Cornelius up even more. He stomped to her and jerked her arm, forcing her to face him. She still refused to meet his eyes.

If Davin could leave the driver to save the girl from Cornelius's forced attention, he would.

The other two women cried out and started toward Cornelius and their companion, but he ignored them. Instead, he grabbed the girl's chin and forced her to look at him.

She met his gaze, whether intentional or not.

Cornelius stiffened. And silenced.

The companions gasped.

The driver mumbled something, drawing Davin's attention away from what was happening. The once deathlike grip on Davin's arm weakened even more. Davin adjusted his position to increase the pressure on the wound. The flow of blood had slowed considerably, but he couldn't be certain it was due to his efforts or if the man was near death. He could feel the man's pulse beat in time with his own.

Thum-thump. Thum-thump. Thum-thump.

An angry roar broke through the air. Davin returned his attention to the others. The three women now clung to each other as Cornelius pried a thick stick from the underside of the overturned coach. He climbed over the rubble and wreckage to where Davin could barely make out the silhouette of a heavyset man propped up against and under debris.

The stick appeared to be of good shape and size to use as a lever to free the trapped man, but Davin didn't believe that was Cornelius's intention. Not after seeing the man deliberately change course on a galloping horse so as to run a helpless man over.

He was right.

Cornelius slowed as he approached the older man. Instead of wedging the stick under the wreckage, he raised the stick high above his head.

"This is all your fault!" He let out a guttural roar and brought the stick down with all his might. It made contact with the injured man's head with a sickening crunch.

The women stumbled back as one, clutching to each other. They scrambled away, toward Davin.

Cornelius continued with his savage attack with single-minded focus. Over and over, he swung the stick until it splintered and broke. He threw the bloodied wood aside and grabbed another piece.

The women continued their careful retreat, picking their way in Davin's direction while simultaneously watching the massacre. None gave him any notice.

Davin could not watch and not help. "Over here," he hissed, not daring to release the pressure from the man's side.

The tallest woman, the blonde who had been limping, locked eyes with him.

Davin barely had time to suck in a breath before time stood still.

Everything around him fell away. Silenced. Stilled.

Only he and this angel of a woman existed. Here. Now.

A vision appeared before him. A peek into her soul, he was sure. Soft. Peaceful. Beautiful beyond imagining. A place of true serenity.

He could reside in this space forever.

The young woman's mouth dropped open. She pressed her hand to her cheek.

He longed to touch that cheek as well. Was it as soft as it seemed?

Then, something within clicked.

And Davin was changed forever.

CHAPTER 11

A S THE REVEALING SLID INTO place, all that existed was Lillia and this stranger. The accident, Cornelius attacking his uncle, Sophie and Hannah holding tight to her, the sharp metallic scent of fresh blood intermingling with dirt . . . they existed, but like a far-off dream.

The only thing that mattered was this man.

Absently, she noted the shape of his chin, the straight lines of his nose and brows, the way the breeze ruffled and tousled his dark hair that was now misted by the light drizzle coming from the sky. Every detail became ingrained in her memory, and she knew she would always be able to pick him out from any crowd.

The Revealing held her like a dance, smooth and graceful. It toyed and teased and eased into place. When time finally resumed its frantic pace, Lillia felt a sense of peace and belonging.

Until she realized the beating sounds had stopped. Cornelius now stood above the battered and bloody remains of his uncle, heaving deep breaths as if he couldn't get enough air. He lifted his eyes to the sky and howled, primal and raw.

There was a connection with him as well. One that pulsed with heated emotions strong enough to strangle her.

Fear coursed through Lillia, and she once again met the stranger's gaze. He glanced down to the unmoving form in front of him.

The driver. He was dead. His blood stained the ground and the stranger's hands and arms.

This stranger had tried to save him.

He gave Lillia a long, searching glance, then pointed to where Cornelius continued to howl over and over again, his cries growing more anxious and loud.

The stranger then pointed toward the trees on the other side of the road, away from the wreckage and carnage. Lillia looked at Sophie and Hannah. They crept toward the trees, keeping low to avoid detection.

Tears streamed down Sophie's cheeks. She scrubbed at them once they entered the relative safety of the woods. Her blinders had been lost in the accident, as had Lillia's and Hannah's. There had been no opportunity to retrieve them. Sophie would have to avoid being around too many people at once to avoid overwhelming her senses, but any ill effects she did experience would ease in time.

The loss of Lillia's blinders was far more serious. Extreme caution had to be taken to prevent another accidental Revealing.

Two more men lost to her gift.

It was her worst nightmare come to life. There would be no coming back from this. She would be lucky to merely be sentenced to isolation. There were far worse punishments for a Gifted who abused her gift.

She would mourn that later. For now, they had to find safety, both from Cornelius and the beasts that had caused the crash. Their howls had been more bone-chilling than she'd imagined.

Even more so when Cornelius joined them as if he, too, was one of them.

Cornelius deserved to be Snatched, that was certain. If he was that dangerous once Revealed, what crimes had he dared to commit beforehand? Had that been the reason his uncle was so insistent on their leaving Lakewood as quickly as possible?

Speaking of Snatched . . . where was Adam?

Lillia plucked at the sleeve of the stranger who led them deeper into the woods. "There was another man riding up top. Did you happen to see him? Is he—"

"He didn't make it."

The stranger didn't slow to give her his response, though Lillia wished he would. Both because she needed time to sit with her grief, and her leg hurt horribly, though she was certain it wasn't broken as she was able to walk on it. It was all she could do to keep up with him. Her limp grew more pronounced the farther they went.

She fell back to join the others. Sophie kept close to Lillia's side. She watched the stranger, her eyes wide. Almost as if she was searching for something. Her meager gift could have been manifesting some sort of aura. It was possible since manifestations were strongest when someone was experiencing strong emotions.

Crashing and banging came from the direction of the coach. "Ladies." Cornelius's weedy voice sang an eerie tune. "Where have you gone? What have you done?"

The hairs on Lillia's arms prickled and rose. She had no desire to speak with the man. She'd seen how he handled those he believed to have caused him harm.

"We must hurry," she urged. Her leg protested, but she ignored it. She would have time to see to her leg after they'd found safety. And a haven from the increasing wind and drops of rain that had begun to fall.

They continued to flit through the trees, stepping as lightly as they could to avoid the cracking of a branch or brushing up against anything that would betray their location.

Cornelius called again, his voice growing fainter as they stealthily hurried away from him. The wind picked up, and snow began to fall, aiding in their efforts to conceal their actions. Though if it began to stick, the fallen snow would betray them for certain.

The connection between Cornelius and Lillia thrummed wickedly, hot and red. If she focused hard enough, she could pinpoint his precise location. From all accounts, he likely could do the same, if he knew how to harness that ability. One of the earliest teachings Lillia had received had been to mask that connection in case a Snatching went wrong, and she found herself in danger.

Never had she expected to use that skill.

She allowed the others to guide her through the trees, trusting they would not lead her astray. She turned her attention inward to that pulsating cord of awareness within her own mind. It writhed violently.

Bit by bit, ever so slowly, Lillia willed a mental wall into place around that connection. She had to work stealthily enough to not draw attention to it, or they were as good as found. The wall would not hold forever, but it would buy them the time they needed to find help.

Hannah pulled Lillia and Sophie a distance back from the stranger who led them. Close enough to still follow, but far enough away to allow for a private conversation.

"What do we know about him?" Hannah asked in hushed tones. "Do I need to Snatch him? Or just the monster we left behind?"

It was a fair question and one Lillia did not yet have an answer for. Lillia responded in the same fashion, keeping her voice low so it wouldn't carry forward. "I'm not certain. We've only just met him. What do you think, Sophie?" The Soulseer must have some inclination one way or the other, no matter how weak her gift was.

Sophie had yet to stop watching their guide. "I think we can trust him. He won't lead us astray." She nearly tripped over an upraised root but caught herself in time. "His, er, aura looks to be . . . nice."

Lillia would have to ask her to clarify later. "Nice" would not hold up in a trial, but it would suffice for now. "And you, Hannah? What do you think? He is Revealed."

"There was no question about that, Lil." Hannah reached up and yanked a pin from her hair and tossed it aside. Her carefully coiffed styled was now more like a rat's nest. "The second he steps out of line, I'll Snatch him before he can think twice."

"But only if he deserves it." Lillia didn't need any more trouble. Soulmaker help them, if Hannah Snatched an innocent man, Lillia wouldn't be the only one in confinement. "Truly deserves it. And not merely because he annoys you."

"He should know." Sophie wiped away another tear, though her voice remained steady. "That he's Revealed. That he does deserve."

Sophie had a valid point. "You're right." Lillia ducked under a low-hanging branch. "I'll tell him once we arrive wherever he's taking us."

"You'll do no such thing." Hannah pulled the last pin from her hair and tried to run her fingers through the tangled curls without success. They remained tight against her head. She shook her head in disgust. "If you tell him now, everyone will know what happened. We'll all be thrown in prison faster than you can blink. But if we can fix everything before we tell the Guild, we may be able to salvage this."

Heavens, that would be nice. Lillia would love to remain a free woman, if at all possible. Mama would prefer that as well. Soulmaker knew what Lillia's imprisonment would do to the Pennyworth name. If they couldn't remedy this, Lillia would have to deal with Mama's ire as well as the judicial side of things. She wasn't certain which would be worse.

Lillia exchanged glances with Sophie. "Perhaps we wait until we know more?"

The Soulseer gave Lillia a long searching look, not unlike the one she had given their mysterious guide. Whatever she saw there must have swayed her mind. She sighed deeply. "I suppose we can wait. But we must tell him as soon as possible. It isn't right keeping such a thing from him."

As Lillia opened her mouth to agree, she stumbled over something in her path. Her injured leg could no longer support her weight, and she tumbled to the ground, involuntarily yelping in pain. She reached out with both arms to cushion the fall. Pain blossomed in her palm and the end of her lack as she made contact with the debris-strewn forest floor.

Their guide stopped and turned back to them. When he saw her on the ground, he hurried to her side. She felt the moment he spied her lack, sensed the shock and confusion. She didn't need to share a bond with him for that. His repulsion was evident in the way he initially pulled away, though he recovered quickly enough to help her up.

Lillia's leg now screamed with pain. She would not be able to walk another step forward. She leaned heavily on their guide, who now held her left arm to keep her from falling over. That he continued to do so without recoiling in disgust raised her opinion of him. Perhaps she'd read him wrong a moment ago. Anyone would be taken aback upon seeing a missing appendage. She herself had done so before.

"Are you well?" Sophie asked. "I'm assuming the house ahead is our destination. I can see it through the trees over there."

"You'd be right about that." Their guide turned to Lillia, those eyes of his meeting hers and nearly taking her breath away. "Are you able to support yourself?"

"I'm afraid not." What a sight she must be—a one-handed

woman with an injured leg. Based on the rumpled and torn appearances of her companions, she likely appeared as battered and bruised as well. "Could we fashion a crutch of sorts? One I can manage one-handed?" They were in the woods. Sticks were plentiful here, she assumed.

Their guide shook his head. "There's no time." The snow fell thicker and heavier, lending credence to his words. He pointed in the direction they were heading. "It's not far. I'll carry you." Without warning, he swept Lillia off her feet and into his arms. His eyes widened, and he sucked in a breath. "Forgive me. We haven't even been introduced."

Yet he did not put her down again.

Lillia forced the fluttering of her stomach back down. She'd never been so close to one of the opposite gender before, save her own father. She hadn't imagined being held like this to feel so right.

Or so good.

"I'm Lillia," she blurted, cognizant of how closely both Hannah and Sophie were watching. They could see her emotions written all over her face, she was certain. In her rush to speak, she failed to give her last name. She did not regret the action. Lady Pennyworth was well known, even in places she'd never visited before. Lillia, however, could be anyone.

The anonymity called to her. Lillia, the girl. Not Lady Pennyworth, the Truthtaker.

Her guide and rescuer chuckled. "A pleasure to meet you, Lillia. I'm Davin."

Davin. A strong and handsome name for a strong and handsome . . .

Even her thoughts trailed off when she saw the knowing smirk on Hannah's face. Had Lillia spoken aloud? Nothing in her companion's body language either confirmed or denied it.

Her face burned with humiliation the remainder of the journey to the house. It nearly distracted her from enjoying the proximity of this man, who spoke her name with such tenderness she could have swooned on the spot.

Nearly. But not quite.

CHAPTER 12

THE REMAINDER OF THE WALK home was both the longest and the shortest Davin had ever experienced.

On the one hand, trying to escape Cornelius and his murderous rage had been terrifying. Davin couldn't move fast enough. He knew at least one of the women was injured, but he couldn't bring himself to slow down, though he knew he should. All he could think was to get them to safety as quickly as possible, the consequences be damned.

But then Lillia had fallen.

Why he had picked her up without even knowing her name, he could not say. Only that he was eager to hold her in his arms. To hold her close. Ever since their eyes met, he'd felt something. A connection of sorts. Deeper and more profound than any other he'd ever known.

It was a relief when they walked through the doors, and he was able to set Lillia down on the sofa in the front parlor. Though accustomed to hard labor, his back protested, and his legs felt shaky. The snow had wet his clothing and hair, leaving him thoroughly chilled. Thankfully, the fire had been recently stoked, so the room was warm and cozy.

Davin's arms ached fiercely. He hadn't noticed how tired they were until he was freed from Lillia's weight, slight as she was. He shook them to restore the blood circulation and to warm up his hands.

The other two women warily followed him into the room, slowly migrating toward the hearth. They watched him as they would a stray dog.

Their caution was understandable. He was a stranger, and he had led them to his home in the woods while being hunted by a madman. He would be cautious too.

"Are any of you injured?" Davin asked. "Enough to require a doctor?" From where he stood, he could see a few scrapes on their faces, mingled in with the dirt. The shorter woman with dark hair held her upper arm, but he couldn't tell if that was for comfort or to help ease pain.

The more plump girl shook her head. "I believe only Lillia is in need. I can see to her wound to ascertain how bad it is."

That was good. Davin was good with animals, but not so much with people. He sat next to Lillia on the sofa and waited. He wanted to be ready should they need anything.

No one moved. All three women watched him with curious expressions.

Lillia was the one who spoke first. "Davin, my injury is to my leg."

"Yes, I know." That was why she couldn't walk, and he had to carry her. He was well aware of where her injury was.

When he still didn't move, the dark-haired girl rolled her eyes. "You need to vacate the room, idiot. For decency's sake."

It took longer than it should have for what that implied to sink in. "Ah. Yes. Of course." He stood and tugged at the bottom of his coat. His hands came away feeling gritty and damp. "I'll go, uh, change into something more suitable for . . . things." Yes, that would be for the best as his mother would be home at any time, and she would not like to see him dressed as a stable boy. And he wanted to look his best for Lillia and the others.

He was halfway to the door before he realized he didn't know his other guests' names. He turned to ask and got as far as opening his mouth when the dark-haired girl spoke again.

"I'm Hannah. That's Sophie. We'll talk later. Go change your clothes and prepare rooms for us. And get some hot water started so we can wash up."

Yes. That was good. It was all good.

Davin hurried to comply, wanting to give them time to perform the examination, but also eager to return.

Gads, why was he such an idiot all of a sudden? It was as if he was the one who'd been tossed about in a tumbling coach.

A mere half an hour later, Davin returned to the parlor dressed and desirous to learn what was determined about Lillia's injury. He'd ordered rooms prepared and hot water started, though the cook grumbled about the inconvenience. He'd thanked her for her time and tossed a few coins to her. That had brought a rare smile to her face.

"I don't think we'll need to do that," Lillia was saying as he walked through the door. "He seems to be fine." Her leg was now propped up on a chair, and her split skirts hung loose, revealing the thick winter breeches underneath. A strip of fabric served as a bandage over what Davin surmised would be the wound. Though the fabric was dark in color—likely torn from the hem of one of the ladies' dresses, a darker stain was already seeping through. Not enough to cause immediate worry.

Davin sighed with relief, drawing the attention of all three women. "So, it is not life-threatening then?" He had been worried about that.

"Thank the Soulmaker for small mercies." Lillia tugged at her skirts to cover her breeches and her bandage. She struggled to reach for the other end of her skirt, which had fallen out of reach of her one hand. Davin took the seat to her left and reached down to hand her the end of the fabric, almost without thought.

She looked at him quizzically but didn't say anything. Once her skirt was arranged to her liking, she leaned back on the sofa and gave him her full attention.

"And you? How do you fare?"

That was an odd question considering he wasn't the one who was injured. "I'm well. Thank you for asking." Almost belatedly, he remembered they were not alone in the room. "And are you well, Hannah and Sophie?" He congratulated himself for remembering their names. It wasn't proper for him to address them so informally, but they hadn't provided anything other than their given names.

Neither had he, now that he thought about it.

Both ladies, who now sat in chairs opposite the sofa, merely stared at him for a moment.

"I'm well," Sophie said slowly. She watched him in a strange, unblinking manner that left Davin feeling uneasy. Was she attracted to him? She was pleasant enough to look at, with those sweet round cheeks and expressive eyes. His first impression of her of being plump was unkind. She was more full-figured than her companions, but it was fetching on her. If he didn't already find himself drawn to Lillia, he could find himself attracted to her as well.

Hannah raised a single eyebrow. "Never better." Her tone indicated otherwise. "Though I'm starving. Did you happen to call for food while you were gone?"

Thankfully, Cook had already begun to prepare a tea tray. She'd offered only after Davin had given her the coin. It was amazing what a little appreciation could produce.

Davin beamed with the self-satisfaction of being on top of things even before they were requested. "It should be here soon."

One of the kitchen maids came in, bobbing a quick curtsy before she spoke. "The rooms are ready, sir. And I've got enough hot water for the ladies to wash."

"Finally," Hannah grumbled. She stood and stomped toward the door. "Show me where to go. And direct a tray to come to my room. Or you'll find out how much of a beast I can be when I'm hungry."

The maid's eyes grew wide. She hesitated until Davin waved her to follow.

Sophie stood as well. "Would you like me to help you to your room?" she asked Lillia. "I can help you wash."

Lillia shook her head wearily. She'd settled deeply into the sofa and leaned her head against the back of it. "I can wait. Go freshen up, then come help me. I'd like to eat something and rest a moment before we attempt the stairs."

There was a flash of indecision on Sophie's face before she gave a tired smile. "Very well. I'll return as soon as I can."

An awkward silence descended upon the room once Sophie left. All the questions Davin had for Lillia suddenly evaporated, and he couldn't recall a single one.

Davin became painfully aware how close Lillia was. And how empty the room had become. His leg bounced uncontrollably. He cast about for something to say. "You are well, then? Besides the leg?"

He'd asked that already and felt more the fool for doing so.

"I believe I am. Though I would feel better if a doctor looked at my injury. The cut is deep enough to be concerning." She rested her hand across the end of her other arm, hiding it from view. When she noticed his attention on it, she tried to rearrange the fabric of her skirt to hide it even more.

His tongue spoke without volition. "Don't do that." He touched her hand, gently tugging it to reveal the end of her arm again. "Please don't feel the need to hide it. Not from me."

Lillia covered her arm again. "It's hideous," she whispered

as she turned away. "Mama says no one wishes to see my deformity. That it marks me as less. I normally have a false hand to conceal my lack, but the lacings broke. Then, the hand broke, and it needs to be repaired, and I don't have a spare. I could have stuffed a glove, but that looks even worse." She trailed off and bit her lip. "Forgive me. You didn't need to know all of that."

"Your mother is wrong." Davin would shake some sense into her mother right now if he could. "And anyone who thinks that you having one fewer hand makes you less than them is a fool."

She gave a tight smile and tugged at her sleeve, still not meeting his eyes. "My papa used to say the same thing."

"He sounds like a very wise man." A man Davin very much would like to meet, if only to ask why he allowed his daughter to think she was anything less than lovely and strong and good. From what little he'd seen of her character, that was precisely who she was.

Lillia sniffed. She rubbed her nose with the back of her hand. "He was. But he's gone now."

Gone. Like Davin's father. He pulled out a handkerchief and handed it to her. "I lost my father too. He was killed a few years ago. Likely by the same creatures that caused your accident."

Lillia turned her big, beautiful gray eyes toward him. Gray like a stormy sky. "I'm so very sorry." She plucked at her sleeve, pulling the lace at the ends to cover the end of her arm. "What was he like?" she asked.

That was something few people had asked. Davin had to think on that for a moment before answering.

"He was kind. And hardworking. And brilliant." Davin leaned forward and started gesturing with his hands. "He had this idea. One to breed horses for the northern lands using the native horses to strengthen their bloodlines. Ones that could withstand the coldest months with thick coats and wide hooves to allow them to walk on the ice and through the snow. He wanted a breed that could forage like a deer too, so he wouldn't have to rely on storing hay and grain through the long winters. He had this theory of how to get them to reproduce so his breeding efforts would last more than one generation. I used to sit on a stool in the stables and watch him work. He'd inspect each foal after it was born, looking for thicker coats and sturdier frames. He fed them less and less hay until they no longer depended on it. Generation after generation, he handpicked the traits he wanted in the purebreds and he'd breed them again. He even believed that having the mares foal late would help their offspring better adapt to the harsh weather."

"That sounds remarkable." Lillia turned slightly toward him. "Was he successful?"

"He came close." Davin had helped him with that last attempt. It had been Davin's idea to breed Serenity's mother with a native stud captured near Midway. That had been the most successful pairing yet. Until Serenity's foal, of course. Father's theories had been correct. He just hadn't survived to see them come to fruition.

"Someday"—Davin leaned back on the sofa next to Lillia—"I'll have an entire herd of cold-hardy brood stock. Then, I'll be able to take control of my own life. Have my own home. Be free."

He very nearly regretted saying those words aloud. Only Sam knew of Davin's future plans, and the man-of-all-work would never tell another soul. Years of friendship and working side by side with the quiet servant assured Davin of that.

Yet he almost felt relieved telling Lillia. Unburdened. Like sharing the load of that secret freed him of some of the weight.

"That's a beautiful dream. I wish you good fortune in your endeavors." She smiled. Her sigh sounded like a mix of hope and sadness. "To think, such a success would be so beneficial, not only for you, but so many others."

"Yes. Precisely that." Davin grew excited again. "Travel between Lakewood and New London and the south would not be entirely dependent on the weather anymore. Horses are faster and more agile than muskox. A sturdier breed could also be put to work on farms here in the north. We wouldn't have to rely solely on the farmlands in the south to get through the winters. And if the horses become plentiful enough, even the lowliest farmers and workers could have access to them, rather than having to settle for donkeys or pull their loads themselves."

"It would be like the stories from the motherland." Lillia's eyes brightened.

"But better."

A quiet cough from the door interrupted their conversation. Sam stood there, tray in hand. "Tea?"

Lillia turned her head away and covered her eyes with her hand. The poor girl. They'd gotten so exuberant about his plans. Her embarrassment was charming.

Davin directed Sam to leave the tray on the table, then to check on the other two ladies. If Sam was back, it likely meant that Mimi was back as well. She must not have known they had guests, otherwise she would have already descended upon the parlor to pry gossip from Lillia. It was only a matter of time before she did.

"Shall I pour?" Davin asked when Sam had retreated. "Or would you like to do so? I can pull the table closer so you don't need to stand."

Lillia gave him another curious look. She did that often. "If you don't mind doing it. I'm feeling rather sore."

Of course she did. She'd been in an accident. How much more of a fool could he be?

He prepared her cup as per her directions, then handed it to her, only belatedly realizing he didn't know how she managed a teacup and saucer with only one hand.

She set them on her lap, using it as a temporary table as she lifted the cup to take a sip. The smoothness of her actions indicated frequent practice in that regard.

"Would a tray be of use to you?" Davin asked after a minute or two. "One you can set your saucer on. Perhaps some cakes too?"

Lillia touched the saucer on her lap with the end of her lack. "That would be helpful, thank you. It's what I do at home. Mama insists on my using my false hand to hold the saucer. To maintain appearances. It's not always easy. More often than not, I end up spilling tea on myself."

"I'm beginning to not like your mother."

"She means well." Lillia dipped her chin ever so slightly and sighed. "She only wants the best for me."

"But it should be on your terms, not hers."

There was the slightest fluttering of her lashes. It was the only indication she disagreed with his statement. "Perhaps."

"No. Not 'perhaps.' You should be able to be your own person. To follow your own path. What is it you want, Lillia? Who do you want to be?"

That was more bold than Davin had intended. He had only wanted to encourage her to think of herself rather than cater to the whims of others. But now he found he was deeply intrigued to learn the answer.

He wasn't the only one surprised by the question.

"I don't think anyone has ever asked that of me." Lillia blinked a few times and ran her finger along the delicate handle of her teacup now balanced on the saucer in her lap. "I'm not certain I know. My life has always been planned for me."

As was Davin's. But he was determined to break free.

And with the Soulmaker as his witness, he would help Lillia do the same.

CHAPTER 13

L ILLIA WOKE WITH A START, not knowing where she was at first. Her world seemed to be an explosion of pink and ruffles. She fought the over fluffed blanket that had twisted around her to take in her surroundings. Pale pinks dominated the room in every fabric and texture possible. It was a small fortune of colors, and none of it felt cohesive. The cumulative effect overwhelmed her already exhausted brain.

She rubbed her eyes, keeping her palm and the end of her arm pressed against her face. A headache raged, centered behind her eyes. It made it even harder to think. Her entire body ached as well, even in places she didn't know could ache.

She must have fallen asleep after Sophie helped her wash up. They were waiting for the doctor to arrive to ascertain the extent of their injuries. Lillia had laid down for what she thought would be a moment. How long had she been asleep?

Sophie was nowhere in sight, which was good. Lillia hoped her sweet companion had gotten some rest herself. Hannah likely had. She was still exhausted from her Snatching at the trial yesterday.

At least, Lillia believed that had been just yesterday. There was no telling how long she'd slept. Davin hadn't given her a time frame as to when to expect the doctor. She may have come while Lillia was slumbering.

Alone with her thoughts for the first time in days, Lillia lay back and stared at the ceiling. She longed to pace, to work through everything in her mind, but her leg still hurt. She didn't want to risk reopening the wound.

Oh, merciful heavens. The accident.

The memory of the tumbling carriage slammed into her mind, and she groaned. Once again, as it had the moment of occurrence, the scene played out as if slowed. Some details remained hazy, while others were as sharp as broken glass. Every sound, every emotion, as fresh as when it happened. It was a miracle none within the carriage had perished. Not initially.

And Soulmaker take her now. She'd unintentionally Revealed a man.

Two men. And nearly a third.

It was her worst nightmare come to life.

She needed her blinders. Even just the lenses. If they could find her bag, her spare pair could be there, fully intact. If someone could . . .

Yet Davin did not know she was a Truthtaker. How could she ask him to retrieve an item that would reveal her secret? If he learned who she was, he would learn what she had done to him. She needed to tell him. Eventually. Sophie was correct that he had every right to know.

Hannah was right as well. Cornelius was out there somewhere. He needed to be apprehended and Snatched before he hurt anyone else. If she was reported, it would only delay that process and who knew how many people could and would be hurt in the interim.

Lillia groaned again, not caring if anyone heard. Curse this injured leg!

There was a soft knock at the door, and Sophie slipped in, closing the door behind her. "You're awake."

Sophie wore borrowed clothing as Lillia did. It was a blessing they no longer had to wear the clothing they'd been in when they crashed. But where the borrowed dress and breeches hung a little loose and short on Lillia, they were a bit tight and long on Sophie. Still, she could not complain. They were clean and, for the moment, safe from harm.

"I woke a moment ago." Lillia patted the bed beside her. "And I'm grateful for your company." Having Sophie there kept Lillia from losing herself in her spiraling thoughts.

Sophie sat next to Lillia and leaned her head back against the headboard. Her eyes were red and puffy and her nose swollen. She sniffed. "I've been a terrible companion."

"Nonsense." There wasn't a thing Sophie had done that could make Lillia think that.

"I have been, though." Sophie pressed her hands to her stomach. "I should have Seen what Cornelius was capable of. I should have insisted he not ride with us. He was the reason our coach overturned, howling like that and spooking the horses." She sobbed softly. "And I should have found your blinders as soon as I realized they were gone. Davin is Revealed because of me."

"If anyone is at fault, it's me." Lillia took Sophie's hand, giving it a squeeze. "I'm the one who didn't repair my blinders. I knew they were loose. They fell off in the accident because I was neglectful. And then I was the one who was careless in where I looked. Both with Cornelius, and then with Davin."

"But how could you not? I would have done the same. Anyone would."

Lillia ached too much to disagree further. Her sweet friend was hurting. It wouldn't do to continue to rehash the past. She needed Sophie to find her strength so she didn't have to rely solely on her own. "What's done is done. How are you faring?"

Sophie wiped away a tear. "Besides being a watering pot almost nonstop, I'm well enough. Both body and ego bruised horribly, but I shall live. I'm nearly seeing cross-eyed without my blinders. I can't look at anyone right now. Thank the Soulmaker there aren't more people here, or I'd be as incapacitated as you. I'll let the doctor look over my injuries, though. There may be something she'll see that I can't."

"Do you think she'll be Gifted?" Lillia hoped she would be. The best doctors were Soulseers who were strong enough in their gift to See what ailed their patients. That ability was why the medical profession had quickly gone from male-dominated to nearly all women after the Arrival. There was the occasional male surgeon or practitioner, but they were rare indeed.

"Perhaps. We'll know soon. Davin called for her right after he helped you up the stairs."

"Helped" was a relative term. The stubborn man had carried Lillia, despite her protests. She had to admit, her protests had been weak indeed. There was something comforting about being in his arms. Something that made her middle erupt with an entire flock of butterflies. If butterflies flew in flocks. Or was it called something else?

Sophie reached into her pocket and pulled out a long piece of cloth. It looked to be a thin scarf. Or a cravat. The edges were hemmed and finished, so it wasn't torn from something else unless Sophie had taken time to sew it up. Sophie rubbed the ends between her fingers. "I think it best for you to wear this over your eyes. Until we can find your blinders or get you another pair. I've seen at least one manservant here. There are likely more."

She didn't need to remind Lillia what could happen if they didn't take precautions. "Thank you, Sophie. Could you help me?"

Lillia sat up fully and allowed Sophie to first brush and braid her hair, then tie on the blinding cloth. The first Truthtakers had worn similar cloths over their eyes until it was discovered that tinted glass and lenses kept men safe from a Truthtaker's gaze. If the precaution was good enough for her ancestors, it was good enough for her.

The cloth was soft and thin enough Lillia wasn't completely blinded. Light and dark filtered through, as did general shapes as long as there was enough contrast with the surroundings. The cloth did render her more helpless than she would have liked. Particularly in a strange new place with people she didn't know. It did help ease her headache. A blessing indeed.

"Hannah has set out to scour the wreckage." Sophie finished tying the cloth and sat back. "I tried to stop her, but she insisted you need your blinders. I said nothing, only because I agree that it would be more dangerous for you to continue to go without than it is for her to brave going there so soon after the accident. She took that one servant with her. I think his name is Sam. She seems to have taken a liking to him."

Sam. That was the servant Lillia had nearly Revealed, wasn't it? The one who had brought in the tea tray? He seemed reserved but steady. Quiet as a Snatched, but still in possession of his wits. The exact opposite of the fiery Witwraith. "That is quite the combination. I hope he returns intact."

They both laughed at that. Sad, soft laughter, but smiling and laughing felt good. Wrong, considering the gravity of the situation, but still good.

"Truthfully, he seems like a good man." Sophie grew quiet. "One meant for more than this place allows."

That last bit was murmured so low that Lillia didn't believe she was meant to hear. Curious. Had Sophie Seen something in Sam's aura then?

There was another knock on the door. Lillia turned toward

it, though she couldn't see anything. The bed shifted as Sophie left it to allow whomever was there entry.

A woman entered, based on the light steps and soft swish of a skirt. Likely Davin's sister, whom Lillia had yet to meet.

The woman was soon followed by Davin himself.

Lillia knew who it was without him saying a word. The connection between them strengthened with every step he took. If she had been paying attention earlier, she likely would have felt him approach her room.

"Are you well, Lillia?" he asked. He stood as near to her bedside as was proper. Her headache, which had lessened with the blinding cloth, lessened even more with his proximity. As did her perpetually damning thoughts that condemned her every move. She would keep him by her side every second if she could.

That selfish wish would have to wait. "I am well enough. Though my leg pains me." She touched the blinding cloth. "And I have a fierce headache. The cloth eases it somewhat." It wasn't entirely untruthful, and it would stave off most questions.

She sensed him nod. A vague feeling of the motion more than anything. This link between them was a curiosity indeed. Davin coughed lightly. "Doctor Thurst is downstairs. I wanted to make certain you were awake before I sent him up." There was the barest hint of contempt in his voice.

Lillia refrained from gasping out loud, but only just. "Him? You have a male doctor?"

"We do." Davin did not sound pleased. The contempt was more pronounced. "He is the only doctor in the area since the last Gifted one died. He isn't the most capable, but he'll do until you're able to return home."

There was an unspoken question there, one Lillia was loath to answer. She hadn't told Davin where they were from. Only that they were visiting. Having been on the coach heading toward New London limited the options, but there were options, nonetheless. She didn't want him to surmise her identity yet. Not until she figured out a way to tell him everything.

"Thank you."

"I'll fetch him." It must have been the sister speaking, as Lillia didn't recognize the voice. "Before Mimi convinces herself she's the one who's ailing." She didn't stay to introduce herself or to clarify who Mimi was. Another sister? A cousin perhaps?

"Mimi is our mother." Davin answered her unspoken question. He sounded closer. Or perhaps that was merely Lillia's imagination. She wished she could see more than vague shadows through the cloth. Davin shuffled his feet. "She can be eccentric."

Lillia could relate, though she would never say such a thing out loud. "I heard Hannah took one of your men back to the coach. Do you know when they'll return?"

Davin gave a small scoff. It sounded like he shuffled his feet again. "Any time now. I told her it wasn't safe with that madman on the loose, but she insisted. There was no arguing with her, not even when she ordered Sam to join her. He looked as if he was marching to his death but on the arm of a pretty girl. Poor man."

"With Hannah on the rampage, I'm more worried about Cornelius than I am about her." Lillia didn't laugh at her own jest. The incident had just happened. Her joke was in poor taste. She regretted the words as soon as they left her mouth. From the lack of response, the others likely felt the same.

The tromping of feet in the corridor was followed by a heavy thud, like the dropping of a bag on the floor.

"Good day, Davin," a cheerful male voice called. "Where is this mysterious patient of mine? Not you, I assume? I was rather surprised it wasn't your mother again. I know my charms tend to sway the ladies, but she may enjoy them a little too much, if you catch my meaning."

"Not Mimi." Davin's tone was flat. "But our guests—"

"Mimi?" Dr. Thurst chuckled. "Is that what she's calling

herself nowadays? I suppose I should check on her on my way out anyway. While I'm here. To see how she's doing after her last appointment, of course."

"And take more of our coin in doing so, I'm certain," Davin said shortly. "As for our guests . . ."

Dr. Thurst sputtered a bit. His sounds grew closer. Lillia wished she could remove the blinding cloth to see this man, but that was impossible. Besides, she needed to keep her lack from showing. A one-handed woman was not common, and while she didn't believe Davin would tell tales, this man certainly would.

Lillia waited while the man prepared himself for her examination. She longed for someone to sit with her. Perhaps hold her hand. She could never ask that of anyone. It was a childish request.

"I understand you were in that accident I passed on the road." Dr. Thurst hummed to himself. "Sad affair that. Three dead. From what I see, you managed to escape the worst of it."

That depended on what he defined as "the worst."

"Yes, my friends and I are grateful indeed." Lillia pulled her skirt over her lack, then patted her injured leg. "My leg was not nearly so fortunate, though. I've got a deep cut. We've managed to staunch the bleeding, but I wanted expert opinion on the injury."

"They were not expecting a male doctor."

Davin's comment left a pause in the conversation. One that Dr. Thurst quickly filled.

"Yes, well, back before the Arrival, only men rose to become doctors." His words had taken on a more condescending tone. "Women could only serve as nurses, a generous role, if you ask me. Men are far better suited for these sorts of things."

An old-fashioned belief, to say the least. This man likely called Gifted witches when he thought he could get away with it too. A staunch Conservationist then. Lillia would have to tread very carefully with him.

When the doctor bade Lillia to reveal her injury, she did so cautiously. She and Sophie had agreed it would be easier for the doctor to examine the injury if Lillia did not wear breeches. They did not want to disturb the bandages to do so, though, so they had cut the breeches off above the injury. The remnants of that article of clothing were now only good for the rag bin. Or as tinder for a fire. Pity. She'd liked those breeches. Cutting them off had been painful in more than one way. Lillia had hated doing it.

Well, Sophie had done so. The angles were far too difficult for Lillia to manage on her own. Bless the Lady Regent for assigning Lillia a companion.

Sophie's reassuring touch on Lillia's arm settled most of Lillia's nerves, and she pulled the skirt up to right above the knee. She hoped it didn't reveal more than she wished, though with Sophie's watchful eye, she trusted everything was aboveboard.

"I'll just remove this bandage." Dr. Thurst placed a hand on Lillia's leg below the knee. She nearly jerked but forced herself to remain still.

A gentle tugging on the bandage, then a release of pressure as the bandage was freed.

"It's bleeding again." Sophie squeezed Lillia's arm. "Should it be doing that?"

Dr. Thurst's voice held a placating quality, one he likely reserved for "hysterical females." He explained as if speaking to a child. "All is well. Only a little trickle. We'll clean it up. But it does look like she'll need a few stitches to help keep everything in place." A cloth was pressed against the wound, and Lillia groaned in pain. Dr. Thurst ignored her. "You, girl. Hold this in place while I ready my needle."

A needle. Applied to Lillia's skin. She would be lucky indeed if she didn't faint dead away. "Don't leave me," she said to Sophie.

"I'm right here." Sophie took her hand from Lillia's arm, and the pressure on Lillia's wound changed.

"I'm here as well." Davin's voice came from across the room.

"But he's facing the wall," Sophie whispered. "Otherwise I would have made him leave."

"I heard that."

Sophie and Lillia giggled.

"A bit of levity in these situations is always good." Dr. Thurst sounded closer again. His heavy hand rested on Lillia's leg without warning. This time, she did jerk. "Settle down, girl. Unless you don't want me to get these sewn straight."

"Forgive me." Why was she breathing so quickly and so hard? She felt as if she'd run a mile.

"I'm here." Sophie's hand returned to Lillia's arm. She took Lillia's hand and held it tight. "Squeeze as hard as you need to. I'll be all right."

The piercing pain of the needle being inserted into Lillia's skin over and over felt like an endless torment. A hell upon the earth. By the time the doctor announced he was nearly done, tears ran freely down Lillia's cheeks, and her hand cramped from holding Sophie's for so long and so tightly.

"Brother!" Davin's sister called from the door. "Sam and that other girl are back. There's something you should see." When there was no response from Davin, his sister clapped her hands. "Urgently!"

Sophie leaned in close and whispered into Lillia's ear. "The blinders. If Sam found them first, he'll know who we are. I must go see."

Or See. Yes, they needed the Sight of a Soulseer to judge the response and to manage the situation. Hannah alone may not be enough.

"Go. I'll manage here well enough on my own." She wouldn't, but the well-being of them all was far more important than her temporary discomfort.

"Only a couple more stitches, and we'll be done here." Dr. Thurst hummed quietly as he worked. A song Lillia didn't recognize. It was lilting and simple. Lighthearted.

The combined reassurances must have convinced Sophie. She patted Lillia's shoulder and was gone. Lillia could no longer feel Davin's presence either. Not unless she strained.

All that remained in the room was the doctor and herself.

She gritted her teeth as the needle entered her flesh once more. Then, there was some tugging, sharp as nails.

Then, relief.

"That should do it."

Every muscle in Lillia's body melted at those words. She was done. It was over.

"After a couple of weeks, you'll want a man of medicine to remove those stitches." He emphasized the word *man*. "But it should heal quite nicely with very little scarring."

"Thank you." Lillia wasn't certain she actually breathed those words aloud or merely thought them.

"I'll replace the bandage, and we'll be done."

Lillia lifted her leg enough for Dr. Thurst to wrap it. Then waited for him to remove his hands so she could lower her skirt again.

Except his hands remained on her leg. Higher than she would have liked.

"Those eyes of yours. They're well? A headache perhaps?"

"Yes. A headache." Lillia tried to pull her skirt down, using the back of her hand to nudge his hand away. "I should be fine after a good night's rest."

Still, his hands would not budge.

Lillia swallowed hard and forced herself to speak more loudly. "Doctor Thurst, please remove your hands from my leg."

"You seem to be favoring your left arm as well. Perhaps I should take a look." One of his hands left her leg but then latched on to her arm. At this angle, he was practically lying on top of her.

Lillia could not hide her lack any longer. She pulled her arm away and used it to push Dr. Thurst back. "Leave me be!"

"That is what you were hiding? Your deformity?" His other hand finally left her leg. "What else are you hiding, wench?"

He snatched off her blinding cloth before Lillia had a chance to stop him. Light flooded into her vision, and she locked eyes with the doctor. "No!" she cried. She squeezed her eyes shut, but even as she did so, she knew it was too late.

The Revealing took. Far faster than she ever believed possible.

The doctor's filthy presence slid into her consciousness. Not nearly as foul as Cornelius, but dirty just the same.

She took advantage of his shock and confusion to roll off the bed and onto the floor, trying to prevent slamming into her leg and injuring it further. Her skirt tore as she yanked it from under the doctor's weight. Unfortunately, the man now stood between her and the door. And based on how he was staring at her, it would be very difficult to get past him to cry for help.

There was only one thing to do.

She screamed.

CHAPTER 14

THE SCREAM CAME FROM LILLIA'S room. Davin ran faster than he believed possible, up the stairs and down the hall to the open door. Lillia no longer lay in her bed, but stood on the other side of it, holding out her hand to Dr. Thurst.

The so-called "good doctor" advanced on Lillia. He snarled at her, oblivious to Davin's presence. The carefully crafted mask he wore had been cast aside, only to be replaced by something darker and more sinister. "You'll pay for that. I'll show you your place, woman." He raised his hand as if he was going to strike her. She flinched and stepped back toward the wall.

Davin was across the room in a flash, though he could not say how he moved so quickly. He took hold of the doctor's raised arm to hold him fast. "What is going on here?" he demanded. "Doctor Thurst, what do you think you are doing?"

"I'm teaching this wench a lesson." Dr. Thurst gave himself

a shake. "I mean . . . why would I say that?" He blinked hard. "She rejected my advances. I . . . I . . ."

"Your unwanted advances." Lillia hobbled back almost until she touched the wall. "He tried to take advantage of my injured state to force his attentions on me."

That was one of the most foul things a man in Dr. Thurst's position could do. He was in a position of authority and trust. Davin pulled the man farther away from Lillia and addressed him directly. "Is that true?"

The doctor had the audacity to meet Davin's gaze unflinching. He even lifted his chin in defiance. "It is my right. My due. I helped her. She should help me in return." Dr. Thurst leered at Lillia, his gaze lingering on her body. "Others have done so. Quite willingly. Someone like her should be grateful for my attention, considering her disfigurement."

Lillia hid her missing hand behind her skirt, which was now torn. She nearly clung to the wall, pressing herself against it as if willing it to swallow her whole. She stared at the ground, not daring to raise her eyes to meet his. What had this man done to her?

Davin's grip on the doctor's arm tightened. "She's no more disfigured than you or I. Less so, if you take into account your actions this day." He would drag this toad outside and teach him a lesson. Several times over. How had he let such a man into Bradford Lodge? How had anyone fallen for his falsities and preening? The more Davin thought on it, the more livid he became.

It was then that he noticed Sam standing in the doorway. Lillia's two companions stood behind him.

Their presence tempered his ire. A good thing, as his thoughts had taken a darker turn than he would have liked. He moderated his thoughts and his tone. "Sam, take the 'good' doctor to the woodshed and lock him in. We'll take him to town to speak with the magistrate. He'll be brought to justice for his sins."

"Not only against me." Lillia still wouldn't look up. Davin didn't blame her. "He said this isn't the first time he's done this. There are others, Davin. Others who didn't fight back."

Dr. Thurst did say that, didn't he?

Davin paused to consider his next words. "We'll put word out and encourage others to speak up. He cannot be allowed to get away with this." Yes, that felt right. Perhaps not as good as it would feel to enact justice himself—with a little help from implements from the stables—but it would be the right thing to do.

"Oh, he'll be punished for his sins." Hannah stepped around Sam. There was an evil glint in her eye. Eager, but in a horrifying way. She rubbed her hands together. "Rest assured, he'll get what he deserves."

How such a small-framed woman could be so menacing, Davin did not know. Only that the intensity in her eyes reminded him of a predator stalking its prey. He would not want to encounter Hannah in a dark wood alone. It would be better to face the night beasts.

Sam took hold of the doctor's other arm, and they wrangled him from the room. Sophie and Hannah waited until they passed, then hurried in to care for Lillia.

"What is going on?" Mimi stood at the bottom of the stairs, looking toward them. She held a handkerchief to the corner of her mouth. Her bottom lip trembled. "What are you doing with our dear doctor?"

Davin did not want to deal with his mother's dramatics right now. "Leave it be, Mother."

Her eyes narrowed. "Mimi. You are to call me Mimi." Her voice took on a steely tone. "And you'll answer my question, Davin. What are you doing with Doctor Thurst?"

At the sound of his name, Dr. Thurst began struggling even more. He leaned toward Mimi, pushing away from Sam's and

Davin's grip. "I am being forced against my will, madam. As lady of the house, order these men to unhand me!"

His lies convinced the gullible woman. Small wonder. She believed anything anyone of importance told her. Mimi placed her hands on her hips and shook her head. The dyed feather in her hair bounced with the movement. If the moment hadn't been so serious, Davin would have laughed out loud at the ridiculousness of it all. "Davin," she said in as stern a voice as she could manage, "you will release him. Immediately. And then apologize for your behavior."

Davin readjusted his grip on the doctor's arm. He had no patience for her antics today. "I'll do no such thing, Mother. He attacked our guest. He will be taken before the magistrate, and he will pay for his crimes."

"Attacked?" His mother took a half step back and clutched her handkerchief to her chest. The staggering wasn't as exaggerated as usual. She must have been truly shocked. "That cannot be."

"It is." Davin and Sam managed to get the doctor down the stairs without incident, thank the Soulmaker. "He tried to take liberties with Lillia while caring for her wounds. And according to him, it isn't the first time he's done so."

"It's not." Abigail now stood next to their mother. "He has tried to do so with me as well."

"With you?" Mimi grew quiet. They all did. This was news to Davin as well. "He has tried to . . . with you?" There was a degree of hurt and betrayal in the gaze she turned to Dr. Thurst. Her voice was small. "With my daughter?"

Davin needed to know the answer too. Had this man really . . .?

"Of course, with her." Dr. Thurst laughed scornfully. "Did you honestly think you were the only one?"

Silence. Davin could hear his pulse inside his head. Thrumming and getting stronger.

Those words condemned the man as surely as a Truthtaker-induced confession. Davin would see this man brought to justice if it was the last thing he did. Whether it was done through the authorities or by his own hand.

"Come, Sam. To the woodshed. We'll be sure to make his bindings especially tight so he has no chance to escape." The temperatures would drop too low to leave the man there overnight, but Davin did not intend to wait that long to fetch the nearest magistrate. He would send word to the inn the Gifted had stayed in as well. If they were lucky, the Gifted would still be there and would be willing to conduct another trial now rather than wait until Dr. Thurst was transported to New London.

Several scrappy incidents and a fist to Dr. Thurst's jaw later, Davin and Sam succeeded in tying up the vile man. He was deceptively strong for someone who lived a life of relative luxury.

For a moment, Davin was tempted to test Serenity's towing ability using the doctor as the test weight, but he didn't want to risk the foal. That and Sam convinced Davin the lack of circulation in the doctor's hands would hurt abysmally once he was freed. As would lying on the cold hard ground for a couple of hours. A pittance of a punishment to be sure, but it was enough to allow Sam to secure the doctor in the woodshed. Davin set one of the stable boys to watch to make sure the man did not escape. Then, he returned to the house.

Abigail and Mimi now sat in the parlor in front of the fireplace. Their mother, for once, was silent. She stared at the flames, her hands clasped tightly in her lap. The giddy light in her eyes had been extinguished. Her shoulders slumped. There were more lines about her face. Everything about her felt wilted. Aged.

"How could you, Mother?" Davin asked as he marched in. He knew he should show grace and understanding. He should bite his tongue and allow his mother and sister to handle the situation. But for the first time in his life, he could not bring himself to do so. "Letting a man such as that into our home? Putting my sister, your daughter, in danger like that?"

"I didn't know." She shrank into herself further and further with each word he spewed. A shell of what she had been.

"Didn't know? Or didn't want to know?" Davin didn't know which was worse. Nor did he know why he was nearly shouting. He never shouted. He never so much as raised his voice. It wasn't his place to speak his mind.

He couldn't stop.

"Enough!" Abigail rose to her feet and met him nose to nose. "She's already suffering from this, Davin. You don't need to make it worse."

"*She's* suffering?" Davin thrust his hand toward the stairs. "What about Lillia? Doctor Thurst attacked *her*. She trusted him to help her, and he attacked her. An injured woman in his care. Who knows what would have happened if no one heard her scream?"

Mimi sniffed. "That isn't like him." She wrung her hands together. "He's never been violent like that. Not with me."

Abigail turned toward their mother. Her voice softened slightly, but she did not give any ground. "No, Mimi. He was never violent. He didn't have to be. He took liberties because he could. Because no one tried to stop him. Because he was the doctor, and who would ever believe he would abuse his station like that?" She shook her head. "Why do you think I never wished him to attend to me?"

"See!" Davin's voice continued to rise in volume when he should have been trying to control it instead. He couldn't bring himself to care. "Abigail agrees with me!"

"Stop shouting at me!" Mimi shrieked. She pressed her hands against her ears and started rocking. "Why are you shouting at me?"

Those words stopped Davin mid-thought. He'd almost started in on her again, the rage dictating his words and his actions. The emotions boiled in his veins, spilling over into his communication and actions.

But he wasn't this person. He didn't want to be cruel and vindictive.

He opened his mouth, then closed it again, uncertain what he should say or do. He took a couple of steps back. Then blinked. His words . . . his actions. They had been appalling. Ungentlemanly.

Angry.

Abigail stared at him. Truly stared at him, her eyes as wide as saucers. As if seeing him for the first time. She lifted a hand toward him. "Why were you shouting?" She furrowed her brows. "You never shout, Davin. Not ever."

He didn't. He didn't shout, and he didn't know why he started.

Abigail squinted and took a step toward him. She tilted her head to the side. Frowned. "There's something different about you, brother." She took another step forward. "Something I don't quite . . ."

Mimi stared openly at her daughter. "Are you . . . Seeing him? Is that what you're doing? Is that why you're looking at him like that? Why you get your headaches?" She half rose in her seat, then sat back down. "Abigail, are you really a Soulseer? Do you See his soul?"

A Soulseer. No. Not Abigail. Not Davin's sister. She couldn't be.

Abigail tugged at her sleeves, then tugged on her hair. She looked everywhere but at Mimi. "I think so."

This didn't make sense. How could she be a Soulseer? She'd never been to New London. Never been through the Gifting Ceremony like their mother had been. Their mother, who came to Lakewood soon after not receiving her gift. Who married Father and settled down and began a family.

Sophie walked into the parlor, guiding and supporting Lillia, who had reinstated the cloth over her eyes. Lillia limped heavily. She still wore the torn dress, though some effort had been made to repair the damage.

Sophie lifted her chin to look in Abigail's direction. "I suspected as much." She helped Lillia to a chair. Lillia sat and leaned back, breathing deep. Sophie took the seat next to her and spoke to Abigail again. "A sister in the Gift can usually recognize another sister in the Gift."

Her meaning initially escaped Davin's understanding as he was still processing the idea his sister could be Gifted. But when both his mother and sister exchanged shocked expressions, he thought on the words spoken.

The realization took longer than it should to settle in. As if his mind refused to accept what his ears had heard.

"Do you mean to say," he said slowly, still processing as he spoke, "that you are a Soulseer as well, Sophie?" His tongue struggled to form the words. He remained in denial, yet the truth stared him in the face.

Abigail. A Soulseer. Gifted as their mother had always longed to be.

And now their guest was also Gifted. The guest Davin had invited to their home. Saved from a madman. Led through the woods.

"Right as rain." Hannah emerged from where she'd been lounging in the corner to join them. "Took you long enough."

Davin hadn't seen her sitting in the shadows. Her dark hair, which had been pulled up earlier, now hung free. Loose. And wild.

He knew that hair. He'd seen her before. And recently.

The memory slammed into him so hard he nearly stumbled.

"Witwraith."

Davin wasn't sure if he said it first or if Abigail did. He grasped about for the back of a chair for support only for his hand to land on the one Lillia now retained.

Lillia. Who averted her gaze whenever Sam entered the room. And now wore a cloth over her eyes. Who hadn't wanted to look at the doctor.

She had looked directly at Cornelius.

Cornelius. Who had then beaten his uncle with a stick he pried off the underside of the wrecked coach.

And then she looked at Davin, before everything changed.

Before this strange connection to her formed. This awareness of her presence. This sense of familiarity. Of knowing.

Davin jerked his hand back as if the chair was molten iron. He scuttled back, putting distance between himself and Lillia.

This could not be. He could not be. "Truthtaker!"

Lillia reached toward him, but then lowered her hand. She pulled at the edge of her sleeve, but when it refused to cover the end of her arm, she covered her lack with her hand. Her uninjured leg bounced shakily. "I am a Truthtaker, Davin." She sounded anything but pleased to admit the truth. Sad. Disappointed. Small.

Mimi gasped, then rose only to lower herself into an unpracticed curtsy. She wobbled as she bent. "My lady."

Abigail quickly followed suit. Her curtsy was no better. There was no need for formalities here in Lakewood. No reason to learn how.

Davin could not breathe. His lungs forgot how to take in breath and expel it again.

Truthtaker.

There was a Truthtaker. Here. In his house. A Truthtaker without her blinders.

Without her blinders.

Without her . . .

Davin legs gave out, and he fell to the floor, his knee smacking against the floorboards with an audible thud. The room seemed to spin about him. He did not know which way was up.

He'd seen her eyes.

Her bare eyes.

Her . . . eyes.

A Truthtaker's eyes.

Was he . . . could he be . . .?

"Yes, Davin." Lillia's shoulders slumped, even as she lifted her chin. The bottom edge of the cloth wrapped about her eyes was dark with damp. The connection he shared with her trembled. Shuddered. Like it was holding back grief-stricken wails. Lillia took a deep breath and released it slowly. "You've been Revealed."

And with that, all of Davin's well-laid plans crumbled into a pile of ash and manure.

CHAPTER 15

THIS WAS NOT HOW LILLIA wanted to tell Davin. Not about who she was or that he'd been Revealed. That was a conversation she'd wanted to lead up to. Sit down over a cup of tea and calmly discuss what happened and what it meant. She wanted to decide how and when, not have it all thrust upon her. How else could she explain the doctor's sudden escalation in his nefarious behavior?

Lillia ran her hand across the tapestried fabric of the chair she sat on. The pattern of the raised threads brushed against her fingertips. If she pressed hard enough, would the threads leave ridges?

Would Davin have believed her if she'd said, "He attacked me, Davin. Even though he's never been known to attack anyone in that manner before. Out of nowhere. With no provocation whatsoever."

Even a child would see right through that.

He had to know. They all had to know. Which was why Lillia

had Sophie help her down the stairs. And even then, the actual telling of the truth hadn't gone as Lillia had imagined.

She could see from under her blinding cloth. More feet and bottom edges of things and rugs and wooden floors than anything else. That small peek of the world allowed her to walk without tripping on anything, and for that she was grateful.

It also allowed her to see when Davin dropped to the floor after learning who she was and what she had done. She saw him smack his knee against the ground. Even glimpsed the shocked expression upon his face until he moved out of her limited line of sight. It mirrored the emotions she felt through their connection.

She didn't blame him. It was a lot to take in.

She wanted to join him there on the floor. Weep and wail and bemoan her fate and his. Cradle his hand in hers while they grieved what was lost. Mourn what they would no longer have.

She could almost hear what people would say of her.

The one-handed witch had Revealed yet another innocent. Ruined yet another life. All because she couldn't control her gift. The old punishments wouldn't be enough for one such as her. She should be locked away where she couldn't harm another soul again. Then, when she was finally blinded by her gift, left alone to suffer and dwell upon what she had done.

She deserved anything and everything that happened to her.

Soft conversations whispered in the parlor. Conversations she was not invited to, ones she could not quite make out.

They were talking about her. And what she'd done. She knew it.

She might as well pen a confession to the Lady Regent herself and be done with it.

The light steps of a child perked Lillia's ears. They hurried across the wooden floors, changing in tone and tempo when the child stepped upon a rug. Lillia tamped down the feelings of self-pity and woe long enough to listen.

"Mister Bradford, sir?" The child sounded like a young boy.

He didn't seem to be concerned his master was on the floor. Rather, he sounded frightened, and not from anything he'd encountered since entering this room. That fear had preceded his coming.

"Yes, Ben?" Davin's voice sounded strained. Lillia wanted desperately to tear the blinding cloth off her face to see what was happening, but with this young boy here, she couldn't even raise her head to peer underneath the blindfold. How could she live with herself if she Revealed a child?

The boy sniffled. "He's escaped, sir. The doctor. He's gone."

"No." The word escaped Lillia's lips. She clenched her hand, rubbing her knuckles across the embroidered cushion. The room suddenly felt too hot and too cold at the same time. She wanted to scream. To yell. To rage. To sob.

The doctor was a Revealed man. He could no longer control his impulses. He'd attacked Lillia once. There was no doubt in her mind he would try again. If not with her, with someone else.

"How did this happen?" The strain in Davin's voice lessened. Hardened. He stood. There were the sounds of hands against fabric. He must have been brushing off his clothes.

"A bad man." Ben sniffled again. "He snuck up behind Michael, he did. Grabbed him and threw him aside. Michael hit his head. It's bleeding. Marm says it looks worse than it is, but Michael's hurt!"

"What about the bad man, Ben? What did he do?" Davin showed more patience than Lillia would have in the situation. Well, perhaps she would be the same, but she didn't feel that way now.

"He's the one who freed the doctor." Ben's voice quivered, but whether from fright or from crying, Lillia could not say. "Said the beasts should run free, and he howled! Mister Bradford, he howled like the night beasts! I never was so scared in my whole life!"

That sounded like Cornelius. Soulmaker help them, Cornelius was here. He must have seen Davin and Sam lock the doctor up in the shed.

"What of Michael? Where is he?" Davin's shadowed figure crouched down next to the boy. He reached to take the boy's hand. Again, Lillia longed to lift the cloth. She needed to see Davin's face. To read the emotions there. Their connection wasn't enough. Davin must have been subconsciously masking what he was feeling. Likely intuitively as Lillia had yet to explain how to do it.

Another sniffle. "He's with our marm. He was bleedin', so she's patchin' him up. He was scared, too, Mister Bradford. He didn't even want to kick me for followin' him out to the shed. Marm says he'll mend. But Mister Bradford, what if that bad man hurt him somethin' fierce? Who'd kick me for followin' them then?"

This wasn't right. Cornelius had injured that boy, a mere child, for simply being in the wrong place at the wrong time. It was a miracle it wasn't worse. Cornelius had proven he was capable of terrible things. Attacking the helpless. Targeting the weak.

This was Lillia's fault. She caused this. She released the beast. She needed to fix this. Now.

"We need to find him." She had no notion if anyone was listening, but it felt better to say the words aloud. No one else said something, so she continued, the words tripping over themselves in a rush to leave her mouth. "We need to find Cornelius and the doctor, and we need to Snatch them before anyone else gets hurt."

"Now we're talking," Hannah said from somewhere to Lillia's left. "I think I can handle them both."

"It's nearly dark, though." That was Sophie, the voice of reason. She stood behind Lillia. "We'll never find them if we can't see where we're going."

"At first light, then." Lillia couldn't allow them to wait any longer. A good night's rest would be good for them all. Assuming any of them could sleep. "We'll need someone who can track. And a way to restrain them. Perhaps a weapon of sorts."

"Leave that to me." Davin cleared his throat. There was shuffling from his direction. He stood farther away than Lillia would have liked. "We've got what you need."

Hannah stepped close enough that Lillia could see her feet from under the blinding cloth. "Sammy and I can track. I've got experience. He's got the brawn."

"And I have your blinders."

This from the sister who wouldn't speak to Lillia earlier. Lillia could have cried with relief. "Mine?" She would give anything to see the world around her. This taste of her future was quite enough. All Truthtakers went blind eventually. Only when their eyesight was gone were they safe in public without the protective spectacles upon their faces.

A cruel irony, that.

She reached out in the direction she believed the sister to be, not truly believing. The cool metal and glass of a pair of blinders pressed into her hand. She held them where she could see them, not trusting until she knew the truth.

They were hers. And they were intact.

Thank the Soulmaker. She was now freed.

She quickly donned them and breathed a deep sigh of relief.

With blinders firmly back in place on her nose, she could do anything.

With blinders on her nose, she could even face down the doctor and Cornelius. Or at least, track them down so Hannah could Snatch them.

She would show them why a Truthtaker was so feared.

"But sir!" Ben cried out. He scrubbed a fist across his face. "The bad man and the doctor . . . They took horses. You can't catch up to them now."

"Horses?" Davin asked. He exchanged a glance with Sam. "Which horses?"

Ben scrunched up his nose. "The big one that likes to bite at me. And Serenity."

Davin paled. "Not Serenity." He pressed his fist to his forehead. "She's nearly at her time."

That didn't sound good. "Your mare? She's expecting?" Lillia asked. It was no wonder Davin was concerned.

Davin began to pace. "We need to get her back, Sam. I need that foal. My future depends on it."

The foal. The doctor. Cornelius.

Merciful heavens. What a disastrous mess this was turning out to be.

CHAPTER 16

THEIR HUNTING PARTY INTO THE woods was a dismal affair. Davin had been to funerals with more life than this. The Gifted, for that's what they were, walked together, speaking softly and often over the top of each other, while Abigail walked alongside them, silent. The tones and gestures of the Gifted hinted at urgency.

Davin walked in the lead, Sam at his side. Neither spoke as they tramped through the dead leaves and fallen pine needles. The snow that had fallen the night of the accident had since melted, but the bite in the air promised more to come.

Serenity was out there, about to give birth. He had to find her. The two Revealed men needed to be found as well. Both had proved to be extremely dangerous, more so now that their inhibitions were lost.

Or taken from them. Like Davin.

It still didn't feel real. How was he supposed to react to learning he'd been Revealed? Parents used the threat of calling for a

Truthtaker to get their naughty little boys to stay in line. Davin knew he'd been on the receiving end of it a time or two himself. The mere suggestion had kept him out of more mischief than he managed to find.

And now, his boyhood nightmare had come to life.

He'd always imagined being Revealed feeling differently. In his musings and imaginary play, he'd thought he'd feel angry all the time. Rage about like a lunatic or turn into a foaming, rabid beast. That's what all the tales seemed to portray.

That's what Cornelius seemed to become.

Davin felt none of that.

Mostly, he still felt like himself. Except he felt as if all eyes were on him, waiting for him to snap. Waiting for him to prove he was as horrid and dangerous as Cornelius and Dr. Thurst. Waiting. Always waiting. Watching for him to mess up.

The attention—imagined or not—left Davin's muscles tense and tight. He stepped carefully, noticed his every blunder and misstep, looked to see if anyone noticed. Being Revealed was one thing. Being Snatched was another. He'd seen firsthand how the touch of a Witwraith stole a man's very soul.

That would not happen to him. He wasn't going to give them the satisfaction. He wasn't going to give them a reason to Snatch him.

Not all men who were Revealed were Snatched. That's what everyone said. Not all men proved to be dangerous enough to resort to such an extreme form of punishment. Just the worst of the worst.

A lot of Revealed men were sent to work in the mining fields or on the farms down south. Davin didn't know of any that were allowed to keep their old life. They were likely too unpredictable.

Davin could understand the caution. He couldn't control his impulses. He'd learned that quite handily. Words and actions sprung into being before he could stop them. Anything he thought, he did.

Which meant he would have to learn to control his thoughts. Change the way he viewed things. If he could figure this out, maybe he could be the first Revealed to remain free. He would prove he was deserving of such a privilege.

As he walked, each step became a mantra.

"I will not be Snatched. I will not be Snatched. I will not be Snatched."

"I hope not." Lillia now walked beside him, matching his pace, though she favored her injured leg. "I'd rather not lose you to that."

Davin slowed to accommodate her injury. "I did not realize I was saying that aloud." Another thing he'd have to be more conscious about. He'd found himself speaking his thoughts far more often than before. "Forgive me, Truthtaker."

Lillia scrunched her nose. "I'd rather you continue to call me Lillia. 'Truthtaker' sounds too formal." She hugged her muff close. The bonnet she'd borrowed from Abigail didn't have as deep a brim as hers from the trial did. It allowed Davin a better look at her profile. He took advantage of the opportunity to study her as they walked.

Calling her by her title had seemed fitting. Not just because she was Gifted, but because she had the grace and elegance of a highborn lady. High enough Davin should not think of her as "Lillia," but as Lady Pennyworth. Being Revealed meant that Davin lost the privilege of being called Mr. Bradford. He didn't feel right calling her by her given name. "Is that proper? Considering your station and the fact that you Revealed me? Does that not make me less?" He could not produce a better word for how he felt in her presence. Less. Less than who he was. Less than who he could have been.

And even less when she was not near.

That galled him. How could he still feel like this when he knew what she was? When he knew what she did?

"What will happen to me?" Again, his words formed before his thoughts could catch up. He lifted a pine branch out of the way, holding it until Lillia passed as well. The question had plagued him all night. He'd slept poorly as a result. It had been a relief when the sun finally peeked above the horizon.

"I wish I knew." Lillia pulled her hand from her muff to touch her blinders, retrieved from the wreckage along with most of her belongings. However, the blinders were no longer merely spectacles with tinted lenses. At some point yesterday, someone had fashioned a strap that held the article more firmly in place. Someone would have to physically rip them from her face for them to budge.

Still, Lillia touched them often, as if to reassure herself they weren't going anywhere.

Davin thought the addition of the straps ingenious. If her blinders had been equipped in such a manner previously, would they have fallen off in the accident? Would Cornelius have been Revealed? Would Davin?

The endless "what-ifs" would haunt him if he let them.

He cleared his throat. "What will happen to you?" It was something else that plagued him, almost as much as the uncertainty of his own future.

Lillia would not have done any of this on purpose. Yes, he'd only known her for a short time, but there was nothing in her character that would point to deliberate negligence or ill intentions.

Quite the opposite, in fact.

And this connection he felt to her was as if he'd known her his entire life. He could almost sense her emotions, her intentions. He knew her nearly as well as he knew himself. Even that wasn't enough. He wanted to know more.

Lillia pulled her hand back into the muff she carried. The

chill in the air warranted the warmer dress. Davin was wearing a scarf and thick mittens himself. He did envy the layered cloaks Lillia and the other Gifted wore. The different layers could be detached to allow the wearer to don them longer throughout the year. Or to remove layers upon entering a building. Even the most well-built homes could be drafty during the winter months.

"I'll likely face some sort of punishment." Lillia blew out a breath, and it misted in the air. "How severe may depend on how quickly we rectify my mistake." She glanced at him and quickly looked away.

Davin looked to the path ahead. More than one mistake. That's what she meant. He was a mistake that needed to be fixed.

He didn't know how he felt about that.

Davin slowed even more, and the wild-haired Witwraith pushed past him to walk ahead with Sam. She didn't bother to apologize.

"Sammy boy." Hannah walked at a remarkably quick pace for someone so short. "What sign have you found? Or are you too busy sightseeing to look?" She took Sam's arm, holding tight enough the man couldn't get away.

Davin watched the interaction between the two. "She's a strange one." He wished the words unsaid almost immediately. The comment could have been taken poorly by anyone. It was in particularly poor taste speaking that way about one of the Gifted. "Sorry. I didn't mean that."

Lillia shrugged. She watched Hannah and Sam for a moment. "She is strange, Davin. But I like her. She's honest about who she is."

She was that. Davin thought about that for a time before he decided he respected that about her. "And unapologetic."

"I think that's what I like most of all." There was a sense of longing in her voice. Davin wouldn't have caught it if he wasn't so in tune with her emotions. Lillia watched as the Witwraith jokingly scolded Sam, who withstood it well. The longing in her voice was now written on her face.

Davin knew that feeling. "You envy her, then?" If she did, he did as well. Or he would have. Before. Did he have a choice to be anything but unapologetically himself now?

"Perhaps a little. I could never be that free."

Nor could he. That sort of freedom could get him Snatched.

"What do you mean, you lost the sign?" Hannah crouched down and touched the ground. She reached up and jerked Sam down with her. "What is that, then?"

"It's not them." Sam's calm, steady manner never faltered. He was unflappable. Davin envied that in the man. "These belong to someone else."

"Who?" Hannah crept forward, eyes trained on the ground. She lifted her scarlet blinders and stowed them on top of her head. They nearly disappeared in the curly mess of hair she allowed to hang free. "I thought you said this was night beast territory. Who would be out here?"

"No one we need to concern ourselves with." Sam plucked a tuft of fur from a branch's snare. He rubbed it between his fingers, his brows deeply furrowed as if deep in thought.

Hannah ignored him. "There's something strange about these tracks. They're human. I think. But they almost look beastly." Hannah leaned close to Sam, peering at the fur in his hand. "What sort of creatures are these supposed night beasts? Are you certain these aren't from the Revealed?"

Sam traced the edge of one of the prints. "No. The men we're tracking never took off their shoes." He pointed to another set of tracks nearby. "You can see their tracks there. Though they don't go anywhere. The trail must have been obscured by these other tracks. I'll have to search to see if I can determine which direction the men went."

"And leave these others to the beasts?" Hannah started to

follow one set of the strange tracks, but Sam stopped her and pointed to something else that drew her interest.

"What do you know of the beasts?" Lillia asked. She stood closer to Davin than he realized. He started to step farther away but found he didn't want to. So, he didn't.

"No one who encounters the beasts lives to tell the tale." Davin knew that from experience. "My father was one of them." He didn't care to revisit that memory, no matter how much it might help. Father's death had been the end of Davin's happy memories at home. With Father gone, the only happiness Davin found was in the stable with the horses.

Sam continued to argue with Hannah. His normally calm voice raised ever so slightly. "They're of no danger to us. We need to find the—"

Sophie shushed him. "Wait." She held her hand out to quiet them all and lowered her blinders. "I See something."

The emphasis drew Davin's attention. Sophie's ability to See was far different than normal sight in a way Davin would never know. Still, he squinted, trying to see where she was looking. There was nothing around them but trees and darkened undergrowth.

Yet where there should have been the usual sounds of the forest, all was still. Quiet. Not even the birds sang, as if they, too, were holding their breath.

Sophie pointed. "Over there. There's something over there."

Davin peered where she indicated. He could only see trees and straggly shrubs.

"And over there." Abigail pointed in another direction.

Davin looked in that direction. Still nothing.

A snap cracked through the air, like a branch breaking. Davin inched closer to Sam. "What do you think?"

Sam didn't respond. He stepped closer to Hannah, his tall frame overshadowing her petite one.

"Who's there?" Lillia called. She now held a thick stick in an awkward fashion. Her grip would fail if she were to swing it at someone. It would only serve to deter the most inexperienced of attackers.

If it was the Revealed men, the rest of them were prepared. Both Davin and Sam carried cudgels. They had ropes in their packs, if it came to that. The Witwraith was terrifying on her own. And Sophie had shown herself to be rather scrappy as well. The only one Davin would worry about was Lillia with her injured leg. He would have insisted she stay back at the lodge, but they needed her to help find the two Revealed men. Her internal connection with them had confirmed they were heading in the right direction. Without her, they could have been wandering aimlessly for hours before coming across the trail.

"Who's there?" Lillia repeated when she didn't get an answer..

A rustle. Another snap.

"The b-b-better question is," a halting voice called from somewhere in the trees, but from another direction, a direction Sophie still watched, "who are you?"

The voice was deeper than Cornelius's and was without the doctor's light country accent. This wasn't one of the Revealed.

Sam and Hannah edged closer to where Davin and Lillia stood. Sophie and Abigail joined them as well. They pressed together, facing in different directions. Davin felt like a muskox, circling together to protect the weaker members of the herd.

"We're surrounded." Sophie's eyes widened. She turned one way, then the next. "So many souls. How did we miss Seeing them before?" She winced and touched her temple. Her blinders balanced on the tip of her nose, allowing her to peer over them. Whatever she was Seeing was intense.

"I only See a few." Abigail shielded her eyes as she would from the sun, though they stood in dappled shadows. "And the ones I do See are faded and washed out. Are you certain you're Seeing their auras correctly? I'm a Visual, not an Aural like you. I can see things you can't."

It wasn't time for the two Soulseers to establish dominance. Abigail may have had the strength, but Sophie had the experience and training.

Davin strained to see something. Anything at all.

"How many, Sophie?" Lillia held her stick out like she was wielding a weapon. The weight looked to be more than she could bear, so she cast the stick aside and held out her hand instead. Davin had no idea if it was part of some secret Truthtaker gift, but he wasn't about to question it.

Abigail blew out sharply. "Not as many as she thinks, Lillia. You know she's weak in the gift. She hasn't the strength to—"

The mysterious voice spoke again. "M-m-more than you think. As many-any-any as is needed." The words were broken and explosive, as if the speaker struggled to force the words out. "And considering how many . . . any . . . any visitors we've had, our pre-pre-precaution is warranted."

Davin focused his attention on the direction the voice came from. There was something there. He could almost . . .

Lillia gasped. She turned to Davin, eyes wide.

"I can sense him," she whispered. "Why would that be?"

"Sense him? Like you can sense me?" Like Davin could sense her. This connection between them. An awareness of the other.

Lillia nodded. She turned back toward the mysterious voice. "Who are you?" Lillia called out.

Davin needed to know too. If Lillia could sense this man, did that mean he'd been Revealed too? Who else had Lillia encountered without her blinders? He felt a prick of jealousy.

Instead of a response, there was only the rustling of leaves and a snap of a twig—a reminder that this man was not alone.

A figure emerged from a thick stand of pines, as if materializing from nowhere. At first, it appeared to be the body of a man and the head of a wolf. But as it got closer, the light filtering through the branches revealed more details. Broad shoulders narrowing to a trim waist, the torso clad in mottled leather.

What had first appeared to be a wolf's head was actually the head and skin of a wolf fashioned into a headpiece. Rather than boots or shoes, the man wore soft leather slippers, simple in style and design.

He stopped several yards away and folded his arms across his chest. Dirt smudged his face, darkening the lines around his mouth and eyes. Not a young man, but not old either.

Lillia sucked in a breath. "I know him." It was barely a murmur, almost too quiet to hear. Lillia pulled her arm from her muff, revealing her lack, and held it out in a reaching manner. "I'm certain he's . . ."

The wolf man stopped and took a small step back, his face registering emotion for the first time. "No. It-it-it cannot-not-not-not be." His already bumpy speech worsened, each word a struggle. His face contorted with visible effort as he tried to form the words, almost as if something kept him from spitting them out. Something unseen.

Lillia took a step forward but turned her head back toward Sophie. "What does his soul look like?"

Sophie shook her head. "It's strange. Hazy. Hard to make out. They all are. I've never seen souls like this before."

"They almost appear deformed." Abigail's lips twisted in disgust. "So many of them. Everywhere."

Then, they truly were surrounded as Sophie had said. "Men or beasts?" Except Davin didn't need an answer. He already knew.

Hannah picked up the stick Lillia had discarded and held it like a club in front of her. "Whatever they are, they'll bleed all the same."

Several men emerged from the thickest parts of the surrounding woods. Men of different shapes and sizes, all wearing hides from wolves, coyotes, large cats, and even a bear.

These were the so-called night beasts, Davin was sure. Men disguised like the predators from the hunting grounds. Hiding their true forms with furs and paint. These men had terrorized Lakewood and its residents for years. They were the reason few dared to leave their homes after dark.

They were the reason the horses had spooked and the coach had wrecked.

"How many?" Davin asked. He positioned himself between Lillia and the first man, but she stepped from behind him. He tried again, but with the same result.

Abigail's lips moved as she silently counted. "Twelve. No, wait. Thirteen."

"No. More than that." Sophie pointed past the man in the bearskin. "There are others deeper in the trees. Possibly more farther on."

Abigail didn't reply, but her jaw tensed. She was not pleased.

So many men. These beasts of the night.

Yet why hadn't they attacked?

Men continued to appear until at least thirty men encircled them. Stared at them. Some moved smoothly, while others jerked with every motion. There was something odd about them. They resembled puppets on a string. Almost as if they were—

Hannah hissed and ripped her blinders off her face. "Snatched!"

Lillia shook her head and stepped forward. She'd never looked away from the first man. Tears shimmered in her eyes.

"Papa?"

The man she addressed stepped closer. "Lilli-bug?"

DAVIN ALLOWED LILLIA TO WALK ahead with her father as the previously Snatched man led them through the woods. The trail wove between trees and backtracked upon itself. Likely to keep the group from being able to determine precisely where they were going.

Sam walked by Davin's side. Resolute. Stoic, as usual.

But not a trace of worry. No concern. Davin studied Sam's face, watching for any indication he was feeling even the remotest amount of uncertainty.

Nothing.

"You weren't surprised when they showed up." Davin kept his voice low to keep the conversation between the two of them alone. "It was almost like you knew they would be here. And what they were." Something else came to him. More a recollection than anything. "You tried to dissuade us from coming this way."

It was a question rather than a statement of fact. A question that Sam allowed to remain unanswered for several steps.

Davin's thoughts ran away with him. Imaginings of Sam being part of the night beasts. Of him colluding with them. Conspiring. Plotting.

Had he been responsible for Father's disappearance and subsequent demise?

Almost as soon as that thought materialized, Davin dismissed it. Sam would never be part of such a thing. He'd loved Father nearly as much as Davin did.

"My father is Snatched." Sam spoke the words slowly. Uncertainly. He looked to Davin without turning his head. Gauging Davin's response.

Being Revealed, Davin couldn't conceal his true feelings even if he tried. So, he didn't.

Nor was he surprised. Which surprised him.

Strange that.

"Snatched and part of this group?" Davin couldn't bring himself to call them the night beasts out loud. Speaking it would make it true, and he couldn't let it be true. Not yet. Not until he knew the truth about his father.

"Yes."

They tramped through the trees in silence as Davin processed. Sam had come to Bradford Lodge at a young age. Far too young to be Snatched himself. Though it would explain the man's quiet and reserved nature.

"I'm not Snatched."

Davin mentally smacked himself in the forehead. He must have said that last bit aloud. Again. Sam's tone had been tight, as if Davin had delivered a low blow to the man's ego. The implication was mildly insulting, not that he thought about it.

Davin grinned at his friend to make peace. "Come on, man. It's an honest assumption." He bumped his shoulder against Sam's. "Can't seem to get you to string more than three words together at a time."

The slightest twitch of Sam's mouth nearly transformed into a smile. For most, it would have been questionable. For Sam, it meant he was amused.

Ah, good. All was forgiven.

Sam's father being Snatched didn't explain how Sam came to be where he was now. A child had to have more than one parent. Davin lifted a finger in the air, but Sam responded to the unasked question. At least, Davin believed he hadn't asked it, but considering how often he spoke his thoughts, he couldn't be certain.

"My ma died when I was born." Sam rubbed his neck. His gait gained a small hitch, then evened out again. "Da was all I had."

"And then he was Snatched."

Sam nodded mutely.

"Do you know why?"

Sam shook his head. He must have been young indeed to not have any recollection of the happenings. And then to live amongst the silence of Snatched. Men who performed tasks with perfect obedience.

It explained everything. Sam's quiet nature. His reserve. And the times he would disappear for hours on end. Davin had thought Sam was out hunting or checking on fences or the muskoxen or something.

"Does he know who you are? Lillia's father. Does he know you?" Davin looked ahead to where Lillia walked with her father. Their reunion was nothing short of miraculous. Were all Snatched the same way? Able to speak, but choosing not to? Was it all a facade? A trick, just as the night beasts were?

"It's real," Sam said huskily. "No trick, Davin. It's all real. And yes, he does."

The sincerity and deep remorse in his voice silenced Davin's questions. At least out loud.

Internally, his mind spun faster than before.

What were they walking into?

CHAPTER 17

A RIPPLE OF UNCERTAINTY AND UNEASE lapped at the edges of Lillia's consciousness as she sat next to the fire with her papa and the others in the camp the Snatched called home. The fire was kept small to keep the smoke to a minimum, and the hide-covered tents were camouflaged with branches and leaves to help keep them hidden. There were muskoxen kept in crude, temporary pens nearby. Creatures used as much for their ability to haul as they were for their soft underfur that could be spun into wool far warmer than sheep's wool. Packs and baskets had been piled under a canvas shelter nearby to keep them safe from the weather.

The entire camp was meant to pick up and go at a moment's notice. All the better to hide its existence from the world.

What Lillia felt, as she sat surrounded by men who shouldn't be there, weren't *her* emotions, though she was feeling more than she could ever express. Rather they were the result of the connections she shared with the men she'd Revealed. Feelings and sensations belonging to other people. It felt like being in a room full of people who kept talking over each other, demanding to be heard. Some voices were louder than others, but they were all there. All speaking at once.

Four bonds with four separate men. Those bonds muddled together in a mangled mess inside her mind. She'd suppressed two of them to keep Cornelius and Dr. Thurst from somehow using their connection to track her down, though she herself was using those bonds as a sort of divining rod to give their search direction. Those bonds felt distant and muted. Even then, they were dirty and foul.

Papa's bond was feeble and weak. She almost had to strain to sense it, though the longer they talked and spent time in each other's company, the stronger it got, almost like a cord being rewoven.

But Davin's bond blazed bright and hot. Even the thought of it sent a flush through her cheeks and her heart racing. She couldn't focus on it, or it would consume her. His emotions had been easy to sense, as intense as they'd been when they discovered the night beasts were mere men.

Not just men. Snatched.

It seemed impossible. Yet here she was, surrounded by Snatched who walked and worked on their own with only Papa to guide them. Papa. Who had been Snatched.

It was nearly too much to take in. Lillia was glad to be sitting down, otherwise she might be crushed by the weight of it all. Sitting here, on a fallen log, feeling the heat of the fire penetrate her clothing to warm her legs and arms, feeling everything around her, it grounded her. Kept her sane.

Davin now sat on the other side of the fire on another log, talking with Abigail. Hannah and Sophie sat close by. Lillia was glad Davin had given her space to process everything. And space to speak with her father. He and Abigail had much to discuss too. It wasn't just her world that was turned upside down. She would have to speak to them later to fully understand the implications.

Papa's story both fascinated and saddened her. After she'd Revealed him, he'd been put into service at a work camp, one designated for the newly Snatched to teach them how to perform the most basic of tasks, and for Revealed to see what could happen to them if they stepped out of line.

There had been an incident where a woman had tried to take advantage of one of the Snatched for her selfish purposes, to attack someone she believed wronged her. Papa had fought the Snatched and won but was painted as the instigator of the incident. He'd been sentenced and Snatched on the woman's word alone.

Nothing had been done to the woman. That made Lillia's blood boil. If she ever found this woman, only the Soulmaker above would be able to stop Lillia from finding a way to Reveal her. True, it wasn't possible, as only men were susceptible to a Truthtaker's gaze, but Lillia would figure it out for Papa's sake.

Once trained, Papa had served as Snatched for a Soulseer on the outskirts of New London. So close to Lillia, yet she had never known. His mistress had been kind but neglectful. His duties with her had been more relaxed, and instructions were vague. Under her care, Papa had grown thin and sickly. But with the autonomy her neglect provided, he became more aware, more in control of his actions. He learned how to break free of the mental block that had kept him catatonic to address his basic needs lest he die from his mistress's neglect.

When the woman died from a wasting disease, Papa was removed from her home and had been passed on to the Lady Regent's court as one of her personal servants at her request. Her Majesty had been the one to discover he could hold conversations and act for himself, though in a limited capacity. She'd nurtured that ability until she brought him to this place in the heart of the Lakewood forest and put him in charge of other Snatched to teach them to think and act for themselves.

This revelation hit hard. The Lady Regent had known of Papa's fate when she assigned the Lakewood trial to Lillia. She'd known where Papa had been. What had happened to him. Yet she said nothing to Lillia. Not a word.

Sophie hadn't known. Not if the shock on her face had been authentic, which Lillia believed it to be. It seemed the Lady Regent had kept this particular secret from the very messenger-turned-companion she'd assigned to Lillia for this journey.

Had the Lady Regent known what would happen? That Lillia would discover the truth? Find her way to the camp where her Papa resided? Had she wanted Lillia to know?

To be honest, this camp was a curiosity. Lillia couldn't help but want to learn more. According to Papa, it had only been a few men at first, huddled together in a single tent. But over the years, their numbers had grown. To keep from being discovered, they had to invent a fear, something to keep people from wandering too far in their direction.

Thus, the night beasts were born.

"Your Snatched have been attacking people to keep your secret hidden?" This was the part Lillia didn't fully understand. She was told the night beasts were brutal and terrifying. That no one saw the beasts and lived. Considering the terrible creatures that roamed the land in the Outer Regions and in the hunting grounds—large cats with teeth like sabers, mammoths, and bear-sized beavers—it was completely believable that some of those animals would have found their way closer to civilization. Their bones were scattered across the landscape, bearing witness to the expanse of their territories. The walls of New London and the manmade chasms along the Southern Road couldn't keep the creatures out completely. Breeches of those barriers happened often enough to warrant armed guards who patrolled the lengths.

But for the Snatched to attack and even kill to hide who they were . . . she could not fathom it.

"No." Papa's answer was firm, though his voice was not. His stammer became more evident the more agitated he got. "We do not-ot-ot attack. Never. These men were accused-used-used of violence when they were Snatched. We do not pro-pro-promote it now."

"Not even to protect your secret?" It was the greatest secret Lillia had ever known.

An indiscernible look flashed across Papa's face. He poked at the fire with a stick he pulled from a nearby pile. "We have rules. About everything. Including that."

"But what if someone gets too close? What if someone finds out? Then what?" She had to know. Something about this conversation bothered her. Davin's father had been killed when entering the woods. Had he stumbled upon these men?

Papa shook his head. "I tell someone." The way he emphasized the word "someone" made Lillia think it wasn't just anyone.

"Who?" She meant to ask who he was reporting to, though she had her suspicion. Sam seemed far too familiar with both the camp and the Snatched for this to be his first encounter with them. Papa seemed to interpret her meaning differently.

"I did not realize-ize he would be tried." Papa continued to poke the fire, but he stabbed something too hard, and his stick snapped in two, leaving the end to burn in the flames. He tossed the other end in as well. "I only meant-eant-eant to stop him from telling about us."

"Tried? As in a trial?"

"I was told-old to watch for an opportun-un-unity. I did. When his wife-ife-ife was killed and her lover was burned as well . . ." The words sounded like they were becoming more and more difficult for him to speak.

This sounded far too much like the trial Lillia had conducted.

She clenched her skirt, then released it. Then adjusted her muff. Then hugged it close. "You mean this was about Adam?"

Papa stopped trying to speak and merely nodded.

"He found you?"

He nodded again.

Oh, dear. Pieces of this puzzle were starting to fall into place. "Was he going to tell someone?"

"I don't know." Papa rounded his back and sat with his elbows propped on his knees. "My orders were to report any-one-one-one."

He wasn't meant to make a judgment call. Despite his increased cognitive ability, Papa was still Snatched. Without further proof of his ability to make sound decisions, Lillia likely wouldn't have trusted his decision-making abilities in this matter either. But to stage an entire trial to keep one man silent? A man who was unjustly Revealed in a rushed trial, then Snatched before the truth could come out, and then killed before he could join these men.

None of this made any sense. And yet it all made perfect sense as well.

If word got out that Snatched men could be healed, there was no telling how that information would impact society. Snatched men were considered the lowest of the low. Dangerous and vile. Meant to serve those they'd preyed upon. Being Snatched was viewed as a merciful punishment. To save them from being put to death, as they would have been in Mother England. It was a proper punishment for their crimes and a safeguard in case they were wrongfully accused or accidentally Revealed, as Papa had been.

And Papa had been aware the entire time. Aware of what he was told to do, where he was, who he was.

The entire time.

All the Snatched were.

And he'd been so close for so long. Within the same city for most of Lillia's life, and she hadn't known. Had Mama? Had anyone?

"I'm so sorry," Lillia whispered. She couldn't bring herself to speak the words any louder, though they were engraved on her heart. "I'm so very, very sorry, Papa." She pulled her lack from her muff and fiddled with the lace on the edge of her sleeve. "I shouldn't have come to your study that night. I should have stayed in my room. I should have—"

"It wasn't your fault." Papa took her hand, then the end of her other arm in his larger, rougher hands. He ran his fingers over her lack as he did when she was younger. He was the only one who did so. Others were too scared, too repulsed. The small flap of skin there, the one that was almost formed like a tiny finger if Lillia squinted just right, that was the favorite part of her arm when she was little. She'd told Papa once, and he'd always made sure to give that spot extra attention as if he, too, believed it to be the best. "I shouldn't have been-en-en-en experimenting without taking precau-au-autions. I knew better."

"What sort of experiments?" Papa had worked for and with the Lady Regent, Lillia knew. With the Gifting Ceremony. The monarch had said as much.

Papa shook his head. "I cannot-ot-ot say."

Or wouldn't say. Lillia would ask later. When there weren't other ears to hear the conversation. When there was more time for a long overdue conversation. She rested her head on Papa's shoulder and watched the flames. This was what she should have had. This closeness. Conversations. Time together. Someone who saw her for who she was, not for what she wasn't.

"I missed you, Papa." More than she could ever say. Lillia pulled back to take in the sight of her papa's face. She needed to commit every feature, every line to memory. Who knew when she would see him again?

She remembered so little of him. He'd been an important man, though she couldn't recall why. The Lady Regent had known him. Had he worked directly with her? Or merely with the Guild? What were his duties? How had he helped? And why him?

She had a million questions to ask but couldn't speak a single one. She was too afraid it would break the spell, dispel whatever magic had allowed for his moment. Her papa. Here. With her.

As they sat, Lillia studied what she could see of the camp around them. For so many people, the atmosphere was muted and strange. Everywhere, men worked silently. Some hauled or chopped wood. Others mended or sewed. A couple were working on other things she couldn't see from where she sat.

Every single Snatched was engaged in a task, no matter how small. Like ants on a hill.

She'd learned quickly that only Papa and a couple of others spoke freely. The rest either chose not to speak or hadn't progressed that far yet. Instead, they communicated in halting sign language. Simple signs that said more than words could. Some could only sign a couple of things, others much more. Some of the signs made sense. Waggling fingers in an upward motion meant "fire." Miming drinking from a cup meant "water." There were others too. Ones Lillia hadn't yet deciphered. But she would. Anything to better understand her papa's world.

The silence and the shadows from the dancing light lent an eerie feel to the camp. The setting sun cast an otherworldly glow to everything the light touched. Lillia stored this, too, away in her memories.

A young woman approached the fire. She was the first woman Lillia had seen here. The only one. She held a small babe in her arms, though she was little more than a child herself. She waved at Papa, then pointed to the side where she then waited.

"Papa," Lillia asked as Papa started to stand. "Why is she here? With a baby?" In a camp full of men, nonetheless.

Papa held up a finger to the girl and sat down again. The girl nodded and stepped back, turning her attention to the infant in her arms.

Papa ran a hand over his head, leaving his hair standing on end. "She had nowhere else to go. The babe."

She was unmarried, then. Despite how far society had come since the Arrival, the old-fashioned values and beliefs around intimate relations outside of marriage still persisted. "How did she come to be here, though?" Unmarried mothers could appeal to the local magistrate and receive aid, thanks to policies and laws enacted by a previous Lady Regent. Lillia had seen it happen in New London when one of the servants at the Academy found herself with child. She'd been placed in a position that allowed her to raise her child while working, as the father had not wished to remain.

"The doctor."

"Doctor Thurst? He brought her here?" It would make sense that the doctor had been the one to deliver the child. He seemed to be the only medical professional around. Or had been. Before Lillia came along.

Papa shook his head. "The doctor is the fa-fa-fa—"

This one was easy to deduce. "The father? But he's married." And then Lillia's interaction with the newly Revealed doctor resurfaced in her memories. She wrapped her arms around herself. "But he doesn't need to be married to her to father a child. Nor did he need the girl's permission. And the girl couldn't go to the magistrate for this because . . ."

Because the doctor was a valued member of society.

"Did she deliver the babe here, then?" The girl seemed awfully familiar with both the camp and Papa.

Papa nodded. "Quite the lear-ear-earning experience." He gave her a crooked grin. "Not one I recommend." He patted Lillia's knee and pointedly looked to where the girl waited.

The girl needed him. Lillia patted his hand to let him know she understood.

After Papa left, Davin took his seat, leaving Abigail to sit by herself on the log across the fire. The newest Soulseer frowned now that she'd been abandoned. She looked at Hannah and Sophie, but they were deep in conversation with each other and didn't seem to pay heed to anyone else.

"What was that about the doctor?" Davin asked. He didn't seem to notice the glares sent his way by his sister. Lillia would have to speak with Abigail later, to make sure she was cared for. Being Gifted and inducted into the Guild was an overwhelming experience, no matter the age. It changed how the world viewed a woman. How a woman viewed herself. It changed a life's trajectory. There would be a time of grief, to mourn what was lost. And a time of adjustment to discover what was gained.

Lillia filled Davin in as best she could. Fathering a child and leaving the young mother to care for it on her own with no aid from him was abhorrent. "Another reason to find him and bring him to justice," Lillia said. She snorted softly. The sooner she was rid of the connection with such a vile man, the better.

"That poor girl." Davin pulled a stick from the nearby pile as Papa had done. He poked at a log in the fire. It shifted and sent a spray of sparks flying upward. "I never knew Doctor Thurst was capable of that. If I had, he would never have been allowed in my home, regardless of what my mother said."

"I know." Lillia swallowed hard. She didn't want to think about what had almost happened to her. Each time she did, it felt like she was in that room again, trying to escape. Her heart pounded, and her hand trembled. It was more than she could handle right now.

Instead, she wanted to be here. Now. Sitting next to Davin. A fire crackling in front of them. Stars above them. Papa somewhere nearby. Her friends close enough Lillia could speak and be heard.

Sophie had moved to sit next to Abigail and was now instructing her on Soulseer matters. Or was trying to instruct.

Abigail argued more than she listened. She turned from Sophie and waved her away. "Just because you can't See what I can as a Visionary doesn't mean you have the right to tell me what I can and can't do. You're not even strong enough to be anything but a companion."

Her outburst startled a young red-headed Snatched man, who had come to add more wood to the dying fire. He made a face at Abigail, then pressed his hand to his chest and gave Sophie a quick bow.

The Soulseer companion smiled shyly and nodded her head in return.

Abigail watched the interaction with mouth agape. "That is not what I meant . . . I mean . . . I was only . . ." She hmphed and crossed her arms. When no one paid her any heed, she stood up. "I'm going for a walk. Somewhere else. Alone."

She marched away, heedless of who was in her way. The young Snatched barely dodged out of her way in time.

Sophie watched her leave, lowering her blinders for a moment before pushing them back up on her face. "Forgive her," she said to the red-headed Snatched. "She's dealing with a lot all at once. I'm certain she'll be more civil when she's had a chance to think things through."

"Or maybe she's been spoilt for too long." Davin gave a small shake of his head and cringed. "I shouldn't have said that out loud."

He'd spoken nothing but the truth, from what Lillia had seen of his sister. Spoilt, but not rotten. There was a core of goodness in the girl, if she would allow it to shine through.

Hannah made a face at the red-headed Snatched. "Careful, boy. You don't want to cross me." Lillia had missed what had happened to provoke the diminutive Witwraith, even playfully. Sophie grinned, which meant it was nothing serious.

Hannah pulled her blinders down to peer over them at the red-headed Snatched.

His face lit up with a wide grin. He tapped his face near his eyes. "Al-al-al-already Sn-sn-sn-snatched." He struggled to speak each syllable, his speech far more bumpy and strained than Papa's. That he could speak was a miracle.

Sophie giggled. She ducked her head and gazed up at the young man through her lashes. He directed his smile toward her. It was difficult to see from this distance, but it looked like Sophie was blushing.

"I want to see that baby again." Hannah stood abruptly and pulled Sophie to her feet as well. "Come on, Soph. Maybe we can hold her."

Sophie seemed reluctant to leave her spot by the fire. She glanced several times at the red-headed Snatched. He looked at her, too, nearly dropping the piece of wood he was holding when he caught her watching him.

As Hannah dragged Sophie away, Sophie glanced back one more time, grinning when she spied the red-headed Snatched watching her go.

"That's almost as odd a pairing as Sam and Hannah." Davin broke his stick and tossed the pieces into the fire. "I've got to stop saying everything that crosses my mind."

Lillia chuckled. The warmth blossoming in her chest had nothing to do with the flames. "I sort of like it. I never have to wonder what you're thinking."

"Yes?" Davin elbowed her gently. "And what about you? Do I need to wonder what you're thinking?" His lips curled up in a soft smile. One that Lillia could look at forever.

Except thinking about a young man's lips was not something a Truthtaker should do. Not even when that young man was no longer susceptible to Lillia's gift. It wasn't proper. It wasn't right.

Though that did mean she could go without her blinders when no one else was around. If they were to become more than friends someday.

That was a possibility now, being more than friends. Or had

been before she Revealed him. As a Gifted, could she still court him? Since she was part of the Guild?

"I was thinking." There had to be something she could say to keep from admitting the truth. "I was thinking that we need to come up with a plan. To find Cornelius and Doctor Thurst."

That had not been on her mind at all. Not until that very moment.

Davin smirked at her. "That's what you were thinking, huh?" He tapped his head, then pointed to hers. "This works two ways, you know."

The link between them. And how Lillia could sense him. He could do the same.

He knew she was lying.

Soulmaker, take her now.

Sam shuffled over to the other side of the fire and sat heavily. He hung his head.

"What's with him?" Lillia asked quietly. Sam had disappeared almost as soon as they'd arrived. This was the first she'd seen of him since.

Davin threw his stick into the flames, sending sparks flying. "Sam grew up here." He looked toward Sam, a curious expression on his face. "His da was one of the Snatched. Sam didn't have anywhere else to go, so he came here."

"Here?" Lillia had thought he'd seemed familiar with the place, but she had thought him only the contact Papa used to communicate to whoever was in charge. "He was raised by the Snatched?"

"Yeah." Davin took a long deep breath and let it out slowly. "I guess he was found on our lands, foraging or something. My father took him in. He's been working for us ever since."

"Did you know?"

Davin didn't respond, but the link between them grew heavy.

"And now?"

Davin scuffed his boot in the dirt. "I don't know. He kept this from me. From all of us." He pulled his foot back and huffed out a breath. It misted in the chill of the air. "I understand why, but . . ."

"It still hurts."

"Yes." Davin hung his head. The dancing light lit up his features. Emphasized the emotions written on his face. "He thought he could find my father here. But my father wasn't Snatched. He was killed. I saw his remains."

"Cornelius." Papa sat back down on Lillia's other side. His business with the girl must have been completed. Lillia looped her arm through his. "The only true beast in these woo-oo-oods. He killed. For fun."

"Hold on." Davin leaned forward to see past Lillia. "Do you mean to say that Cornelius has been the one attacking people? Not you?"

Papa gestured to the other men in the camp. Their movements were like a musicless dance. The men busied themselves with a multitude of tasks, which Lillia had originally assumed to be related to the daily maintenance of the camp. As she watched, though, she realized there was so much more.

One man whittled a stick into a chess piece. Two finished pieces sat at his feet. Another man tied grass and straw into a broom. Yet another was treating a deer hide, stretching it across a frame to cure. And there, almost out of Lillia's line of sight, a man sewed a muff, much like the one she wore.

"We seek to live. Not kill."

"You trade these items for supplies. In town." Davin pointed to the man who was whittling. "Abigail gifted me a chess set like that one for my birthday."

"Yes." Papa rubbed his hands together and blew on them. "Trade. To live."

Trade. Not attack.

"Cornelius was behind the deaths then? He must be found." Lillia's heart felt like it would pound out of her chest. She may have accidentally Revealed the man, but he was proving to be a monster unlike any she'd tried. The doctor, while not as vicious as Cornelius, needed to be stopped too.

Davin leaned forward and rested his elbows on his knees. "The sooner, the better."

"We tried. When he rode the coach to leave."

The howls that had frightened the horses, those had been Papa and his men? "You tried to stop the coach? To stop Cornelius? But how did you know it was him?"

"He attacked. The child."

The child who had been killed after the trial. Not merely killed, but butchered. That had been Cornelius as well.

Lillia turned to face her papa fully. "Papa, could you and your men help us find them? You know the woods far better than anyone, and we could use the extra manpower." Cornelius would not go down easily.

"No." Papa clapped his hands on knees and stood. "These are now men of peace."

Men of peace who still needed someone to tell them what to do. Most of them, anyway. They likely wouldn't know what to do with the two Revealed men when they found them anyway unless they had detailed instructions.

Perhaps it was better this way.

Papa furrowed his brows. "Tomorrow, I will lead you to the ed-ed-edge of our land. To where they went."

It was more than Lillia could ask for.

"Thank you, Papa."

Tomorrow, then. Cornelius and Dr. Thurst could no longer run free. Soulmaker, help her find the strength to see this through. She would need all the help she could get.

CHAPTER 18

JOSIAH PENNYWORTH WAS NOT WHAT Davin expected. For one, the man could speak and act for himself. No one told him what to do or how to do it. He simply did what needed to be done. On his own.

A Snatched man, doing those things. It was unfathomable. Incredible. Mind-boggling. And a whole host of adjectives that continued to revolve in Davin's mind.

Secondly, Josiah was far more attentive as a father than most. Save Davin's father, who had included both Davin and Sam in nearly everything he did. Should Davin have children, he could only hope to be half the father his own father was.

That fatherly compassion extended to the Snatched in Josiah's care. Davin saw it in the way he slowly and patiently explained how to perform tasks, such as preparing beds for their guests, cooking and serving the meal, and even in walking from one place to another.

It was perplexing how normal it seemed. When nothing here

was normal. Not in the least. Davin pondered on it until his thoughts drifted to the task on hand. He wasn't clear on how things would play out. Lillia, Hannah, and Sophie had been close-lipped about the details.

"We set out at first light, I suppose?"

Lillia startled when he spoke. She'd been watching her father as he spoke in that hand language with Thomas, the red-headed Snatched boy. "Oh. Yes. Tomorrow. First thing."

He didn't blame her for being distracted. If he had the opportunity to spend time with his father again, he would do it in a heartbeat. There was also so much to take in here. This camp ran on its own rhythm. Every rote, every ritual seemed perfectly timed, as if it had been choreographed and rehearsed a thousand times. Perhaps it had been.

"Do you want to go with him?" Davin pointed in Josiah's direction. "Talk to him some more?"

Lillia looked at him again, this time fully meeting his eyes through her blinders. "I think I do. Do you mind?"

"Please go. Take all the time you need. I can wait here." Or anywhere really. So long as she was happy. He had to mull over everything anyway. Sam having been raised by these Snatched men, while it made sense, still felt far too big to take in all at once. And Serenity. She was too close to her time to be carrying a rider. She needed to be home. In her stall. Safe. Davin wanted to be able to think it through without having to worry about being mentally present.

Davin felt Lillia's beaming smile as much as he saw it. "Thank you, Davin. I can't tell you what this means to me. We can talk later. You and me. About everything. We can figure it all out. I promise." She fluttered her hand and bounced her knee as she spoke. "Thank you!"

Contentment settled in as Davin watched Lillia hurry to catch up to her father, as she looped her arm through his and laughed lightly.

This was what he wanted. To see her happy.

"It's too bad Father isn't here." Abigail made her way around the fire to sit next to him. So much for a quiet moment to think. Davin scooted over to give her more space. She tucked her skirts back to keep them from the flames. "Though it's a miracle her father is."

That it was. Though, from what he'd gleaned from his conversations with Lillia and the others, it may have been less of a miracle and more of an orchestration. What he wouldn't give to have five minutes alone with the Lady Regent. He had a million questions he'd like her to answer.

"Are we to stay the night then? Here in this mudhole?" Abigail wrapped her arms around herself, despite the warmth radiating from the fire. She gestured to where they could see the tops of trees and clouds high up in the sky. The light had dimmed too much to see anything more. "This isn't my idea of ideal accommodations." She wrinkled her nose as the Snatched cook lumbered past, carrying a half-full stewpot. This man, while seemingly autonomous, had received extensive instruction from Josiah twenty minutes ago. Instructions the man now followed precisely, never wavering. He must have been relatively new here.

"Nor mine." Truthfully, Davin would love to crawl into his own bed. Not as much as he wanted to see this through, though. Abigail was not as dedicated to their mission as him. "But the day is late, and we don't have time to return home."

"There is time. It's only nearly dark. Not fully. The night beasts are the only reason we wouldn't want to be out of doors at night, and they're not going to do a thing to us." Abigail kicked at a small rock at her feet. "But she would rather be here with him. And I suppose we have to do as they say since they're officially Gifted. Which I would have been by now if Mimi had sent me to the Academy when I was younger."

"At which point they would have discovered you already had

your gift, and our mother would have been put under investigation for having been with child when she went through her Gifting Ceremony." That was the only explanation for Abigail's naturally occurring ability. Davin had puzzled it out on his own last night. Mimi had all but confirmed it with her evasive answers when he'd asked. Even when confronted with the truth, his mother opted to dance about it. "Which you know very well, otherwise you would have spoken up about your gift sooner."

Abigail's silence confirmed his assertion.

He had enough. "I have to find Serenity." The only trace they'd found of the mare was the trail the Revealed men had left. Her hoofprints were there, but she'd been pushed too hard. At some point, her feet had begun to drag.

Chasing them now would push her even farther. It was better to wait until first light when they could see better. Plan better.

Davin couldn't take credit for the plan. Sam had to talk him through it several times over before Davin stopped trying to track down the idiot savages who stole his horse. This impulsivity thing was going to get him in trouble if he didn't figure out a way to control it. Or guide his thoughts. There had to be a way to direct his impulses to keep him out of trouble.

Abigail huffed. She'd never liked Serenity or any of the other horses. "You'll forget that mare soon enough when you're shipped off to the mining fields."

A fact Davin had tried to forget. "Perhaps that won't be the case. If I can show them that I'm of no danger." He stared into the flames, internally begging and praying for an answer. Every idea he'd come up with had come up short.

"Men can't be trusted." Abigail rearranged her skirts before placing her hands in her lap. Thomas brought her a blanket, which she took reluctantly. The red-headed boy grinned at her, despite her scowl. Abigail pursed her lips and continued, though she did wrap the blanket around her. "There's a reason men no longer lead. A Revealed man is dangerous, no matter how they assert otherwise."

The extreme Novationist viewpoint came out of nowhere. "So, you're saying that I can't be trusted as well?" This was the first he'd heard her speak like this. Though he had no idea the topics of conversation that were discussed when he wasn't in her presence. "How sisterly of you. Women shouldn't be the only ones making decisions simply because they can't be Revealed and Snatched."

Abigail barked a laugh. "And I say they should. Besides, I'm not the one keeping secrets anymore, Davin. Not now that you know of my gift. Have you told Mimi of your mare and the foal it carries? Or that you've been making deals behind her back?"

She was far too perceptive with that gift of hers. Davin never should have let her step foot in the stables. "How much have you Seen?" He placed the proper emphasis on the last word, making sure there was no mistaking what he meant.

Abigail's smirk caused Davin pain. Actual, physical pain in his gut. And yet she seemed oblivious of anything but her own agenda. She laughed blithely. "All of it. More than you'd like, I'm sure."

"How much more?" Davin stood and began pacing the length of the log he'd shared with Abigail. The movement kept his thoughts focused on the topic at hand. He had to know which of his secrets were safe, though how he could keep them secret now, he didn't know. A Soulseer for a sister was already proving to be disastrous.

"Besides your plan to run away and leave us in a lurch?" Abigail tapped her chin in an exaggerated fashion. "Let's see . . . how about your feelings for the woman who Revealed you? Do you really believe she'll save you from your fate?"

Until that moment, Davin hadn't realized that was what he'd been hoping for. That Lillia would somehow be able to use her position as Truthtaker to help him avoid being Snatched. Or transported. Or worse.

Yet it was. If he closed his eyes, he could picture being at Lillia's side, seeing her smile, supporting her, and even . . .

Loving her.

That thought startled him, even as it felt right and true.

Davin sat back down. Hard. The log rocked with the movement, and Abigail gave a small squeal. She glared at him as she braced herself to keep from falling back.

Did he love Lillia?

It was too soon for those emotions and feelings to have come to fruition, but he could feel the possibility. He longed for that possibility more than he could ever say.

No words came. No rebuttal. All he wanted was to bask in the all-encompassing sensations that washed over him and filled his soul.

"It won't work, Davin." Abigail's voice broke through his imaginings. "She's a Truthtaker. You're Revealed. You cannot share her path. You never could. Most Revealed are Snatched, no matter what the official documents say. Mimi told me all about it. How Revealed men are Snatched after the trial so they can be controlled, no matter if they're innocent or not."

With that, Abigail successfully brought him back down to earth. "You're wrong." Davin scooted away from her. Lillia was no longer in sight, which hopefully meant she was no longer within earshot either. "You don't know that. Not for sure." Abigail asserted she was a Visionary. Not a Temporal Soulseer. She couldn't See his future. She couldn't know. Even a skilled and experienced Temporal didn't always get it right. They couldn't. There was far too much in the future to be able to See and predict. So much could change. Everything they did, every decision they made could shift the course of their lives away from what was envisioned.

"You'll see, Davin." Abigail stood and brushed off her skirts.

"You'll be sent away, and she'll remain. She'll forget all about you as soon as you're out of her sight."

She wouldn't. Davin couldn't have that. Lillia's visage was ingrained on his very soul. He couldn't bear it if she didn't feel the same. "I'll refuse to go. I deserve the right to speak for myself. I deserve to lead my life on my terms. I've done nothing wrong."

"Nothing except be Revealed." Abigail walked behind him, touching his shoulder as she passed. "I'm sorry, brother."

After she left, Davin dropped his head into his hands. She couldn't be right. He would find a way to break free. He would find a way to be his own man.

He would not go quietly. No one would decide his fate but himself.

He would see to that.

CHAPTER 19

LILLIA BUBBLED WITH EXCITEMENT AS she helped prepare her bed inside the tent she would share with the other women—including Amianne, the young mother. Speaking with Papa, walking with him, simply being with him. It was all too wonderful. She could almost forget the real reason they were there.

"Someone is happy." Hannah was working on the bedroll she'd claimed for herself, nearest the one the young mother shared with her babe. Hannah had shooed Thomas out of the women's tent when the boy spent more time trying to talk to Sophie than preparing the beds. "If you shine any brighter, I'd need blinders over my blinders."

"It's true." Sophie folded a blanket, then tapped her blinders. "I don't need to See your soul to see that." She smiled to herself and giggled softly, a testament to her own bit of happiness.

"I can't help it." Lillia fluffed her pillow, then held it to her chest. "My papa is here. He's alive, he's well, and he knows who I am."

Hannah gave her a mischievous grin. "And there's a certain young man who makes your heart flip and flop in your chest. A young man who sat next to you by the fire and whispered sweet words in your ear."

Lillia couldn't help the smile that formed on her face. "He did no such thing. We talked. Nothing more."

"Ohhhh." Hannah drew out the word. "But you wish he did."

Lillia busied herself with trying to spread out her blanket, but it refused to cooperate. "I don't know what you're talking about." It was a bald-faced lie. Anyone would be able to see right through it, but how was Lillia supposed to admit to feeling something for Davin? Even if she wanted to, she had no idea how to go about it. She'd never had a true friend before. All the other girls at the Academy had whispered and giggled about who they fancied.

Lillia had spent all those years alone, save for her tutors and her studies.

"It's all right." Sophie reached across Lillia to hold the far end of the blanket taut so Lillia could pull it flat. "You don't have to tell us. We'll watch from afar and make our own guesses."

The gentle teasing was accompanied by a wink. Lillia ducked her head to hide the smile she couldn't keep from springing into place.

"That is my brother you're talking about," Abigail said as she came into the tent. "My barely tolerable brother who thinks he's going to prove he doesn't need to be babysat as a Revealed." She sat on the nearest bedroll, one that had already been made up without her help. "He's wrong but won't admit it."

"What if he's not?" Lillia sat on the edge of her freshly made bedroll. She tucked her feet beneath her. "What if I'm able to help him? What if I can keep him safe?'

"From what? From being Revealed?" Abigail scoffed. "It's too late for that, my dear. You decided his fate the moment you looked at him. His fate and your own. You're in no position to help him."

"And if I can?" When did Abigail become cruel? She'd only been indifferent. Possibly distant and high-minded. But not cruel. "If we're able to find and Snatch Cornelius and the doctor and bring them both to justice? And I'm able to convince the Guild I'm of no danger, that what happened was an accident?"

"That's a lot of ifs, Truthtaker." Abigail looked at each of the four bedrolls in turn. Amianne was already lying down with her child in one of them. Abigail pressed her hand against the one she sat on. "There's not enough bedrolls for us to each have our own. One of us will have to double up."

"I'll share with you, Lillia, if you don't mind," Sophie murmured. "We'll stay warmer that way." She finished smoothing the blanket down and pulled another pillow from a small pile in the corner.

Hannah dropped the blanket she was attempting to fold on the bedroll in front of her and flopped on the ground next to Lillia. "You'll have to shove over. I'll share with you too. If we pile the blankets together, we'll be warmer."

There was a flash of hurt in Abigail's eyes. Had she wanted to be the one to share? The momentary expression disappeared. "Fine. I'll take this one over here." She took up the blanket Hannah had cast aside and lay down, facing the other direction.

"ABIGAIL'S RIGHT ABOUT ONE THING." Sophie kept her voice low, likely to avoid waking the others. Hannah had fallen asleep almost immediately, curled up as near as she could be to the baby. They lay shoulder to shoulder, and their combined body heat was enough Lillia had pushed one of the blankets off to let some of it escape.

"What is that?" Everything the wild Soulseer had said irked Lillia to no end. It had come across as mean and spiteful, and she wanted to shake the girl. Partially because she couldn't argue against it.

"The part about you saving Davin." Sophie sighed. "That only works if you save yourself first. And if he can control himself. Revealed often become Snatched, Lillia. There's nothing anyone can do about that."

That's what Lillia was afraid of. But she had to hold on to hope. It was all she had left.

"We'll make it work, Sophie. Somehow, we'll make it work."

Hannah reached behind her to awkwardly smack Sophie without looking. "Save the sappy tears and sentiments for tomorrow. Some of us are trying to sleep." She rolled back over and reached out to take the baby's hand again.

As Lillia lay in bed, staring up at the ceiling she couldn't see in the deep darkness, she turned her focus inward, to where her link with Davin resided. Already, it was a part of her she could not imagine living without.

She closed her eyes and allowed herself to feel that connection. If asked, she could point directly to where he was. That knowledge filled her with comfort.

The thought she could lose that filled her with dread.

CHAPTER 20

JOSIAH LED THEM THROUGH THE woods on a trail only he seemed to know. Davin tried to figure out where it went, or to anticipate the twists and turns in the path, but gave up after a while. This wasn't an area he knew. No one in their right mind went into the night beast territory.

"Can you see where we're going?" he asked Sam, who still hadn't said much after their visit to the camp. The man-of-all-work had spent time with his father last night but had returned to their shared tent in a funk. He refused to speak of it. Davin wasn't surprised. Sam had always kept his thoughts to himself. Still, he would have liked to know which of the Snatched was Sam's father. His friend had been tight lipped about even that.

"No. But I know where we are." Sam looked behind them, toward the Snatched camp. "I could find my way back."

That's right. Sam had made the trip many times before. Davin had nearly forgotten. Sam had acted as Josiah's go-between, delivering messages and even obtaining supplies. All without telling Davin a thing.

"Good. I'm glad." Davin didn't know how knowing where the Snatched men resided would help him yet, but he wanted to keep all options available to him. The girl had found safety and support there. If things went terribly wrong, perhaps Davin could do the same. Then, he and Sam would have something in common. More than just a shared childhood. Would Sam trust him with his secrets, then?

He took a deep breath and let it out slowly. The crisp fall morning air felt cool in his lungs, refreshing and awakening. It spoke of a new life. Of change.

He was ready for change.

Soulmaker, help that Serenity was all right.

"This is where I leave you." Josiah stopped on a ridge. He pointed ahead of him, farther into the trees. In the distance, Davin could see the rooftops of a farm or outbuildings. "If you con-con-continue in this direction, you'll see more signs of the Revealed. My men tracked-acked them this far."

It made sense the Revealed men would be near people. They needed to eat, find shelter, and clothing. That didn't bode well for the people living there. Their first stop should be to check on the family to make sure they were well.

Lillia bid her father a fond farewell with promises to return to visit. Davin suspected she would be here as often as she could. He would help her make her way here each and every time she asked. He would do anything she asked.

Assuming he wasn't Snatched.

"What now?" Davin asked once Josiah had left to return to the camp. "What is the plan?" The Gifted and Abigail had huddled together this morning, heads bent together, before they announced they had a plan. However, they'd been too secretive about it all. Now that they were on the cusp of encountering their prey, Davin needed to know what to expect.

"Find them." Hannah flipped her hair away from her face. "Stop them. Snatch them."

Simple. Yet completely ludicrous.

"Tell me that's not the extent of it."

Abigail gave him a look that had long meant for him to stay quiet. "That's not for you to decide."

The hell it wasn't. "If you're putting my life and Sam's life in danger, then it absolutely is for me to decide." Davin spoke louder than he'd anticipated. His outburst startled a couple of birds from their perches. He silently apologized to them. "We must have a plan that gives us the best chance at success. We can't go in blind."

"Nor can we plan around something we can't anticipate." Lillia started walking in the direction her father had indicated. Her limp was barely noticeable now. She would want to rest her leg soon to keep it from getting worse. "When we get closer, we can scope out the situation and plan accordingly."

"Assuming they aren't lying in wait." Davin jabbed a finger against his temple. "They can sense you coming, Lillia. Just as I can."

That connection made Lillia both an asset and a liability.

She glanced back at him over her shoulder, her blinders barely visible beneath the bonnet's rim. "I know. That's why I blocked their link to me."

That was possible? "If you blocked it, how can we track them? How do we know where they're at? What if they're not where your father said they are? What if they've moved on?" And what if she blocked him? He didn't want to consider it.

Lillia slowed and pulled her muff close. She didn't quite meet Davin's eyes. "Then I unblock them."

"And put yourself in danger?" Either man had reason to want her dead. Cornelius had proved he could and would kill without hesitation. There was no telling what Dr. Thurst was capable of now that he had no inhibitions. If Lillia was determined to risk her life, Davin was as determined to haul her away to keep her safe from harm if he had to.

Lillia's shoulders slumped. Their link felt heavy with resignation. "I have to face them eventually, Davin. Either here or in a courtroom. They can't be allowed to remain free."

Gads! Why wouldn't she listen?

"And I can't allow you to do this, Lillia! Have you even thought this through? These aren't men chained to chairs. They're dangerous, and they're not afraid to do what it takes to remain free. You and your Gifted friends don't stand a chance!"

By the time his tirade trailed off, he was breathing heavily and stomping his way through the underbrush. Any wildlife in the area was likely miles away.

"Davin!" Abigail caught up to him and smacked his arm harder with each sentence she spoke. "That is not acceptable." Smack. "I don't care if you're Revealed or not." Smack. "I don't care how you feel about this plan of theirs." Smack, smack. "You will not speak to a lady like that!"

Davin exploded. "And you don't get to tell me what to do! Not anymore. Never again! You're as bad as our mother!"

Davin knew as soon as he said it that he'd gone too far. The shock on both Abigail's and Lillia's faces felt like a slap to the side of his head. An apology was in order, but Davin didn't have it in him. His emotions still ran too hot.

"You addlepated ninnyhammer." Hannah slapped him alongside the head. "Just because you're Revealed doesn't mean you can act like an ass. Knock it off, or I'll Snatch you myself and be done with it."

Being battered and bruised on every side—and he wasn't only talking about his ego—wasn't something he was willing to put up with from women who were walking into what was sure to be a self-made disaster.

"H-h-help!"

Thomas, the red-headed Snatched, ran up to them, panting

and grabbing at his chest as he nearly collapsed at their feet. Sophie took his arm and held him up, supporting his weight.

He opened and closed his mouth, trying to spit out whatever he was trying to say, but could only manage a strangled cry.

Josiah appeared from the direction he'd come from and came to the boy's side. He must not have gone far. "Thomas?"

When the boy couldn't spit the words out, Josiah held up his hand, then made several gestures. The hand language moved too quickly for Davin to decipher, but even with simple movements, the two men were able to convey an entire silent conversation.

Thomas sucked in a deep breath and clenched his fists. Then, he made exaggerated motions with his hands. Quick. Big.

Josiah paled. He made some more motions. Strong, urgent motions.

Thomas repeated the ones he'd made. Then, he started to cry.

"What is it, Papa?" Lillia asked.

"Gone." Josiah clapped a hand on Thomas's shoulder and squeezed.

Thomas sobbed even harder and fell to the ground. He buried his face in his hands. Sophie rushed to his side and wrapped an arm around his shoulders. He leaned into her and continued to cry.

"Gone?" Davin looked in the direction Thomas had come from. "What do you mean gone?"

Josiah's hands twitched, as if he longed to relay the message via his hand language instead of verbally. Considering how hard it was for him to speak normally, that very well may have been the case.

Sophie lowered her blinders and peered both at Thomas, then at Josiah. "Soulmaker, help us." Her eyes were wide as saucers. "It's bad. Really bad."

"I don't know how you know that." Abigail was studying both men as well. "I can't make out what's going on. Only that they're both upset over something. You can't tell more than that by reading their auras."

Sophie pressed her lips together but didn't respond.

"G-g-gone!" Josiah spat out the word. The effort to speak left him wheezing. He shook his head. "Dead. All dead."

Davin knew he hadn't heard right. "Who's dead, Josiah? Who's all dead?"

"Everyone." Josiah pressed his fists to the sides of his head. "All. Sna-sna-snatched."

"The Snatched?" How could that be? Davin and the others had been there only a couple of hours ago. They couldn't all be dead. While the camp hadn't exactly been bustling—that wasn't possible due to the nature of the Snatched—it had been alive.

Sophie squeezed Thomas's shoulders. "How, Thomas? How are they dead?"

Thomas moaned and rocked back and forth. "B-b-b-b-b-b-bad man. Cor-cor-cor-cor . . ." He couldn't say the rest.

"Cornelius?" Davin supplied. He didn't want it to be true, but something in him screamed the answer.

Thomas nodded and let out a shuddering sob. He leaned into Sophie again and cried against her shoulder.

"No." Lillia's response was barely audible. Her eyes widened. "He couldn't."

After what Davin had seen at the scene of the crash, he had no doubts the madman was capable of such a heinous thing. "Whether he could or couldn't, we need to get back. Now."

Hannah snarled and clutched Sam's hand, dragging him back the way they came. "Come on, Sammy boy. We've got a monster to Snatch."

CHAPTER 21

DEVASTATION.

That's what Lillia expected when Thomas fetched them, when he told them the camp had been attacked.

Yet when they arrived, it wasn't devastation she saw.

It was far worse.

The Snatched men had been downed where they stood. Killed in place. The man who so carefully carved wooden animals and spoons sat slumped against the same tree, looking as if he had merely closed his eyes for a nap. Were it not for the deep red stain that had spread across his chest, Lillia would have believed he was merely sleeping.

The cook who had seemed so proud to serve them only the night before lay on the ground, a ladle still clutched in his outstretched hand. He stared with glassy eyes. The stew he had been cooking over the fire bubbled and burned and blackened with no one to attend to it.

Everywhere they went, the scene was the same. Snatched

men, helpless to defend themselves, killed without mercy. Most likely without warning.

Their animal hides and hoods had been slashed and torn apart. Scattered throughout the camp, as if the animals had exploded into bits.

Papa had been adamant his men would not participate in violence again. These men must not have received instructions on how to defend themselves should they be attacked. He probably hadn't thought it a possibility. Who would dare attack the night beasts? Who would dare venture into their territory?

No one spoke as they made their way through the eerily silent camp. Before, there had been the gentle mumble of men at work. Quieter than it would have been if the men had been whole. But still something. Now, there was nothing.

"They're all dead." Sophie had removed her blinders and was examining every one of the bodies, her actions slow.

Abigail practically clung to her side, following mutely. She didn't offer her opinion or offer aid in searching for survivors. Instead, she merely followed, silent as the men who'd fallen.

Sophie's gift allowed them to move more quickly through the camp. Rather than stopping at each man to determine who lived and who didn't, Sophie could See instantly whether any form possessed a soul.

So far, none did.

"How could anyone do this?" Lillia spoke more to herself than to the others. "He didn't need to kill them. They were of no danger to him."

And yet, she wondered. Cornelius had been obsessed with the night beasts. In the coach, he'd pressed his face to the glass when he heard their howls. He'd howled himself when he killed his uncle. He called to them, begged them to wait for him.

What if he discovered these men had been the true night beasts? His unchecked rage could have led him to do this, stabbing one after another, not bothering to stop until the last man no longer drew breath. Then, taking out his rage on the hides and skins the Snatched had worn to cement their reputation as fearsome beasts.

"I See someone." Sophie pointed toward the tents where they had slept the night before. They seemed to be the only structures that hadn't been slashed or toppled.

Abigail stepped ahead of Lillia and looked to where Sophie pointed. She shielded her eyes, rather dramatically in Lillia's opinion. Exaggerated, as if proving her gift was valid and real. It was the first she'd spoken since they came upon the camp. "I think whoever it is, he's hurt."

Sophie wiped away a tear. It wasn't the first she'd shed. Her eyes were red and puffy. "He's scared. And feeling lost."

Abigail glared at her. She sniffed and shook her head. "He needs help. We need to get closer so I can See more."

"Do we know his intentions?" Lillia's question had been directed more to Sophie, but Abigail was the one to answer.

"I won't know more until I can See him more clearly." She tossed a look of superiority toward Sophie. "I'll let you know as soon as I know more." She strode forward without looking back.

"Who stuck a thorn in her skirts?" Hannah elbowed Sam, who stood near her, as he'd taken to doing even when Hannah didn't make him. He seemed quieter and more reserved than before. No one could blame him. His father was one of the first they'd found.

Hannah rolled her eyes. "Let's go make sure she doesn't fall into a hole or something. I'd hate to try to drag that ego out. It may take a team of muskoxen to do so"

The comment evoked an uneasy chuckle from Lillia. She turned to Davin, hoping to share a moderately amused smile, but he refused to look at her.

As they approached the injured man, there came the sound of faint humming. A familiar song, though it was hummed off-tune. Abigail and Sophie had stopped some distance away and were watching whomever it was.

As Davin and Lillia approached, Abigail held out a hand to stop them.

"It's Doctor Thurst," she whispered loudly. At least, it felt loud here where there was so much death.

Lillia took another step forward. Then another. She could now see the man more clearly. It was indeed the doctor. He sat on the ground, leaning up against the tree nearest Amianne's tent. His face was flushed, his hair in disarray. Most likely inebriated. Empty bottles were scattered about him, as was a bowl with several chicken bones that had been cleaned of their meat. The doctor held a half-eaten loaf of bread in a hand that rested on his lap. He continued to hum his tuneless song, swaying his head to the music he created. His eyes were closed. He smiled softly to himself.

The scene appeared to be that of one who had celebrated a little too much.

There was no sign of Cornelius. Or of the young mother, who Lillia had last seen in her tent, nursing her babe.

The absence of the beast-like madman unnerved Lillia. Based on the devastation left in his wake, he was capable of anything. She would rest easier knowing he was near where they could keep track of him. Stop him before he could do more. After a quick discussion, Davin and Sam each took a direction to scout the nearby area.

Lillia crouched down and crept closer to the doctor. She stared at him, allowing the link between them to be free and unencumbered.

He was injured. Hurting. His connection to her felt limp and nearly lifeless.

The doctor lifted a bottle to his lips, and Lillia froze.

He lifted his head slowly and with great effort, prying his eyes open and looking directly at Lillia. The night had not been kind to him, it seemed, though he had warmed his insides with wine and spirits, if the bottles surrounding him were any indication. The front of his coat was stained dark. He must have spilled his drink in his inebriation.

"The one-handed Truthtaker," he drawled. He tapped a finger against his head before dropping his hand back down. "I feel you here. Did you know that? Strange how that is."

"Doctor Thurst?" Abigail stepped closer. She smiled sweetly, though that smile faltered slightly when he turned his attention to her. "It's me. Abigail. Daughter of your favorite patient."

Dr. Thurst barked a laugh that turned into a cough. "My favorite patient only because she fed my coffers more than most with her imaginary ailments. And she never said no." He lifted the bottle he held in his hand and took a long drag. "If only I could have had a dozen such patients."

Sophie touched Abigail on the shoulder, gently trying to pull her back. Soulseers were meant to See from a distance. Their passive gift did not protect them from danger. Abigail jerked away and glared at Sophie. She gave a little shooing motion, then stepped closer to the doctor.

"But Doctor Thurst, it's me. Abigail. You told me I'm one of your favorites as well." She held out her hand to him. "You told me I was special."

The leer that spread across the doctor's face made Lillia feel as if something slimy had settled upon her neck and shoulders even though his attention wasn't directed toward her.

"You are special." His words became more slurred. "One of my girls. One I wasn't allowed to touch. Your mother would have seen right through me, and your brother would have had my head. Would have sent me to New London to be Snatched. It didn't matter, though, did it? I was Revealed anyway."

Alarms went off in Lillia's head. She could almost see the doctor's intentions. Almost sense what he longed to do. The link between them had been dulled, hidden by her own means, and then by the drink he continued to imbibe, but she could still feel it. And him.

Dr. Thurst turned to Lillia again. He glanced down toward his midsection, then to her. "This is your fault, too, you know. This whole thing. If it weren't for your injury and deformity, I wouldn't have tried anything. Not in that house. But you weren't supposed to be able to fight back." He belched and rubbed his chest. "And Cornelius would be making a mess of things somewhere else. With someone else."

"What are you talking about?" Abigail inched closer to the doctor. Lillia wanted to shout at her, to force her to retreat, but the words wouldn't come. She felt frozen in place, watching a scene unfold and being helpless to stop it.

Abigail was now within arm's reach of the doctor. Far too close.

"Get back!" Sophie screeched, but she was too late.

Dr. Thurst lunged up and grabbed Abigail, holding her close against him. She fought and struggled, but her actions did little against the doctor's greater strength.

The sudden movement spurred Lillia into action. "Hannah, can you Snatch him?"

"Not yet." The Witwraith circled the doctor, her gaze never leaving his figure. The light reflecting from her scarlet blinders flashed red. "I need him to let her go first. There's no telling what would happen if I tried now. Not with him touching her."

"Let me go!" Abigail cried. She continued to struggle, to no avail.

"I will have . . . what's mine . . ."—the doctor's words came out in short bursts—"if it's the last thing . . . I do . . ."

Abigail thrust her elbow into his side, and he roared in pain. He nearly lost his grip on her, but his anger must have given him strength. He jerked her closer, his fingers visibly digging into Abigail's skin.

Almost without thought, without knowing what she was

doing, Lillia took off her blinders. She had to trust that Sam was out of harm's way. She would focus only on the doctor, lest Sam be Revealed. It was the best she could do.

Lillia took a deep breath and allowed the shield she'd placed between herself and the doctor to fall fully away. Even the last bit she'd held on to keep from feeling his slimy, snake-like nature.

Then, she looked at him. Full on. No reservation.

The doctor fought her gaze. His head jerked back and forth, but once his eyes locked on hers, he could not seem to look away, no matter how hard he tried. Lillia mentally tugged on something. She could not say what.

And once again, it was just her and the doctor. All else faded away. Just as when he was Revealed. All his horrible, awful secrets sped through her mind, so fast she could barely register any of them.

She was vaguely aware of movement. Of Hannah and Sophie pulling Abigail away from the doctor's grasp. Of gasps. Of someone shaking her and trying to get her attention.

Whatever she was doing, she couldn't stop. She needed to stop. This connection with the doctor was all-consuming. It was going to consume her.

But she couldn't look away.

It was the doctor who looked away first. He grabbed his midsection and clenched his fist.

"Witch!" A gurgling cough racked his body. "Cornelius was right to want you dead. You and the Bradford boy who stopped him from getting away, who kept me from getting what I'm owed. I'm glad Cornelius is going after him. Him and all he cares for. Good riddance! I wish you all to hell." He choked and coughed violently.

Then, he crumpled to the ground, his eyes rolling back in his head.

The connection snapped.

Lillia came to awareness in a head-spinning rush. Spots

danced before her eyes. Everything felt topsy-turvy and upside down. She wobbled on her feet. Someone steadied her to keep her from falling. Words and images wouldn't consolidate. It all coalesced together in a mass.

"Bradford boy?"

"I don't think he's breathing."

"He's bleeding."

"He's been bleeding."

"How could he do that to me?"

"This isn't about you right now. I think he's dying."

"There's enough blood."

"It's all over me!"

"You'll wash. Help put pressure on this."

"How's Lillia?"

"Dazed. But I think she's coming out of it."

"She'd better. I don't know what she did, but we need to figure out how to use that again."

"Where's Davin? He was talking about killing Davin!"

"Go find him yourself and get out of my way."

"You can't talk to me like that!"

"If I could Snatch you right now, I would."

A lightning bolt of pain smashed into Lillia's skull. She pressed her hand and the end of her arm to either side of her head, trying to ease the pain however she could. It increased until she thought it would destroy her.

Then, as suddenly as it came on, it was gone.

"He's gone." Sophie's voice rang through the haze and the daze, clear as a bell, as if it was the only sound in the world.

Lillia lowered her hand and arm and blinked until she could finally see straight. The scene unfolded in front of her. Blood on all three of the other Gifted, but no injuries to be seen. The doctor lay on the ground, his eyes staring, unseeing.

Abigail stood apart from the rest, holding herself tightly and shifting her weight from one foot to the other. She stared at the doctor's body.

"He attacked me." She let out a shuddering breath. "Why would he . . .?"

"The better question is why didn't he do it earlier." Hannah held out her bloodied hands and inspected them with a grimace. "My guess is because you're the daughter of a lady. He didn't think he could get away with it as easily. He was a predator of easy prey."

"Predators don't always bare their fangs for all to see." Sophie rubbed her bloodied hands on her skirts and grimaced.

Lillia couldn't look away from the doctor, from where he rested on the cold, hard ground.

"How did he die?" Lillia hadn't used any force on him. She hadn't held a weapon. None of them did. And no one had any injuries that she could see. "Where did all the blood come from?"

Abigail turned and twisted to look at her back. It was completely covered in a deep red stain. She shrieked and started to unbutton her coat, her fingers fumbling more than they undid.

"He was injured before we came." Hannah knelt next to Dr. Thurst and touched his chest. "For some time, I think. The edges are dry."

"Do you think Cornelius did this to him?" Sophie examined her hands, using her skirts to carefully wipe off any remaining vestiges of blood there. Without water, she was only moderately successful.

Abigail finally succeeded in removing her coat. She threw it to the ground and stepped away, scowling at the offending article of clothing. "That would explain why his soul was cowering like a dog."

"It wasn't Cornelius. Whoever did this was smaller." Hannah opened the tent flap. "I think I know who it was."

Where was the girl? And the babe? Their bodies were blessedly absent. If the doctor had attacked Amianne, she would have fought back. She had her wits, unlike the Snatched who'd been slaughtered without a care. She could have defended herself and her child, then fled.

Oh, how Lillia hoped she'd fled. If she'd fled, she was safe.

Davin stood next to the doctor's body, frowning down at it. "He's dead, then?"

"He is." And now that all was calm, Lillia could finally slow her thoughts enough to take in the details. The doctor's messy hair, the rumpled clothing, the stains on both shirt and skin. Dr. Thurst did not have an easy road since his Revealing.

She could not bring herself to feel sorry for him. The man had attacked her as well. If he had merely stitched up her leg and left well enough alone, he would not have pulled off her blinding cloth, and he would not have been Revealed.

This had been a vile man. A veritable snake in the grass. One who took advantage wherever he could. Who used his fading good looks to do as he pleased with whomever he pleased. She hoped Amianne was the one who ended his life. Justice served to the most excellent degree. Lillia would not be sorry for his death. Relieved he was no longer a threat to anyone else, but not sorry in the least.

"You did something." Sophie still worked at removing the blood from her hands. "Something a Truthtaker shouldn't be able to do." She lifted her eyes to meet Lillia's. "How?"

But Lillia had no answer. She didn't know herself. She didn't even know what she did, let alone how she did it.

"I have to find her." Davin opened the tent flaps, one by one. "The girl. And the baby. Sam, help me."

They left the small circle, Davin in the lead. Sam followed with Hannah close on his heels. Lillia hoped they didn't find the girl or her child. She hoped the young mother had run as far and as fast as she could.

"He should have been Snatched," Abigail announced loudly.

Lillia couldn't argue with her statement. The doctor deserved nothing less. "Yes, he should have." Though she no longer believed Snatching to be the merciful punishment she once knew it to be. These men must have seen death coming for them. Seen it and had been unable to do anything to stop it. Trapped in the prison of their own bodies.

Abigail continued to voice her thoughts. "What of Davin? What will happen to him if he's not Snatched?" Her eyes widened. "What if he is? He would feel and see and know it all." She began to pace back and forth. "He could be given to someone who would treat him abominably. And he would know it. He would know all of it. And he would be miserable. And alone. And have no way of freeing himself."

The Soulseer was in shock. Lillia couldn't keep up with the girl's emotional swings. High, low. Angry and cruel to panicked and irrational.

"I'll make sure that doesn't happen." Soulmaker, help her, Lillia needed to get Abigail to calm down. There would be time enough for hysterics after Cornelius was stopped.

Abigail came to a stop in front of Lillia. "How? How can you ensure his safety? He doesn't deserve this." She thrust a hand toward the doctor. "Davin's my little brother. He doesn't deserve to die."

No, he didn't. "Not all men are like him." Few were, considering how few trials Lillia conducted in a year. While men generally avoided her, Lillia didn't believe them to all be monsters. Her papa was proof of that. As were Davin and Sam.

"But he is Revealed!" Abigail clasped her hands and held them tight to her chest. "He is Revealed. Just like the doctor. Just like Cornelius. Revealed. He will be Snatched. Mimi told me so. All Revealed end up being Snatched. During a trial or after a trial, when there are no more eyes to see. Davin will be Snatched. And then where will he be?"

"With me." Lillia said it in a rush, like the words could not wait to be freed from her mouth. "I'll care for him." She had no desire to take on a Snatched. She'd never had that desire. Caring for someone too helpless to care for themselves when she could barely care for herself most days. But for Davin, she would do anything. "I'll make sure he's safe. Cared for."

She nearly said "loved." The word hovered on the tip of her tongue. It longed to be spoken. Yet she could not do it. She could not say it until she knew for certain that's what it was.

Abigail went from despairing to elated in the blink of an eye. She wrapped her arms around Lillia. "Thank you," she whispered as she squeezed Lillia so tight she could barely breathe.

"What did the doctor mean about going after the Bradford boy?" Sophie asked.

"It's me." Davin stepped between two of the tents. Lillia hadn't heard him return. Not with Abigail still holding tight. Lillia pulled away so she could talk to Davin.

"I stopped Cornelius from getting away," Davin said. "The day of the trial. He was trying to get away from his uncle. To keep from being sent to New London. I stopped his horse and kept him from escaping. His uncle caught up with him. Cornelius promised to pay me back for that."

Hannah reentered the space as well, the young mother and baby in tow. "Found them," the Witwraith announced proudly. "We're taking them somewhere safe. I might even take them back to New London with me. I could use a companion."

A companion with a small baby to cuddle and coo at. Amianne smiled shyly at Hannah. The arrangement seemed to be to her liking as well. A roof over her head and security for her little one. Lillia could see the benefit in that.

She exchanged a glance with Davin. "Cornelius doesn't know who you are, though. Does he?" Davin's anonymity could keep him safe. For a time. It may provide them the advantage they needed.

Davin shoved his hands in his pockets and shook his head.

"He knew my name, but nothing more." He pointed his chin toward the doctor. "But he did."

Lillia only glanced at the doctor's body. She frowned. That pairing didn't bode well. The doctor and Cornelius had been together long enough for Dr. Thurst to spill all his secrets. He wouldn't have been able to help himself. Considering how much he loathed Davin as well, he may have been thrilled to tell Cornelius all he knew.

Abigail gasped. "Mimi." She clung to Davin's arm. "Mimi. She's home. By herself. What if he comes? What if he does something to her?"

A cold breeze blew, rattling the leaves above and shaking the branches. "We have to get home," Davin said. "Now." He picked up a satchel of supplies they were able to salvage from the wreckage. Papa had insisted.

Lillia had pocketed something of her own. One of the carvings. It was of a dragonfly. One of the wings had lost its tip, but the man had been skilled. Far more skilled than almost anyone Lillia had known. He could have created the articulating prosthetic she'd pined for. Possibly even improved on the design.

"But he's on horseback." Sophie scrubbed the back of her hand against her cheek, then wiped it in her skirts. The fabric was now splotchy with her tears. "He's likely far from here."

"No." Sam approached from the opposite direction, leading two horses. The shaggier one had sides that bulged in an almost painful manner. Neither were saddled. "He's walking."

Walking meant they could catch up to him if they hurried.

Davin touched the pregnant mare's nose. He touched his forehead to hers and closed his eyes. "Serenity."

Lillia knew this horse, though she'd never set eyes on it until now. Knew it as surely as if it were her own. This was Davin's mare. The one he'd banked his future upon. He'd fretted dearly over her as they pursued the Revealed men. That worry had sung across the connection Lillia and Davin shared, like a song that almost couldn't be heard. To find her safe was a victory they needed.

Soulmaker, bless it wouldn't be the only one.

CHAPTER 22

THE DOCTOR WAS DEAD, AND for that, Davin was glad. It wasn't the punishment he would have chosen for the man, but it got him out of the way and out of Davin's—and Lillia's—life. She would never have to look over her shoulder, wondering if he was coming after her. Davin had sensed that she experienced a whole slew of emotions when the doctor took his last breaths, but the greatest of them all was relief.

Amianne confirmed it had been she who had ended the foul man. She'd heard the commotion in the camp as Cornelius attacked and hid. Josiah had given her a knife for protection when she'd joined the camp, but she never thought she would have to use it. Dr. Thurst had found her and her child. He'd recognized her and, according to the girl, had realized he had fathered her child. While Cornelius was killing the others, the doctor tried to rid himself of the evidence of his wrongdoings.

When the doctor attacked, she defended as best she could, stabbing blindly. Her thrust struck home. The doctor doubled over, then fell to the ground. Amianne took her babe and fled before Cornelius could find her.

Now she trudged wearily at Josiah's side. Sophie walked next to her, murmuring kind and supportive words. The girl hadn't stopped crying since Davin had found her and the babe huddled behind a fallen tree. The experience had scarred her, no doubt.

Hannah carried the child, cooing to it and making silly faces. She had removed her blinders, which now sat perched on top of her wild mane of hair. Thomas walked nearby, also making faces at the child, who seemed more interested in the Snatched boy than she was Hannah.

For the first time since meeting the Witwraith, Sam wasn't the primary object of Hannah's attention. He walked ahead, leading the horses who were both laden with what little Josiah and Thomas had wanted to salvage from the camp that didn't fit in the satchel Davin carried. The man-of-all-work often glanced back toward Hannah. His emotions, as usual, were unreadable.

Davin would have to think about what that meant later. After the danger had passed. After Lillia's mission was complete.

After everyone was safe.

Cornelius's actions proved him to be ruthless. A killer of opportunity. He preyed on the weak. He'd freed the doctor for reasons unknown, other than to prove that he could. Perhaps he'd believed it some sort of a game. Perhaps he'd overheard that the doctor had attacked someone and sought for a brother in mind and purpose.

There was no telling what went on in the man's mind. Lillia might have been able to glean something from the connection she shared with Cornelius, but he would never ask her to expose herself to that man's subconscious or conscious thoughts. No one deserved that sort of punishment.

Lillia walked next to Davin. They kept their pace slower to accommodate her injury. She was tiring, that much Davin could tell—both through their connection and by the way she had slowed and favored her leg. She refused to ride on either horse, insisting she could manage. She also admitted she'd never ridden a horse. Trying to do so while injured was not the best way to start. When all this was done, Davin would teach her to ride. Perhaps on Serenity. The mare had a sweet but stubborn temperament. Serenity had taken a liking to Lillia at once, pressing her nose into Lillia's shoulder and trying to walk as close to Lillia as Sam would let her.

Lillia had abandoned her muff. Or had lost it somewhere. It was possible it had gotten blood on it in the mess they'd left behind at the camp. Davin hadn't paid close enough attention to recall. With the cool of the day and the crisp wind blowing, she was likely regretting the loss.

Davin took her arm and looped it through his, tucking the end of her arm in the crook of his elbow to keep it warm. When she placed her hand on his arm, he covered it with his.

She didn't speak. But neither did he.

She hadn't said anything for some time, even when he'd tried to strike up a conversation. After a few minutes, he'd stopped trying.

The way back home had never felt so long. Nor did it feel so cold, but it wasn't the weather that was giving Davin the chills. His thoughts were consumed by the mere idea that Cornelius was on his way to Bradford Lodge. He could even be there already. Mimi was in no condition to defend herself. She didn't know who Cornelius was. The madman could stand in front of her, and she would likely try to share a tidbit of gossip with him rather than run for her life.

When they left, she'd been distraught over Dr. Thurst's confession. She'd threatened to leave for her sister's house but was too embarrassed to endure company. For once, her gossipy nature was silenced. That tended to happen when the subject of the gossip was one's own self.

Dr. Thurst had used her in a most abominable way. Davin likely would never know all the details, nor did he want to.

With Davin, Abigail, and Sam gone, Mimi was alone with only the cook and other servants for company. Or for help.

"He's not himself." Abigail's voice carried in the still air. Davin looked back to where his sister walked next to Sophie. She walked with her head lowered, leaning down toward the shorter Soulseer. "He's going to be Snatched if he keeps this up."

"Hush." Sophie wrapped her arm around Amianne, who had started crying again. "You don't know that," she said to Abigail.

"I do."

Davin turned his gaze back to the trail where Sam was picking his way back home. He moderated his breathing.

They were talking about him.

He glanced at Lillia, but she seemed to be lost in her thoughts. Or trying to focus on where Cornelius was. Or something other than listening in on a conversation that wasn't meant to be overheard.

"He's not that bad." Sophie's higher pitched voice carried even better than Abigail's. Neither of them seemed to realize their conversation wasn't nearly as private as they believed. "He lost his temper, yes. But the Guild won't order him Snatched for that."

"How do you know?" Abigail all but hissed. "For all we know, this is only the beginning." She sighed with exasperation. "At least I know that Lillia will take him on. Then, he won't be lost to wherever the Snatched go."

Lillia stiffened.

She *was* paying attention.

And so was Davin.

He slowed to allow Abigail and Sophie to catch up. Then turned partially so he could speak. "What do you mean Lillia will take me on?" This was news to him. It would have been nice to have been included in this decision. He hadn't even known there was a decision to make. "I've been Revealed for all of three days, and you've already got my future planned as if it's already been decided?" He pulled away from Lillia to walk with his sister. She had the decency to seem cowed, but he wasn't fooled. She'd always believed she knew what was best for him. "I'm not going to be Snatched, Abigail."

"Perhaps." Abigail shook her head. She gestured toward him in a vague manner. "But see how you're acting, Davin. Can you not see how reckless you've become?"

Impulsive, yes. Davin could agree on that. But reckless? Certainly not.

Abigail continued her tirade, heedless of whomever else might be listening. "Being Revealed has changed you. You're not the same. You say and do things you never would have done before. You're not yourself."

"Or perhaps I'm finally acting like myself." Davin was sick and tired of holding back, of holding his tongue. He'd always been the subservient one. He'd always done as he was told. Never caused a scene. Kept small and tucked away lest he be an embarrassment or problematic. This lack of restraint provided a freedom he'd longed for. Who knew it was right at his fingertips this entire time? "Perhaps I'm no longer hiding behind a mask that you and our mother created for me with your expectations and demands. I had to be that version of me. You wouldn't have tolerated anything else."

Threats of being sent away? It was now happening, despite his caution.

Fear of being Revealed? It was already done.

Anything they could have used to hold him down, to hold him back, no longer applied.

"Davin, stop." Lillia slowed, then pulled him into a stop. "That's enough." She spoke with quiet authority. He should have listened. If he had been smart, if he'd had control of his wits, he would have shut his mouth and waited for a more appropriate time to discuss it all.

But it wasn't enough. He had more to say. He needed to speak up. He needed them to know. "And you, Lillia? Playing into her plan to care for me when I'm Snatched? Agreeing to this? How could you not believe in me? Do you really think I'm dangerous enough to be Snatched?"

He desperately needed to know the answer. Because if she didn't believe in him, who would?

Lillia didn't answer right away.

That pause hurt more than anything Davin could have imagined.

"You do believe I'm a threat," he said hoarsely. He needed her to say otherwise. He needed her to tell him she knew he wasn't dangerous.

He needed her to trust him.

"Davin—"

"No!"

His raised voice startled the baby Hannah held. It started to cry. She tried to shush the child, but it only wailed louder.

Davin couldn't do this anymore. He stomped ahead to walk with Sam and the horses. Maybe press on ahead of everyone just to gain space to breathe. He was tired of being watched like he was going to snap. He wasn't dangerous. He knew that. They should have known that as well. Abigail and Lillia especially.

If they couldn't trust him, he would trust himself.

Being Revealed hadn't changed him. It had simply torn down the walls he'd constructed around himself to fit in with what society and his family expected of him. The real version of himself was finally free. He liked this freedom. He liked being able to speak his mind instead of always having to keep it all inside.

He would never go back.

He would never allow himself to be Snatched.

Once free, always free.

CHAPTER 23

THEY STOOD IN FRONT OF Bradford Lodge, staring at the front door. The light was fading, and the cold autumn air had started to bite. Light streamed through a couple of the windows, and smoke wafted from the chimneys, but other than that, there were few indications anyone was home. Or that anything untoward was happening. All they had to do was reach out and open the door.

Still, they stood there.

"He's in there," Lillia whispered. Now that they were closer, she could feel Cornelius. Even blocked in her mind, his presence felt dark and foreboding. It overwhelmed and threatened to overtake her senses.

He'd grown in strength too. Not physically, but in confidence and something more basic and primal. He would be a formidable opponent.

They only had the barest of plans in place. Not even a true

plan, if she was being completely honest. It consisted of three things—find Cornelius, corner and contain him, and Snatch him.

Simplicity in a plan meant there was less that could go wrong, but Lillia had no idea how this would work.

She worried that he could feel her, though. She could feel him. His presence lurked in the darkest corners of her mind. Did he know how to sense her?

She was going to fail. How could a one-handed reject Gifted possibly overtake someone so violent and dangerous? Or even three Gifted? He'd defeat them soundly before Hannah could take off her blinders.

The faintest sound of pounding footsteps drew her attention. The young stable boy, Ben, rounded the corner. He hurried over to them.

"He's here, Mister Bradford! The bad man is here. In the parlor with your marm!" Ben danced from one foot to the other, barely able to stand still. "I told my marm, and she said to find help. But I didn't know where to go. Then, you came along, so I told you. We need your help!"

"Thank you, Ben. You did a brave thing. I need you to do another brave thing now." Davin bent down to bring himself to the boy's level. "You're to take this young woman and her babe back to your house. Your mama and brother and sisters will follow. I'll send word when it's safe to return."

"But Mister Bradford—"

"I need you to keep them all safe." Davin clapped a hand on Ben's small shoulder. "Do you think you can be brave enough to do that?"

Ben sniffled. He rubbed his hand across his nose and nodded. "Yes, sir. I can keep them safe."

"Thomas will go with him." Josiah gestured to Thomas. "He'll know how to best keep them safe. I trust him. I'll care for the horses."

Besides Sam, Josiah was the only other one here Davin would

trust Serenity's care to. He'd seen how the man cared for those in his stewardship. Serenity and her foal would be in good hands.

Davin nodded his assent. "Thank you, Josiah."

Sam made to go with them, then stopped. He looked to be torn. He glanced toward Hannah, then to the horses. Then to Davin. "I'll go to town. Get help. I know who to ask." He handed Serenity's lead to Josiah and lifted the load from the other horse's back. He mounted smoothly and took off down the road at a good clip.

"I'll hurry too!" Ben ran a little ways ahead. He seemed to realize he'd forgotten someone because he stopped in his tracks and spun around to wait for Thomas and Amianne.

Davin nodded to the boy. "Good man. Now hurry."

"Yes, sir." Ben took Amianne's hand and tugged her along. They disappeared around the house the same way Ben had come. Josiah and Thomas followed more slowly, Josiah leading Serenity with care.

Lillia closed her eyes and sighed with relief. The girl and her child would be safe. Serenity was home and in Papa's care. The servants would be out of harm's way.

If only Lillia could join them. If only she could hand this task over to someone else. Someone who was stronger and more capable. Someone who was whole, both emotionally and physically.

There was no one else. Hannah could not do this on her own. Sophie and Abigail could not fight Cornelius or contain him. There wasn't time to send for someone from New London.

"Stop it." Hannah smacked Lillia's arm. She rolled her eyes. "I may not be a Soulseer, but even I can see you're doubting yourself."

Had Lillia been that obvious? She didn't think so. But she'd also been so lost in her thoughts, she hadn't been paying close attention to what was going on around her. "I don't know how to do this."

"Of course you don't. That's why you have us." Hannah smacked Davin's arm too. "And you? Stop being an arse and tell us how to go about this. You know this place better than we do."

Davin rubbed his arm and glared at her. "It's not my opinion that matters here."

"That's a load of manure, and you know it." Hannah rolled her eyes. "Will the two of you start talking so we can get this started?"

Lillia glanced at Davin out of the corner of her eye. She still felt shame in planning his future without consulting him. "I could use help. Some suggestions." She outlined what she had in mind, though as she said it aloud, it sounded even more sad and pathetic than it had in her thoughts.

Davin cocked his head to the side. He paced back and forth a couple of times, then stopped again. "I think . . ." He furrowed his brows. "I have an idea."

"No." Abigail pushed past Lillia to stand in front of Davin. She tried to push him aside as well. He didn't budge. She stomped her foot and looked at Lillia. "We're not following any plan he comes up with. We can't trust him."

Lillia's initial thought was to agree. But she'd made the mistake of not trusting him earlier. He'd been right to be mad at her. She would have been upset too. Instead, she closed her eyes and reached deep within, past Cornelius's foul presence, to where her connection with Davin resided. There was peace here. Peace and safety and familiarity. She leaned into that link, seeking for something, anything that would help.

The only thing she sensed, though, was confidence. And uncertainty.

And hope.

That hope filled her. Buoyed her. Gave her hope as well.

"Hear him out." Lillia opened her eyes again and looked

each of the others in the eye, stopping when her eyes met Davin's. "Let's hear what he has to say."

He stared at her for a long moment. Then nodded. "Here's what we should do."

CHAPTER 24

VOICES CAME FROM THE PARLOR in a house that was otherwise dark and empty. Davin had checked the kitchen and back rooms to make sure that the cook and her children were long gone. There was no need to put their lives in danger.

Mimi's voice filtered into the hallway, bright and clear. She was entertaining as if nothing had happened, though there was a strained feeling to her laugh, one that hadn't been there before. It seemed even one as shallow and callous as her could be affected by what had happened after all.

She laughed again. Whatever she and her guest were discussing must have been amusing.

Davin must have imagined the strain in her voice. Disgust rose within like bile. This woman, this mother of his, who had only ever thought of herself, was laughing and entertaining while her children sought a monster of a man. The monster whom Lillia confirmed was within that very room.

Did the woman care where her children were? Or if they were well?

Did she care about anyone or anything besides herself?

Davin couldn't take it anymore. He couldn't wait a second longer. He strode purposefully into the room, ready to take on anyone or anything . . . and stopped. Even though he knew what to expect, he still found himself staring like a fool.

There, sitting across from Davin's clueless mother, acting as if nothing at all was wrong in the world, was Cornelius. He must have cleaned himself up, as there was no sign of blood or altercation on his being anywhere. His clothes, while somewhat worn and old, were tidy and neat. As was his hair. He chatted easily with Davin's mother, his arm draped casually across the back of the sofa.

Nonchalant. Not a care in the world.

As if he hadn't murdered dozens of helpless men and left them to rot. Or beat his own uncle to death. Or killed an innocent boy in the woods even before he'd been Revealed.

As Cornelius shifted his position, the glint of a knife handle revealed its position under his coat. Easy access. It would only take the slightest of movements to grab it. Cornelius could have it in his hand and at his hostess's throat before Davin could make it halfway across the room.

If Davin were closer to the fireplace, he could use one of the pokers as a weapon. There was a knife in his room, but he'd already stepped into the parlor. Leaving immediately would draw the wrong sort of attention.

His indecision kept him immobile.

Mimi finally noticed Davin's presence. She gave him a faltering smile that morphed into an exaggerated frown when she took in his appearance. Truthfully, Davin had never looked worse. Where Cornelius looked as if he'd been freshly bathed and dressed, Davin's clothes looked like he'd been sleeping in them for a week. He likely didn't smell that great either.

Mimi sniffed and pressed the back of her hand to her nose. "Davin, we have a guest. It won't do to have this gentleman think I have a neanderthal for a son. Go clean up before you're introduced."

Davin's bark of a laugh startled everyone. He composed himself quickly. "We've met, Mimi. In town. Don't you remember? Just after the trial." His gaze flickered from Cornelius's smug expression to the knife.

Cornelius touched the hilt with a single finger. He pressed that finger to his mouth. "But not formally." He stood and stretched out a hand. "How do you do, Mister Bradford? Or may I call you Davin?"

"Of course you may call him Davin." Mimi laughed lightly. She practically wiggled in her seat. Nerves? Giddiness? Davin could not tell. "We're all friends here, Cornelius," she said, then giggled again.

The last thing Davin wanted was for a monster like Cornelius to call him by his given name. The man was a beast. Who could kill an entire camp of men, then casually drink tea and converse in a parlor as if nothing had happened? If it was up to Davin, they'd string the madman up right there in the yard to end him once and for all.

But that knife.

Abigail stepped into the room as they planned, though she was supposed to wait a few minutes longer to give Davin time to get their mother out of there. Davin tried to subtly motion for her to leave again, but she ignored him. Instead, she cleared her throat and blinked furiously. Her attempt to control her emotions failed miserably, and she hurried over to their mother and buried her face in Mimi's shoulder.

Mimi had the decency to appear startled and even concerned. But only for a moment. "Abigail, my dear." She laughed shakily and tried to push Abigail back up to a sitting position. "Do you need to lie down? Shall I take you up to your room so you can recover?"

Abigail refused to be budged. She clung to their mother as if that was the only thing keeping her afloat. Her soft sobs shook her shoulders.

This was not part of the plan. If Davin wasn't successful in extracting their mother from the parlor, Abigail was supposed to sneak her out while Davin kept Cornelius distracted.

Davin glanced toward the doorway. Lillia, Sophie, and Hannah waited in the hall, listening for his signal. A signal he couldn't give until he and Cornelius were alone.

Mimi continued to try to persuade Abigail to leave the room. She made fervent apologies to Cornelius and shot glances toward Davin that held more meaning than he could decipher.

Did his mother know whom she faced? She'd been there that day in town. Did she connect the man who nearly ran Davin down with the man they chased? Or was she as oblivious as usual.

Something was off with her behavior. She was as skittish as a spooked horse. Though it could have been the result of finding out her daughter was Gifted. And that three Gifted women had stayed under her roof.

Cornelius sat back down and crossed his legs. The man was far more comfortable here than Davin would like. "This must be your lovely daughter, Missus Bradford. Abigail, is it?"

Mimi gave a closed-mouth, mirthless grin. She tried again to dislodge Abigail's grip. "She is very much out of sorts." She pushed again and lowered her voice to a harsh whisper. "You must get up, child. Go to your room to compose yourself. Now."

It did not work. If anything, Abigail now clung even tighter. "It's all falling apart, Mimi," she cried, sounding more like a child than the young woman she was. "I just want it all to go back to the way it was. I don't want to go to New London."

Davin prayed Cornelius wouldn't ask what was falling apart.

Abigail wasn't referencing their plan, though that was rapidly unraveling at the seams, but Cornelius wouldn't know that.

Thankfully, Cornelius ignored her comment. "I don't believe I've had the pleasure of being properly introduced to your friends, Davin." He examined his fingernails, as if he didn't have a care in the world. "The ones lurking outside the door. I can feel them there, you know."

This was all so ludicrous. The only one Cornelius would have been able to sense was Lillia. He could only be guessing at the rest. "And why would I introduce anyone to you?"

No, no, no, no, no. That wasn't what he meant to say. He needed to play along until his mother and sister were safe. Yet he could not bring himself to comply. As he stared down this man who had destroyed so many lives, even before Lillia had Revealed him, Davin felt the anger swarm within. The more Davin watched this man, the worse the anger raged. He needed to gain control himself before he made things even worse.

"You're not worthy of their acquaintance, you sniveling, cowardly worm!"

That did not help at all.

"Davin!" Mimi stood up, upending Abigail and leaving her sprawled on the sofa. "That is enough. You'll take your sister to her room this instant. I'll not tolerate this sort of behavior in my house."

Her eye twitched. She gave the most fleeting glance toward Cornelius.

And then she gestured ever so slightly to the door.

She was trying to get them out of the room. Mimi—the mother who pretended he didn't exist until she needed something from him—was trying to save both him and Abigail by sacrificing herself.

The idea that she was that selfless, it was infuriating.

Tension built in Davin's neck and spread to his shoulders.

Heat rushed through his veins. Twenty-four years of tolerating her selfish, ridiculous, neglectful behavior boiled to the surface.

"No."

Mimi gasped.

Cornelius's grin widened. "Oh, this is getting good." He settled more comfortably into the sofa but kept his hand near the hidden knife.

"This sort of behavior?" Davin turned to his mother, no longer caring about trying to restrain himself. He couldn't. It wasn't possible. "The behavior you thought you berated out of me? The behavior where I stand up for myself and speak what's on my mind? That sort of behavior?"

Lillia slipped into the room and touched Davin's arm, then grabbed at his sleeve. If he wasn't so far gone, the touch would have stopped him. "Davin, that's enough." She tried to pull him back.

"I'm not done!" He pulled free and stepped toward his now quivering mother. "You pretend to be perfect, to be this paragon of virtue, but all you are is a self-centered, pretentious fool who only cares about herself."

Hannah yanked off her blinders and met him nose to nose, putting herself between Davin and Mimi. Despite being a head shorter, she seemed to tower over him. "Don't make me Snatch you," she hissed. "Because I will."

Davin blinked a few times. Then a few more. The raging fire within tempered to a mere flicker. He lowered the hand he didn't know he'd raised and took a step back.

This was not the plan. It wasn't what he'd intended. Lillia, Hannah, and Sophie were supposed to wait in the hall. In the moment that it mattered the most, he could not control his words or actions. He couldn't even try. Every emotion that had rolled through him burst from his mouth in angry accusations.

Cornelius stood. He began clapping slowly. "That was brilliant, if I do say so myself. This is the gentry, folks. The ladies and gentlemen who are supposed to be the pillars of our society. Who feel they can make others do whatever they want. Stop others from doing what they want to do. These hypocrites are as messed up and damaged as the rest of us. Quite refreshing."

Too late, Davin realized that by standing, Cornelius had placed himself closer to Mimi and Abigail.

In a flash, Cornelius had the knife out and held it to Mimi's throat. He jerked her close to him and wrapped his arm around her shoulders. She whimpered as the tip of the knife bit into the skin on her neck, drawing blood.

Davin dared not move.

"It's been fun," Cornelius drawled. "But with so many Gifted, including a Witwraith who's out for blood, I'll be taking my leave. I hear there are places in New London where a man seeking a fresh start can disappear without a trace. I had hoped to stick around and make some new friends here. But I think I've overstayed my welcome."

The way he twisted the word "friends" left Davin feeling the man meant something else entirely.

"Don't." Davin reached out a hand, though he didn't know what good it would do. "Leave her be. She has nothing to do with any of this." Despite their differences, Davin didn't wish this on his mother.

"Neither did that woman or her supposed lover." Cornelius leaned closer to Mimi's ear. "You know, the two that Adam Burns was Snatched for. That was my handiwork. And that camp of fake beasts. None of them fought me. Not one. Not even when I plunged this very blade into their chests. They were a disappointment, not deserving of being called night beasts."

Mother whimpered. "I tried to make you leave." She looked to Davin before she squeezed her eyes shut. "I tried to save you and your sister."

And Davin had ruined it all. All because he couldn't control his tongue.

Perhaps he did deserve to be Snatched after all.

CHAPTER 25

EVENTS HAD UNFOLDED FASTER THAN Lillia could process. One moment, the plan was going according to, well, plan. The next, Cornelius was holding Mrs. Bradford hostage—the very thing they had tried to prevent.

"Lady Truthtaker." Cornelius turned his attention to her. Connecting with him visually was just as stomach-wrenching as the mental connection they shared. "We meet once more. I was wondering if we would cross paths again. I believe I need to thank you. Being Revealed is so refreshing. I should have done this years ago."

That was one thing they did agree on. Though Lillia would have preferred for Cornelius's Revealing to have been in a proper trial, where he would have been immediately Snatched and sent to the mining fields to be worked hard until the day he died. Now that she knew he would retain his conscious mind but not be able to do a thing to change his fate, the punishment felt even more just.

"Let her go," Lillia said with more courage than she felt. "She's nothing to you."

Cornelius waggled his blade. "Nice try, Truthtaker. She may be nothing to me, but she's everything to him." He indicated Davin with a tilt of his head. "I swore I would pay him back for stopping me. And while I don't always keep my promises, this one feels so deliciously perfect to keep."

"You'll break this one as well if I have anything to do with it." Hannah no longer held her blinders, having stowed them away somewhere. "You'll be Snatched and taken to the mining camps, where you'll never harm anyone ever again." The threat, despite coming from someone so small, felt ominous. Dangerous. Lillia would not want to be on the receiving end of that promise.

Cornelius laughed and raised his head as he let out a long, low howl. "Snatch that, witch. I dare you." He pulled Mrs. Bradford with him as he made his way to the door. "No? I thought not."

Lillia had to do something. If Cornelius made it to that door with Mrs. Bradford, there was no telling what he would do. He would escape, putting so many others in danger. But not after he rid himself of excess baggage. She had to do something. Anything.

But what? She'd already Revealed him. What more could she do besides help constrain him so Hannah could Snatch him?

Unlike the doctor, Cornelius wasn't afraid to . . .

Wait.

The doctor.

Lillia had done something. She'd stopped him somehow. Using the connection they shared. Right before he died. It had been something strange, but . . .

Could she do it again?

Whether she could or not, she had to try. She closed her eyes and focused on that thread of awareness that linked her to Cornelius. It still lay buried under a mountain of mental clutter, far more than she remembered laying down. She must have subconsciously fortified that blockage to keep him from finding her. But now she needed to lean into that connection as hard as she could. The time for hiding was past.

The first bits of that blockade protested her efforts. Each felt as heavy as stone. It took nearly everything she had. But as she lifted each memory, each idea, each thought, the task became easier and faster. More and more sensation flooded through her brain.

"What are you doing?" Cornelius demanded. His voice shook, but whether it was from fear or laughter, Lillia couldn't tell. She kept her focus on this one task. This one thing only she could do. If she could take hold of that connection, like she'd done with the doctor . . .

Mere moments must have passed, but they felt like hours. An eternity.

Then, the last bit of mental clutter cleared, and the link between Lillia and Cornelius was revealed, an ugly, writhing cord of mental energy. She seized it with two whole and sound mental hands, a manifestation of what she never had in physical form, and willed everything she had into it, into forcing Cornelius to stop. To let go. To hold still long enough for Hannah to Snatch him.

Lillia opened her eyes and met his gaze. Then lowered her blinders to increase her strength, operating by instinct more than anything else. She only barely knew what she was doing.

But it worked.

Cornelius stopped moving toward the door. He stared back at her, mouth slightly agape. "What are you doing?" His voice cracked.

Lillia leaned into the effort, infusing even more energy into it. "Let her go." Though the words were whispered, they carried. Reverberated. Deafened.

Cornelius cringed. His head jerked and twisted, but he continued to maintain eye contact, as if he could not look away.

Lillia pushed even harder. As hard as she could, until she had nothing left to give.

It had to be enough.

Cornelius's hand that held the knife lowered and relaxed. Mrs. Bradford started to cry. She struggled in his arms and tried to pull away.

It was working. It was really working.

Nothing in the history of Truthtaking had ever suggested such a thing was possible. That compelling an un-Snatched man to act was within the ability of any of the Gifted. Yet here, in this parlor, it was happening.

Lillia could have marveled at the miracle of it all. This remarkable and exhilarating thing. They were going to succeed. Despite their original plan falling apart, they were going to succeed!

Until . . .

Cornelius blinked. Then blinked again.

The mental link between them bucked and wrenched itself from Lillia's imaginary grasp with such force it sent her reeling. Someone grasped her arms to keep her from falling.

An evil grin spread across Cornelius's face. "Another nice try, Truthtaker. But I've been waging a war inside my own mind my entire life. Your pathetic attempts to contain me are laughable, to say the least. You're no match for me. None of you are."

He pulled Mrs. Bradford toward the door. She no longer fought him, her face paralyzed in fear. Cornelius leaned in close and licked her face, letting out a low chuckle when she whimpered. The knife he'd held to her throat was now pressed against her side.

Cornelius backed them both through the doorway, slowly but surely. "I wouldn't recommend following," he warned. "Not if you want her to stay intact. No promises, though." He let out another long howl, then laughed to himself. "No promises at all. And when I'm done with her, I'll come for you next, Truthtaker."

Another howl pierced the air, close and loud. Hollow and haunting. Lillia thought it might have come from Hannah, but she didn't look to confirm her suspicion.

In a flash, Davin was behind Cornelius. He wrapped an arm around Cornelius's neck and tried to pull the madman's arm free from its death grip on Mrs. Bradford.

"NO!" Cornelius fought back, tightening his hold. "I . . . will . . . not . . ."

A vindictive gleam flashed in his eyes before he thrust the knife deep into Mrs. Bradford's side.

Lillia expected a gasp or a scream from the woman. Hysterics or any sort of reaction.

Instead, Mrs. Bradford merely looked down at the knife protruding from her side and slumped.

Her dead weight proved to be more than Cornelius could bear while fighting off Davin. He released the woman, letting her slide to the floor in a heap. Davin wrangled Cornelius a few steps to the side. Sophie and Abigail rushed to Mrs. Bradford and pulled her away.

Cornelius fought Davin's attempts to subdue him, but Davin was bigger and stronger. Years of helping in the stables and helping on the grounds had molded him, prepared him for this. He restrained Cornelius, his arms interlocked with the madman's. Cornelius kicked and bucked, but Davin held fast.

"Snatch him!" Davin clenched his teeth and redoubled his efforts to hold the man still. "Snatch him now!"

Hannah hesitated. Her blinders were already off, but she didn't move forward. "If I Snatch Cornelius, there's no telling how it will affect Davin. Lillia, I could Snatch him too."

It was too big of a risk. Lillia had promised to do what she could to keep him from being Snatched. She couldn't do it. She couldn't risk him.

"Snatch him!" Davin pulled back, but Cornelius resisted. They were in a deadlock, one that could give at any moment.

"No!" Lillia cried. She couldn't let Davin go through what Papa had. She couldn't. She couldn't lose him when she'd just found him. She wasn't strong enough. She wasn't brave enough.

She didn't want to be alone again.

"Witwraith!" Davin tried to adjust his grip, but Cornelius fought like a cornered animal, snarling and savage. Davin's hold on him slipped. "Do it. Now!"

There was no other choice. They were out of time.

"Hannah," Lillia cried, though doing so shattered her heart, "Snatch him!"

The despair in Hannah's eyes transformed into a determined glare. She rolled her shoulders and cocked her head, giving the restrained man the darkest of grins. "My pleasure."

Cornelius's efforts to escape increased as Hannah approached. Davin backed them both against a wall and wrapped his leg around Cornelius's to keep him from kicking and injuring the small Witwraith.

Hannah stepped forward and laid a petite hand on Cornelius's chest. She began to speak, her voice low and slow.

Cornelius jerked and fought harder than before. Davin shut his eyes and turned his head away while keeping hold on Cornelius.

Hannah's chanting continued. Her words repeated over and over, though Lillia could not make them out. When it seemed that Cornelius would break free from Davin's hold, he shuddered. Then stilled. His eyes met Hannah's, and he stared at her, mesmerized.

Her chant was then the only sound in the room.

"Your will to mine. Your soul to mine. Your will to mine. Your soul to mine."

Lillia's heart beat in time to those words. She could hear them in her mind, feel them in her soul. What was happening in her mind superimposed itself upon her vision. She could see both the people in front of her and the link she shared with Cornelius. But if she could hear them this deeply, so could Davin. Lillia rushed to him and pressed her hand and the end of her arm against his ears as best she could.

"Your will to mine. Your soul to mine."

Inch by inch, the link between Lillia and Cornelius retreated. It slid from her mind like a snake, twitching and writhing as if in pain.

"Your will to mine. Your soul to mine."

The link, the bond, shrank and withered until it was a mere shadow of what it was. Lillia closed her eyes, but the mental image that was once so clear faded far too quickly for her to make out anymore.

Hannah's chanting grew quieter.

"Your will to mine."

Her words slowed.

"Your soul to mine."

Even slower now. Slow and steady. Calm. Soothing. Hypnotic.

"Your will to mine."

The tension in Lillia's shoulders disappeared. She opened her eyes.

Hannah pressed her forehead to Cornelius's. He relaxed fully. His now unfocused gaze stared straight ahead.

"Your soul . . . to mine."

The last word was a mere breath.

Her task done, Hannah pulled away and took a few faltering steps back. She trembled ever so slightly as she tucked her hands close to her chest.

"Lillia. Your blinders." The gentle reminder from Sophie woke Lillia from the trance.

Lillia hurried to replace the indigo-tinted spectacles. She'd nearly forgotten they weren't on her face. The world went from brightly colored to hues of blue again.

She tipped her blinders down long enough to see things untinted once more. Was it her imagination, or was the red of Hannah's blinders—now on her face again—not nearly as intense as it once was? And the amber hue of Sophie's more dulled?

"Is it done?" Davin asked breathlessly.

At Lillia's nod, he released Cornelius, who barely moved. The newly Snatched man stood at an awkward angle, arms twisted in nearly the same position they'd been when Davin had held him in place.

Davin. Who had risked being Snatched again himself to save Lillia and the others. He narrowed his eyes toward Cornelius, then moved to wrap Lillia in his arms. She laid her head upon his shoulder.

"You're not Snatched?" she asked against his chest.

He kissed the top of her head. "No. I'm myself."

No stutter. No stumbling over his words. He hugged her of his own volition, free of any command or orders. If she wasn't so overwhelmed with everything that had happened, she would cry buckets of tears. Instead, she merely reveled in the sensation of being held close.

"No!" Abigail cried out. She pressed her hands to Mrs. Bradford's side, where Cornelius's knife had pierced her skin.

Blood. So much blood. Just like the doctor when they'd found him.

"I can't stop the bleeding, Davin!" Abigail's words were a half sob. "I can't stop it!"

Davin released Lillia to rush to his mother's side. He tried to pry Abigail's hands away to press against the wound himself, but she fought him off.

"I can get some cloths. Some water too." Sophie scurried from the room without waiting for a response.

Lillia stepped to Mrs. Bradford's side. "What do you need?"

Abigail responded first. "Fix her!" she demanded. She hiccupped and readjusted her hands. "If a Truthtaker can make a man do her will without him being Snatched, she can do anything. Heal her!"

"That's not how it works—"

Abigail didn't allow Lillia to finish. "Then I'll do it!" She pressed harder on her mother's wound and squeezed her eyes shut. Her hair fell around her face, covering her expression with a curtain of tangled curls. "Come on, Mimi. Heal!" She repeated it over and over, the "Mimi" slowly transforming to "Mama."

Mrs. Bradford groaned and arched up. "Abigail."

Abigail crowed triumphantly. "It's working! I can feel it!" She touched Mrs. Bradford's face with a blood-soaked hand. "It's working, Mama. I can save you!"

Something *was* happening. Lillia could feel the energy in the room, though she couldn't see anything. It was impossible to tell if what Abigail was doing was truly healing her mother, not with all the blood.

Before today, Lillia would have said it was impossible to compel a soul-possessed man to do her bidding. Could healing be possible as well?

Lillia reached her hand toward Abigail. "Let me help. I think I can—"

"No!" Abigail's eyes shot open. She swatted Lillia's hand away. "I can do this. I can do this. Without you. Without anyone!"

Sophie returned, cloth and bowl in hand. She stopped in the doorway and stared. The bowl tipped, and water started to dribble out, but she didn't correct it. "What are you doing, Abigail?"

"I'm healing her!" Abigail started her chant again. "Heal, Mama, heal. Please, Mama! Heal!"

"That's not possible," Sophie murmured. "It can't be." She set the cloth and bowl down, then hurried over and pressed her hands over Abigail's. "Take my strength. If you can do this, then do it!"

The energy that had radiated from Abigail now amplified in intensity. Tenfold. A hundred. Something indeed was happening. Something incredible.

Mrs. Bradford whispered something unintelligible. She lifted her hand toward Davin, who clasped it and held it to his chest. They locked eyes.

Her mouth worked a few times before she managed two simple words.

"I'm sorry."

Her grasp loosened and went limp. Her head lolled to the side, and she released a long breath.

The room suddenly felt emptier. The energy that pulsated only a moment ago fell flat.

"No!" Abigail's cry felt savage and raw. "No. I was healing her. It was working!" She pulled her hands from under Sophie's to hold her mother's face. She patted Mrs. Bradford's cheeks, then ran her hands down her arms. "Mama, I was healing you. You can't leave me. I need you! You can't go!"

When Mrs. Bradford didn't respond, Abigail fell across her still form, sobs wracking her body. "I was healing you, Mama," she cried between gasping breaths. "I know it. Why didn't it work? Why didn't you stay? Why did you leave me?"

Davin's brows furrowed, and he stumbled back. He stared at his mother, as if waiting for her to wake. His eyes glistened, but no tears fell.

Sophie sat back on her heels. Fatigue was written on every feature. Her shoulders slumped. She pulled her blinders off and wiped her brow with her sleeve.

"Are you well?" Lillia asked.

"Yes. And no." Sophie rested her hands in her lap. She looked forlornly toward Mrs. Bradford. "I was certain it would work. It shouldn't have. Healing simply isn't possible. Not for a Soulseer. Not for anybody. But for a moment, I thought it was possible."

Lillia had thought so too. She'd hoped so. Hard enough to believe.

Just as she had to hold faith Davin wouldn't be Snatched.

Lillia ignored Cornelius, who still stood silent in the corner. She couldn't look at him. Not now. He stood as a reminder that this could have been Davin's fate as well. Thank the Soulmaker at least one of her prayers had been answered.

CHAPTER 26

MIMI WAS GONE.

Really and truly gone.

Davin had seen the life bleed from her face as he sat on the floor next to her. He heard her last words as she told him she was sorry. He'd watched helplessly as the light in her eyes extinguished, even while Abigail desperately tried to save her with magic she didn't hold.

Mimi's body now lay in her bed chamber, being prepared for burial. Abigail had not left her side, not even to sleep.

And now, Bradford Lodge bustled with activity, while Davin hid away in the stables that had always been his refuge.

Serenity's foal arrived last night, thanks to Josiah's tender care. A strong, beautiful filly with a thick coat and sturdy build. She promised to be everything Davin had hoped for. The filly now rested in the corner as Davin tended to the mother. Both were healthy. Both were safe. His future was secured. Or would have been before everything happened.

He could not rejoice in it. Not like he'd wanted to. All he could think was how much he wished he could speak to his mother one last time. To make things right between them. She'd tried there, at the end. The more he thought on what happened, how she tried so hard to get her children out of the parlor, the more he knew she had tried to make things right.

He sensed that Lillia was approaching before she entered the stables. Somehow, during the altercation with Cornelius, their connection had strengthened. Whether it was the emotions he felt when he held tight to Cornelius while he was being Snatched ,or when he realized he would do anything for Lillia, it didn't matter. He was tied to her. Forever.

Davin didn't turn to greet her. He kept running the brush down Serenity's back, losing himself in the rhythm.

Lillia placed her hand on his hand that held the brush, stopping the motion. She stood so close, Davin could feel the heat emanating from her body. Or perhaps that was his imagination. Either way, he was acutely aware of how close she was to him.

He lowered the brush and switched it to his other hand so he could lace his fingers with hers. He needed this physical connection more than he needed the internal one. He needed to feel grounded somehow.

Lillia leaned against his shoulder. "You're hurting."

He was. He wouldn't be able to say it yet, but he was. Terribly.

"Thank you." Even that was almost too much to utter. "For trusting me. For trying to save me."

To be honest, he didn't know at the time if his plan would work. He'd hoped avoiding eye contact would be enough to keep him safe from the Witwraith's spell while he held Cornelius in place. He didn't know if Lillia covering his ears made any difference, but her efforts had been valiant indeed.

All he knew was that he'd needed to stop Cornelius by any means necessary. The madman had set his sights on Lillia. Only a fool would think that once he gained his freedom, he would have left her alone. Davin's actions had saved Lillia.

If only Davin could have saved Mimi too.

He pulled Lillia closer, holding her as tight as he dared.

"You did your best. No one could ask for more." Lillia sighed contentedly and placed her arm against his chest. Davin covered the end with his hand. It felt right to do this. To hold her like this.

When they first met, Lillia had been so determined to hide her lack from him. Now, she allowed him to see her as she truly was. Both physically and emotionally. He couldn't imagine her any other way.

Voices approached, and people Davin didn't recognize walked past the stable entrance, but no one entered. That's how it had been all morning. The Gifted and an army of people had descended upon Bradford Lodge at first light. Davin didn't know where they'd all come from, only that Sam had relayed the message they were needed.

Sam, who had worked at Davin's side for the past six years. Who had grown up in the Snatched camp. Who had been their liaison and caretaker, along with Josiah. Whose father was Snatched and was now gone.

There was so much there Davin had to work through. So much he needed to understand before things would be right between them again.

"Abigail says she's selling." Davin had tried to talk to her earlier, to convince her to take some breakfast. She'd refused. Then yelled at him, accusing him of letting their mother die. It was only after the elder Soulseer, Lady Madeleine, stepped in and spoke to Abigail that his sister finally told him she was giving up their family home and moving to New London to begin her training.

It wasn't a surprise. He'd suspected she would make her way

to the Guild of the Gifted eventually. With Mimi gone, there was nothing to hold either of them back any longer.

"I know." Lillia wrapped her arms around Davin's middle. "Lady Madeleine told me. She also told me you're also planning on going to New London. Something about working in the royal stables?"

It was an opportunity of a lifetime. One he could not turn down in his condition. "Yes. Me and Sam." Davin would be able to take Serenity and her foal. Lady Madeleine had hinted he could continue his breeding efforts, assuming the Lady Regent allowed it. He'd also be able to see Lillia. Daily, if he had anything to do with it.

Davin hadn't mentioned to anyone he'd been Revealed. As if by unspoken agreement, no one had said anything about it. Not even Abigail in her grief. He suspected Lady Madeleine knew. She was a perceptive one. The elder Soulseer had cornered Davin almost immediately upon her arrival to pry the details from him. He worried he said more than he should, though she seemed to already know the answers to most of the questions she asked.

"What of Thomas and Josiah?" Davin hadn't heard of their fate. There was no hiding who or what they were. Fate would not be as kind to them.

Lillia looked down. "I don't know. I'm to report to the Lady Regent when I return to town. I'll do what I can to help them, but who am I to sway the decision of the Guild? Or the Lady Regent?"

Davin tipped her chin up and kissed her forehead, soft and slow. "You, my dear, are a Truthtaker. Someone who is stronger than she realizes. You will walk into that meeting with your head held high, and you will speak to her as you would an equal." At her raised eyebrow, he chuckled and amended his statement. "A slightly inferior equal. But one whose words hold weight nonetheless."

Lillia pressed her cheek against his chest and held him tight. "And you'll be there."

"And I'll be there." Revealed or not, he would be there for her. With her.

Forever, if she let him.

EPILOGUE

LILLIA WANDERED THROUGH THE PALACE courtyard, lost in thought. She paid little attention to those around her, though some bits of conversations from the varied political groups who gathered, hoping to gain an audience from the Lady Regent, filtered through. Conversations she'd heard a hundred times before.

". . . wanting to build a colony in the south. But who would want to go? The wild mammoth creatures would kill them all . . ."

". . . radical Preservationists. I heard they keep their women subservient. Claim they're the weaker sex . . ."

". . . finally exterminated the night beasts that were terrorizing the area. Good riddance, I say . . ."

That last one gave Lillia pause. She wanted to stop and listen to the rest of the conversation to find out what was being said. There was truth to the rumor. The night beasts were no more, now that the Snatched who were masquerading as those same beasts had been killed. How much did the laymen know about what truly happened?

Two months had passed since that night. Two months of inquiries and questions and interviews from the Guild. Two months of not knowing her fate.

Lillia had Revealed three men. Well, two that the Guild knew of. She and the others had successfully been able to keep Davin's Revealing quiet. For now.

Inadvertent Revealing was subject to severe punishment unless it could be proven that Lillia had not been negligent in her precautions. Hours upon hours of questions, and Lillia still did not know her fate. Her duties had been suspended until all was decided.

"Lillia!"

Mama raised her hand and waved from where she talked with an unfortunate group of Gifted she must have cornered. "Lillia, darling, come and settle a dispute."

As Lillia had no time constraints, she could spare a minute or two. "Yes, Mama?" As she approached, she gauged the responses of the Gifted Mama was now preening for. None currently seemed impressed. A couple wore bored expressions.

Her mother, now sporting the same kind of muff Lillia herself wore, lifted her chin in a proud fashion. "I told them that you had an interview with the Lady Regent, and that she favored you with a ride in her carriage."

"That's correct." Lillia could already see where this was going. The skeptical expressions Mama's companions held turned to speculation.

There was a triumphant gleam in Mama's eyes. "What we were wondering is whether the Lady Regent's Snatched is as handsome close up as he is from far away." She smiled conspiratorially. "Is he?"

This was the hot debate Lillia needed to settle? Whether a man who was Snatched was good-looking or not?

Before the events in Lakewood, Lillia would have sputtered and mumbled something about how the Snatched could be handsome, but she wasn't one to say. She would have allowed these women to intimidate her. She would have allowed Mama to say and do whatever she wished, and Lillia would have obeyed.

Now, she simply didn't care. These things seemed trivial and small.

"Why does it matter if a Snatched man is handsome?" Lillia met the eyes of each Gifted in turn. At least one had the decency to be embarrassed. "He is Snatched. Not an object of affection. Not a piece of art to be admired. He is a man. A human being. And I had more important things to consider during my time with the Lady Regent."

With that, Lillia bid them farewell and continued on her way. Mama sputtered a bit before making her excuses and following Lillia.

"Daughter. What was the meaning of that? You can't afford to make enemies of those women." Mama grabbed Lillia's wrist and pulled her around. "You have enough strikes against you." She gestured to Lillia's muff. "Why would you deliberately make it worse by spouting Novationist foolishness?"

This was getting ludicrous. Lillia had no desire to continue this conversation. She pulled her arm from her muff and raised it to display her lack for all to see. "You mean this, Mama? This is one of the strikes against me?" She made no effort to lower her voice. "My missing hand? This is a reason I am less worthy than others?"

"Put that away," Mama hissed. She tried to wrangle Lillia's arm down and out of sight. "Where is your false hand? I thought it repaired. Do you want everyone to see your deformity?"

"The deformity they already know I have?" Though Lillia no longer thought it as such. "My lack of a hand does not make me any less, Mama. Nor does the fact that I accidentally Revealed my father when my gift first manifested."

Mama gasped loudly. She stepped in front of Lillia and leaned in close. "Keep your voice down, Lillia. People may hear."

"Let them hear." Lillia started to turn away. "I'm tired of hiding in shadows while my secrets are displayed for all to see." She would rather await the Guild's decision away from these petty gossipmongers. Perhaps she would find Sophie or Hannah and see what they were doing. Or sneak away to the Royal Stables to spend time with Davin.

"Well said."

Lillia turned to see who'd spoken and immediately dropped into a curtsy, as did Mama and the other Gifted in the vicinity.

"Your Majesty." Lillia straightened and shoved both her hand and her lack into her muff but did not raise her eyes to meet those of the Lady Regent.

"No need to stand upon ceremony with me, Lady Lillia." The Lady Regent tucked her arm through Lillia's and pulled her into a slow stroll. "Walk with me. We have much to catch up on." Her Snatched companion followed, as mute and stoic as usual.

The whispers began almost immediately.

When they were out of earshot of the others, the Lady Regent chuckled. "We gave them something to gossip about now, didn't we?"

"We?" Lillia risked a glance back to see several people quickly avert their eyes only to scurry to another group of people to start whispering again. She smiled to herself. "I believe you are the cause, Your Majesty."

"As I very well should be." The Lady Regent tapped Lillia's muff with the fan she carried. "The muffs from Lakewood are delightful, are they not? I have one myself. Lady Madeleine acquired one for me while she was there."

"Yes. I was there when she purchased hers." It was strangely similar in coloring to the one the Lady Regent now wore.

The Lady Regent hummed her reply. "I noticed you no longer wear the false hand I had repaired."

Was that disapproval in her voice? Or merely curiosity? Neither truly mattered.

Lillia pulled her arm out to reveal her lack. She held it up and openly examined it. "I suppose I no longer need it. After going without while in Lakewood, I found the hand and the rest felt restrictive. Though I appreciate the repair." The ivory hand had nearly looked new, with only the faintest line where the thumb had broken off. The craftsman had great skill. If Lillia ever had need of such a thing again, she knew where to go. "Of course, I may commission one with articulating fingers. Could you imagine how much easier it would be to hold a teacup and saucer with fingers that can actually grip?" She would have to save up for a time to make it happen, but she was very tempted to do so. What else could such a mechanical contraption do?

She nestled her arm back in the muff. Though the sun now shone, it was far too cold to keep hands—or arms—out for long.

"I was happy to do it. And even happier to see you without it. I do like the idea of the mechanical prosthetic, though. You'd be the one to make the tongues wag with one of those. Well worth the expense just for that."

An unexpected response. "My mother would say otherwise." And had said otherwise. Multiple times.

"She's a foolish woman who doesn't know worth when she sees it."

Something told Lillia the Lady Regent wasn't speaking solely of Lillia's lack of a hand.

They walked in silence for the length of the courtyard. People gawked and stared. Some said nothing, while others spoke in hushed tones or behind their hands to their companions.

It was well known the Lady Regent did not casually stroll. Nor did she openly spend time with any of the Gifted. In fact, the Lady Regent rarely emerged from her chambers except to meet with her advisors in the council chamber or to receive visitors in her audience chamber. It simply wasn't done.

Or hadn't been done until now.

"Why me?" Lillia asked. There was nothing special about her. No reason she would attract the eye of the most powerful woman in the land. She'd hidden in the shadows, shunned and unnoticed until the Lady Regent invited her to ride in her carriage and started the slew of events that led Lillia to where she was now.

The Lady Regent didn't respond for a full minute. When she did speak, it was slow and low enough her voice would not carry. "You have a future. A beautiful future. One few have. A strong Temporal has confirmed it several times over. I want to see it happen." She smiled at a high-ranking Soulseer who passed by. "Your father was also one of my most trusted advisors. I had no doubt his daughter would be as skilled and reliable as he."

"And just as troubled? I'm afraid I'm still awaiting the Guild's decision." That was why Lillia was wandering the courtyard this morning instead of preparing to speak to the girls in the Academy. Her previously assigned lesson times had been reassigned to others for the interim. It left her with nothing to do but fret.

"For you? Or for him?"

The Lady Regent posed a fair question, as both futures hung in the balance.

"Both."

They now walked toward a more secluded part of the courtyard, where there was a bench under a winter-ravaged arbor. The Lady Regent made a small gesture to her Snatched. He assumed a protective stance, preventing any from following them.

They sat on the stone bench, the cold seeping through Lillia's layers almost immediately. She shivered and hoped this conversation wouldn't last much longer. This part of the courtyard, while beautiful in the summer months, saw little use in the winter since it didn't have the open fire pedestals common in the rest of the courtyard.

The Lady Regent set her muff in her lap. "I'm afraid there isn't much I can do for your father. He's known to be Snatched and must act as such for now. He and that young man, Thomas, have been sent to the mining fields. To a section of my choosing."

Lillia's shoulders slumped, and tears pricked at her eyes. She'd suspected as much. Sophie had been melancholic since their return to New London, but wouldn't tell either Lillia or Hannah why. She must have already known Papa's and Thomas's fate.

"I have made certain they will be treated well."

That reassurance did little to calm Lillia's worries. The mining fields were days away. There was little chance of seeing Papa again. "Thank you."

"As for you," the Lady Regent continued, "I have overseen the Guild proceedings myself to ensure certain things will not come to light. Including your young man's current condition."

Those other certain things included a secret camp of previously Snatched men hidden deep in the Lakewood forests. A camp that was no longer, the men within all killed. Lillia understood the ramifications if news of that got out. Everyone knew that once a man was Snatched, he did not recover. That's why Snatching was reserved for only the most vile of crimes.

If people learned the truth . . . Lillia shuddered, thankful her previous shivering could mask it.

"And what has been decided?"

Lillia hadn't wanted to ask the question. These moments could be her last as a free woman. Fallen Truthtakers did not have the option to be transported to the southern farms or put to work in the mining fields alongside the Snatched who weren't handsome enough to serve the Gifted.

She would be placed in isolation, deep within the palace

grounds. Her only companions would be the Gifted and her guards until she lost her vision and no longer could Reveal another soul.

And Davin. If it got out he was Revealed, he could be lost to her as well.

She braced herself, preparing for the worst.

"You are to join Sophie as one of my companions."

Lillia jerked and stared, open-mouthed, at the Lady Regent. "Pardon?"

The Lady Regent tugged at her muff, pulling it on more tightly. "In addition to your other duties, of course. The added responsibilities are meant to help guide you and teach you to better control your gift." She raised her brows. "Unless you'd rather be placed in isolation?"

"No!" Lillia tried to calm her racing heart. "I mean, I thank you for the opportunity. I humbly accept."

She was not meant to be imprisoned. Her thoughts skipped and leaped and refused to settle.

Lillia was free.

The Lady Regent stood, and Lillia hurried to join her. "It's far too cold out here for idle chit chat." The monarch walked back toward the main courtyard. "I expect you in my audience chamber promptly at nine tomorrow morning." She made another gesture to her Snatched, who fell in line behind them. "Sophie can find more appropriate clothing for your new position."

"Yes, Your Majesty." Lillia would wear anything required of her. She would even wear a fool's cap and cape and parade about the streets of New London, if it was asked of her.

As they approached the nearest doors leading to the palace proper, the Lady Regent turned to Lillia. "I assume you would like to tell a certain young stablehand about your news?" She gave the barest hint of a wink. "I'm certain he would like to know as well."

Davin. Yes. Of course.

Lillia gave the Lady Regent a curtsy, then lifted her skirts and practically ran to the stable yard.

She was free. She and Davin. They were free.

She couldn't wait to tell him.

VERITY LEANED HER HEAD AGAINST the window frame and watched the two lovers as they shared a quiet moment. Their budding relationship was a pleasant surprise. A glimmer of light and hope in an otherwise dismal situation.

"Woolgathering?"

The deep timber of that voice was one she knew as well as her own. She turned with a smile. "Always."

Miles placed a fist to his heart and bowed. "Forgive me, Lady Madeleine. I was looking for the Lady Regent."

Verity rolled her eyes at him. She dropped the illusion she wore nearly as often as her own face. "You know very well who I am, you rascal."

"Lady Madeleine" allowed Verity to wander about the palace grounds—as well as other places—without the pomp and circumstance associated with her formal title. She'd assumed the face after slipping from the courtyard to keep from being accosted on her way back to her quarters.

Miles winked at her and straightened, every bit as handsome in the palace livery as he had in his lieutenant's uniform when they'd first met on the *Atlantia* all those years ago. Decades now.

No. Centuries. How had it been that long?

She turned back to the window. Lillia and Davin were now holding hands and walking with their heads close together. Soon, they would be out of her line of sight.

Miles wrapped his arms around her shoulders and kissed the side of her head. "Spying on the new recruits, are you? How scandalous. Should I alert the gossipmongers that their Lady Regent is just as nosy as they?"

"Alert away." She leaned back into his embrace, relishing in the familiar comfort of his arms. If only her reputation was the only thing she had to worry about.

"You're fretting again."

It wasn't a guess. The link between them had deepened until his emotions were nearly intertwined with hers. At times, Verity almost felt as if she could read his thoughts. Heaven forbid he could read hers.

"The gifts are changing, Miles." This wasn't new. Her gifts and those of the original Gifted had evolved. It had happened slowly and gradually, as slow and gradual as their aging, which also remained unexplained.

These new changes were happening far more quickly, and often without warning. "According to Sophie, the new Soulseer almost healed her mother. Healing! I never believed that possible. If she'd been stronger—Gifted wildly as we were, perhaps—I think she could have done it."

"Sophie believes so as well." He placed another kiss on her temple. "She says Lillia and Davin have futures. As does Hannah and Sam. Clear ones."

That was another source of her worries. "Four more. Out of thousands. Hundreds of thousands."

"She seems certain of what she Sees."

As she should be. Sophie was one of the few who gained her gift as Verity and the other originals had. A wild energy had swept her up while she was a child. A doorway of light, as Sophie put it. Her gift was stronger than Verity had ever seen, particularly as a Temporal. She could See years into the future with near perfect clarity, though her Visual and Aural abilities were far weaker.

"Thomas has a future too."

This was news to Verity. "The Snatched boy?" She'd seen

how Sophie looked at the red-headed boy. It reminded her of the schoolgirl crush she'd had on Miles. Verity had dismissed Sophie's attentions as merely a crush, but if the boy had a future . . .

"Should I be worried our daughter is placing her affections where she shouldn't?" There was a hint of amusement in Miles's voice. "Or should I be proud she's following in her mother's footsteps?"

"Falling for a man who's supposed to be Snatched?"

Miles pretended to pull away, but Verity held him in place. He laughed. "Pardon me, Your Majesty. I have never been Snatched." He tightened his hold. "I only pretend to be so for appearance's sake."

"And he's recovering. Like Josiah. Like you did."

At that, Miles did pull away. He stepped to the sideboard and poured himself a cup of tea. "Josiah should have never been Snatched to begin with. What was he thinking, experimenting with energies in his home?" He lifted the cup to his lips but set it back on the saucer without taking a sip. "His experiments attracted the wild energy that Gifted his daughter."

"He was only trying to make them safer." At her behest. Too many young women had gone through the Gifting Ceremony with child. It was a miracle more children hadn't manifested Truthtaking abilities at birth. If they could figure out how to bestow the gifts upon only the girls and not a child they carried, there would be no more accidental Revealings.

"And with his Revealing and subsequent Snatching, we lost our strongest Tamer." Miles took a sip this time. "He can't Tame a thing now. There are too few remaining who can tame the energies, my love."

Too few by far. Only Miles and two others could Tame anymore. Their magicked doorways granted the gifts that their society depended upon. Those gifts paled in comparison to those granted naturally, but the wild energies were far too erratic and dangerous to rely upon.

"What happens when we lose them all?" Verity whispered, more to herself than to Miles. Out of the remaining Tamers, only Miles had a future. Sophie was quite certain in that regard.

Miles poured a second cup and handed it to Verity. It was prepared precisely how she liked it. He always knew what she needed. What she wanted. It was what she loved most about him.

"What if she's wrong?"

Verity absently swirled her cup, watching the tea gently slosh in an almost hypnotic fashion. "About what?"

"What if the gifts aren't merely evolving?" Miles joined her at the window, leaning against the opposite side of the frame. "What if some gifts are replacing others? What if that's the reason so many don't have futures?"

Verity took a sip of her tea, far too lost in her thoughts to taste it. It was an intriguing thought. One that, if true, gave her some degree of comfort. She looked up, past the stables and over the water of Lake Verity to where the pale blue cliffs of ice rose up to the sky.

Gifts evolving and changing. Novationists and Preservationists fighting over each new idea. Guiding and shaping the future of a people that might not have a future.

It was all a far cry from where she started. An innocent young woman, staring out over the sea at an uncertain future of her own.

But where would it all end?

ABOUT THE AUTHOR

LYSANDRA JAMES IS A DREAM-CHASING dragon slayer who thinks she's hilarious (because she is). As a breast cancer survivor, she's a firm believer in using humor to get through difficult times and that stories are the best way to inspire others to overcome the darkness in their own lives. She loves people and often jokes that she could walk into an empty elevator and come out with a friend. Lysandra started writing fantasy to avoid the tedious task of research only to write "displaced history" stories that take people from one time and place and dump them in another just to watch chaos ensue. This involves far more research than she'd ever hoped to do . . . and she absolutely loves it. Who knew?

Lysandra lives in a small town in northern Utah with her handyman husband, three properly geeky sons, a diva house that requires a LOT of attention, and seven typewriters. The typewriters are the least demanding things in her life. Usually.